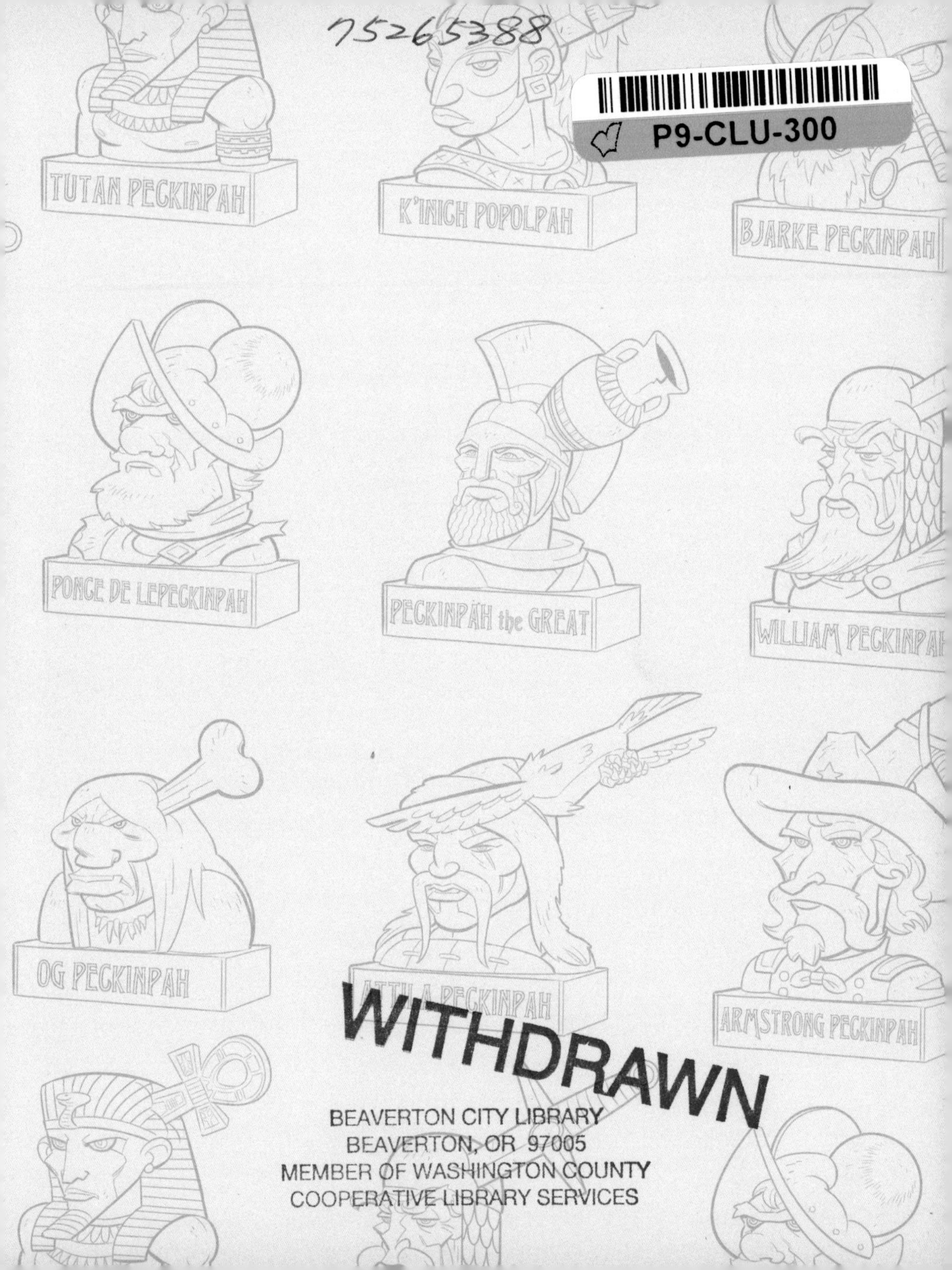
TUTAN PECKINPAH
K'INICH POPOLPAH
BJARKE PECKINPAH
PONCE DE LEPECKINPAH
PECKINPAH the GREAT
WILLIAM PECKINPAH
OG PECKINPAH
ATTILA PECKINPAH
ARMSTRONG PECKINPAH

ATOMIC FRENCHIE

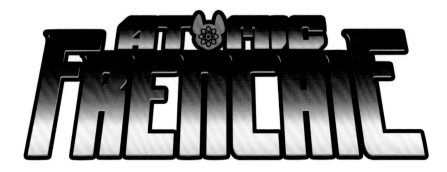

ATOMIC FRENCHIE

The Cow with the Nuclear Heart

Thomas E. Sniegoski and Tom McWeeney

San Rafael, California

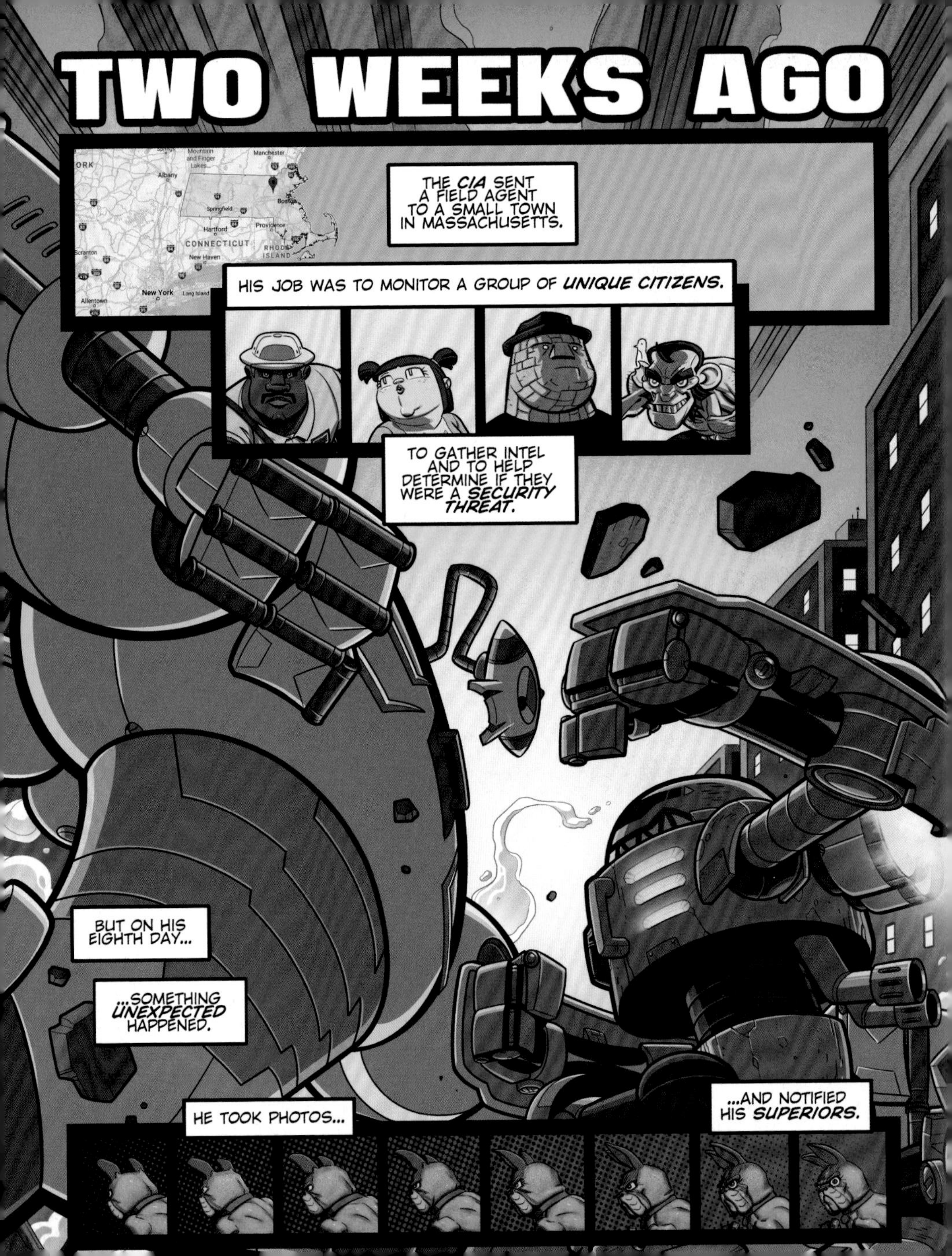
TWO WEEKS AGO
THE CIA SENT A FIELD AGENT TO A SMALL TOWN IN MASSACHUSETTS.
HIS JOB WAS TO MONITOR A GROUP OF UNIQUE CITIZENS.
TO GATHER INTEL AND TO HELP DETERMINE IF THEY WERE A SECURITY THREAT.
BUT ON HIS EIGHTH DAY...
...SOMETHING UNEXPECTED HAPPENED.
HE TOOK PHOTOS...
...AND NOTIFIED HIS SUPERIORS.

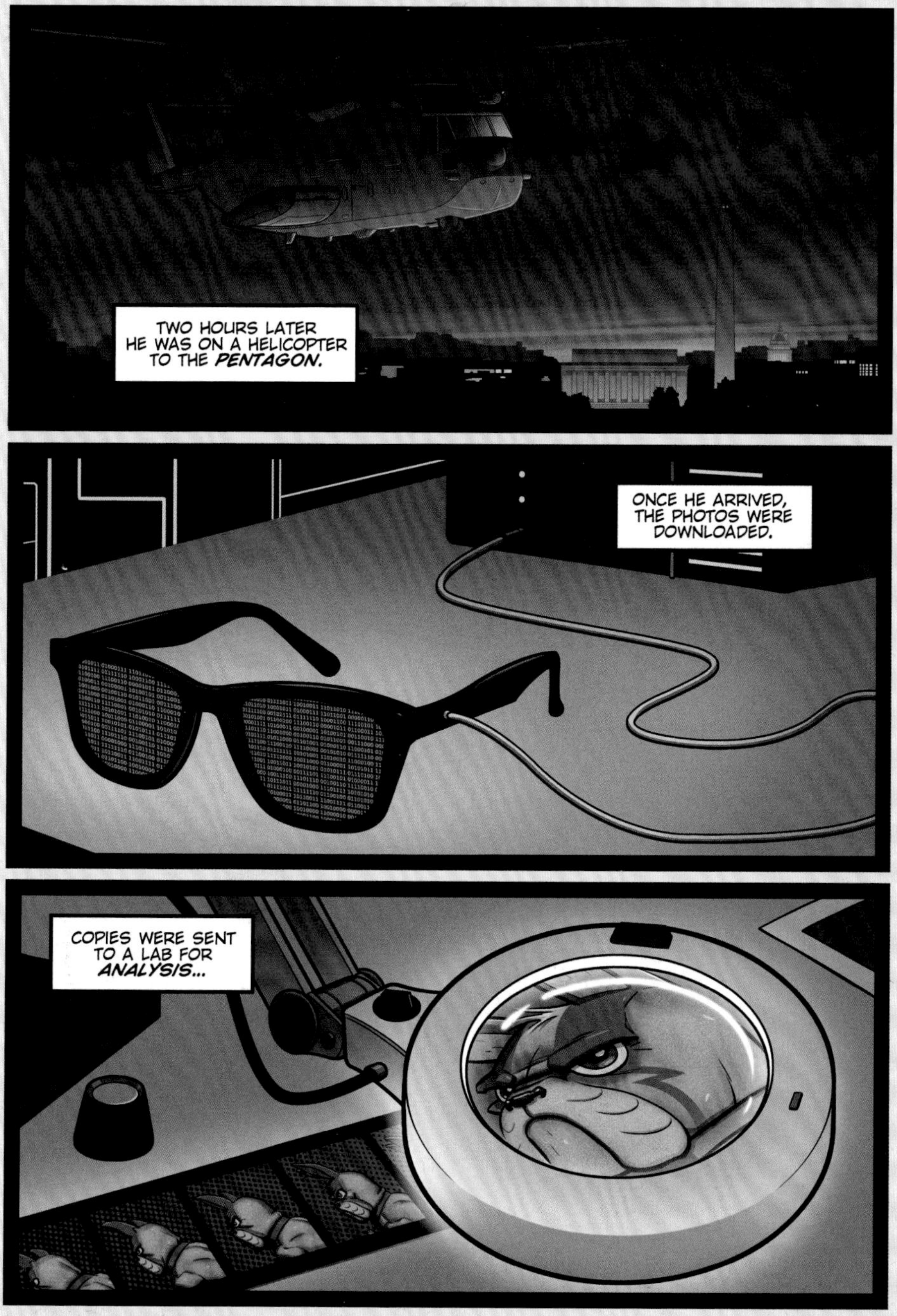
TWO HOURS LATER HE WAS ON A HELICOPTER TO THE *PENTAGON.*
ONCE HE ARRIVED, THE PHOTOS WERE DOWNLOADED.
COPIES WERE SENT TO A LAB FOR *ANALYSIS...*

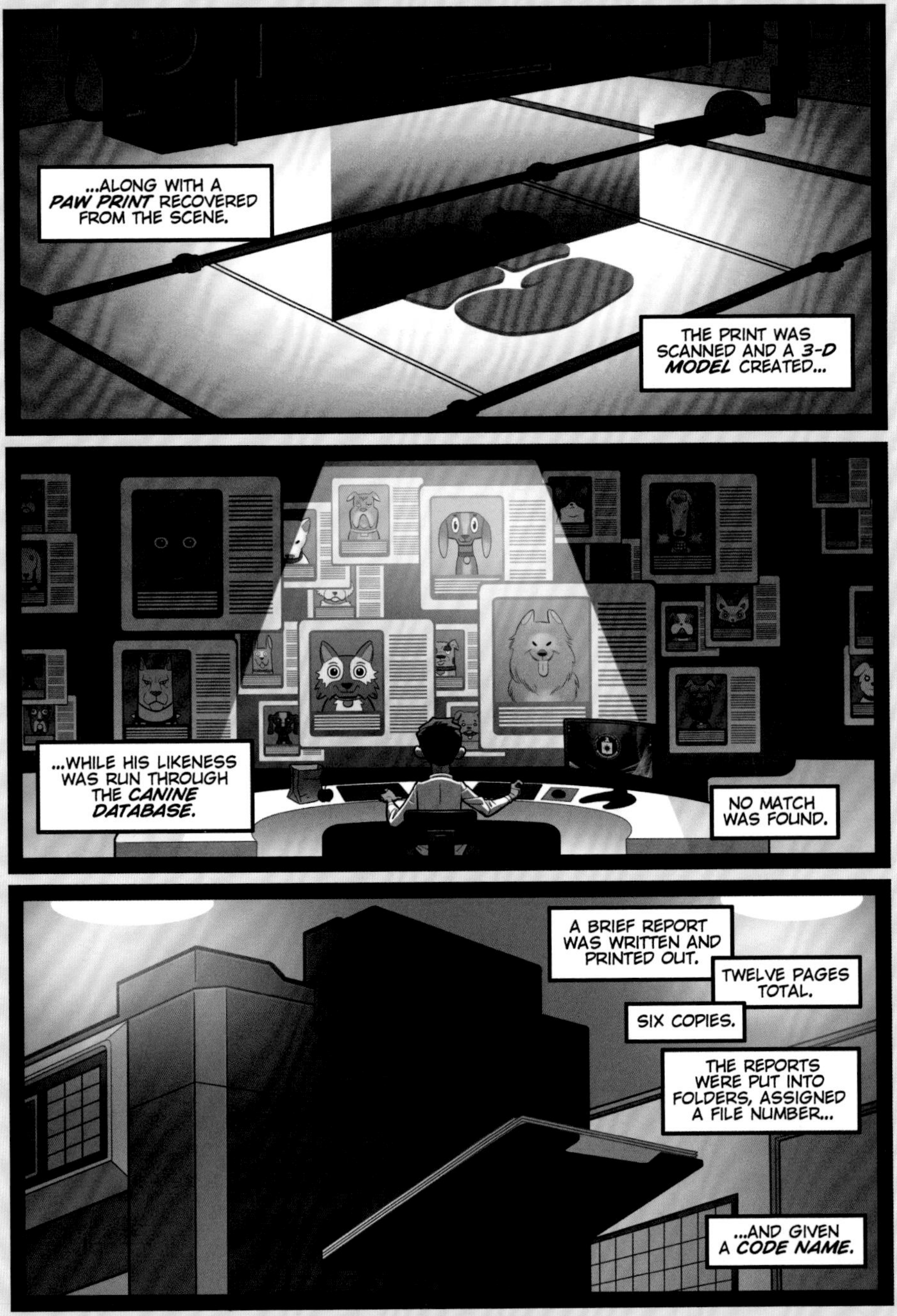
...ALONG WITH A PAW PRINT RECOVERED FROM THE SCENE.
THE PRINT WAS SCANNED AND A 3-D MODEL CREATED...
...WHILE HIS LIKENESS WAS RUN THROUGH THE CANINE DATABASE.
NO MATCH WAS FOUND.
A BRIEF REPORT WAS WRITTEN AND PRINTED OUT.
TWELVE PAGES TOTAL.
SIX COPIES.
THE REPORTS WERE PUT INTO FOLDERS, ASSIGNED A FILE NUMBER...
...AND GIVEN A CODE NAME.

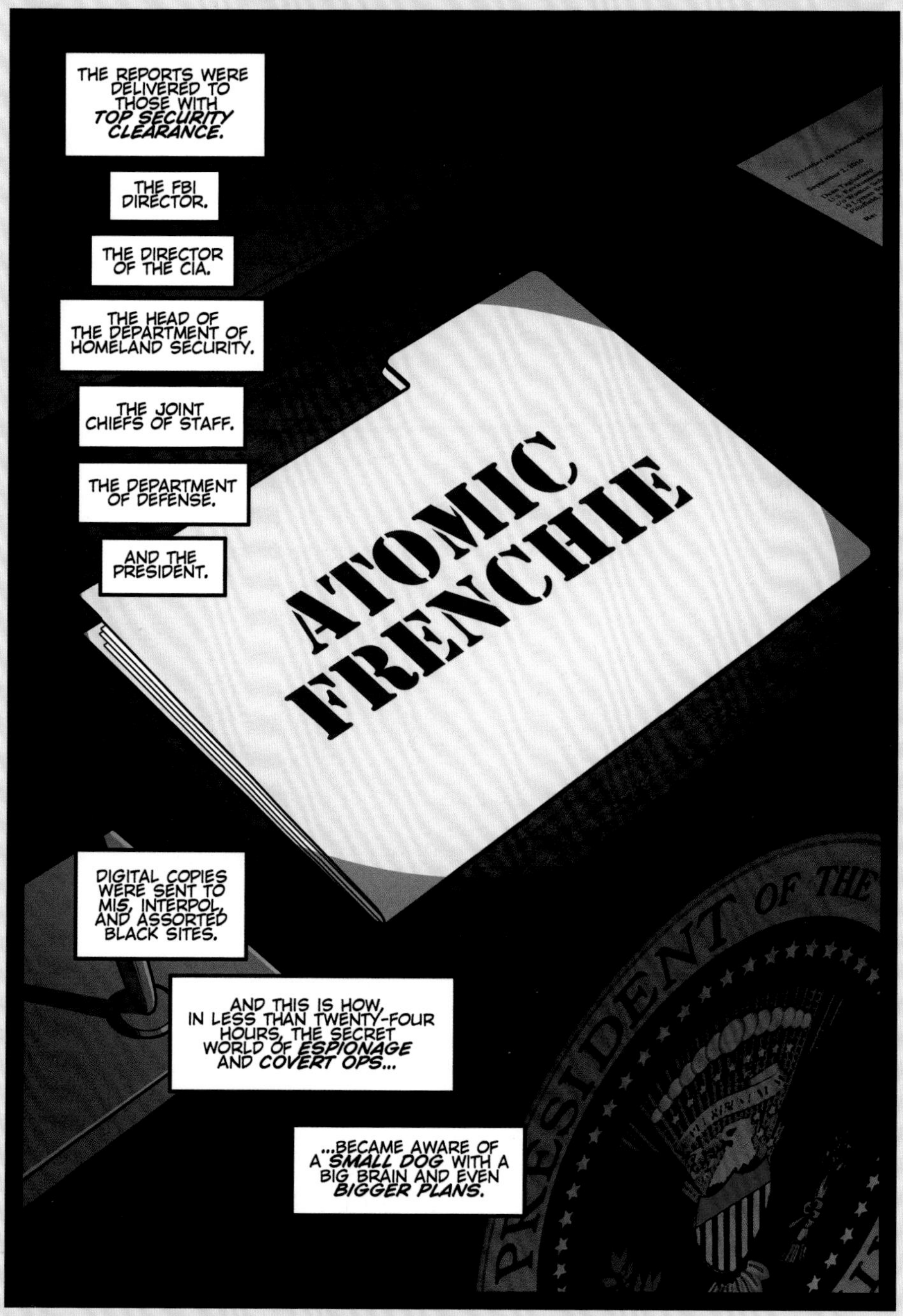
THE REPORTS WERE DELIVERED TO THOSE WITH TOP SECURITY CLEARANCE.
THE FBI DIRECTOR.
THE DIRECTOR OF THE CIA.
THE HEAD OF THE DEPARTMENT OF HOMELAND SECURITY.
THE JOINT CHIEFS OF STAFF.
THE DEPARTMENT OF DEFENSE.
AND THE PRESIDENT.
ATOMIC FRENCHIE
DIGITAL COPIES WERE SENT TO MI5, INTERPOL, AND ASSORTED BLACK SITES.
AND THIS IS HOW, IN LESS THAN TWENTY-FOUR HOURS, THE SECRET WORLD OF ESPIONAGE AND COVERT OPS...
...BECAME AWARE OF A SMALL DOG WITH A BIG BRAIN AND EVEN BIGGER PLANS.
PRESIDENT OF THE

ONE

US ROUTE 50.
NEVADA.
THE LONELIEST ROAD IN AMERICA.

The 1959 Cadillac Eldorado zoomed down the lonely highway, a French bulldog of supreme intelligence behind the wheel.

A Frenchie on a mission.

"I don't know," said OB the box turtle. He was standing on a stack of pillows in the passenger seat and had rolled down the window, stretching his long neck out far enough that he could see the pavement as it passed beneath them. "This road doesn't look lonely to me."

Kirby rolled his eyes and tried to ignore the turtle's inane chatter by concentrating on his driving. He'd had to modify the old Eldorado to accommodate his stature, but it seemed to be working just fine.

"I'll give you lonely," the ghost of Erasmus Peckinpah said from the back seat where he floated wearing nothing but an ectoplasmic bath towel. "Try dating in high school with an IQ well over 150. It was like trying to have a conversation with a tub of butter!"

"I'd think butter would have a lot to say." OB pulled his head back inside the car. "Lonely roads, uncommunicative dairy products—I guess it's these little mysteries that keep life interesting," he mused cheerily.

Kirby glared at Erasmus in the rearview mirror, but the bespectacled ghost ignored the Frenchie's gaze.

"Speaking of butter," the former mad scientist said, "did you know that Ronald Reagan had a deep, abiding fear of butter? Once, during a State

Department dinner, someone missed the memo and put out buttered rolls. It took Nancy and the Secret Service three hours to get him to come out from under the table. He was curled up in a ball and crying like a baby. True story."

"That's kinda sad," OB said.

Kirby had heard enough.

"What saddens me is having to endure this insipid prattle while attempting to concentrate on the road," the Frenchie snarled, squeezing the steering wheel tighter in his little paws.

"Sorry, K," OB said. "Didn't mean to prattle."

"Yeah, Kurt," Erasmus said, leaning forward from the back seat. "I just can't help myself. I come from a long line of prattlers. In fact my great-great-great-great grandfather Aloysius Peckinpah was known for being one of England's greatest—*armadillo*!"

"Your great-great-great-great grandfather was an armadillo?" Kirby questioned, his eyes still on the rearview mirror.

Erasmus had floated farther into the front seat and was pointing a long, twisted finger out the windshield and at the shelled animal they were about to run over.

"No, armadillo!"

Kirby looked through the windshield just in time. Quickly, he yanked the steering wheel to the right. The Eldorado's tires shrieked, tossing up a cloud of dust and rock as the car drove onto the shoulder of the road and careened past the armadillo. Kirby turned the steering wheel back to the left, and once again the car was traveling the smooth surface of the highway.

"That was close," Erasmus said. "Good driving there, Klint!"

"If you hadn't distracted me . . . ," Kirby began.

"Jumpin' Jahosafats!" Erasmus exclaimed. "The cryo-chamber!"

And the ghost was suddenly gone, floating through the back of the car to check on the attached trailer that held the cryogenic freezing chamber containing the mad scientist's frozen body.

"Jeez, hope it's all right," OB said worriedly. Again he stretched his long neck to peer around the front seat toward the trailer at the back.

"I'm sure it's fine," Kirby said. "My mastery of the road is beyond reproach."

Erasmus came back, his body emerging from the seat.

"Everything looks fine. Wouldn't that be a kick in the head if something happened and I started to defrost?"

Kirby acknowledged the ghost with another glare in the rearview mirror.

"Can you imagine coming all this way with my corpsesickle of a body for nothing and having to turn around?" the scientist asked.

Kirby could not even begin to imagine the enormous waste of precious time that would have caused—time that could have been used to achieve world domination. He forced his enhanced brain to tune out the latest yammering of his passengers and thought about how this mission would eventually bring him to his most auspicious goals.

32 HOURS AGO:

Using a special key, Erasmus opened a secret door in a wall at the far end of the laboratory under the garage to reveal another, far heavier door, like the kind used for bank vaults.

The kind used to protect things of incredible value.

Erasmus said that he'd locked away all of his greatest ideas behind the second door. Things far too important to leave lying about.

Things that Kirby could put to good use.

"Open it," Kirby demanded of the ghost.

"Not so fast, short-stuff," Erasmus said. "There's a matter of great importance that you are going to take care of for me. Then, I'll be more than happy to open her up and let you have first crack at anything you find inside."

The ghost of Erasmus Peckinpah paused to let his words sink in, as OB, who had been standing next to Kirby, quickly pulled himself into the protection of his shell, sensing danger.

"You wash my back, and I'll wash yours," said the ghost.

Kirby looked at Erasmus, his annoyance on the rise, but he quickly tromped it down. He would play along with the ghost—

For now.

"What would you like me to do?" Kirby asked mildly.

Erasmus smiled, rubbing his ghostly hands together in anticipation. "Kirkwood, I thought you'd never ask." The ghost floated to the combination lock in the center of the vault door. "Just let me get this bad boy open . . ."

He blew on his fingers before reaching out and grasping the dial. "Five to the left . . . ten to the right . . . six . . . then four and . . ."

From within the thick metal door came the sound of mechanisms unlocking, and then the door slid silently open.

"Bingo!" Erasmus said, as a wave of cold fog rolled out from inside the vault.

"It's freezing!" OB shrieked, popping out of his shell and retreating from the icy wave.

"Yes," Kirby said. He didn't move. "What's the reason for that?"

"It's what I'm going to need your help with," the ghost said, peering around the thick, steel door and motioning for them to come forward. "Come take a gander."

Kirby approached the door, reaching out and pulling it open wider. What he saw within was not at all what he'd expected.

"Explain," the Frenchie ordered the ghost, who hovered beside a large, metal container.

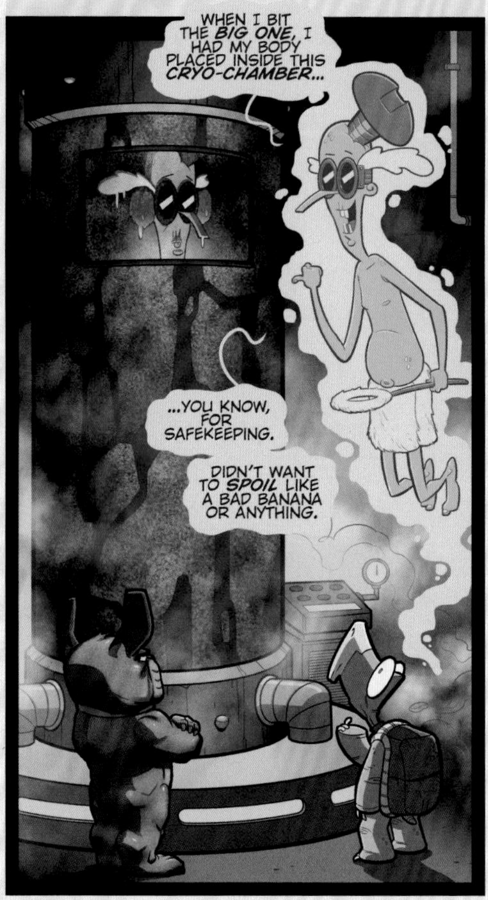
WHEN I BIT THE BIG ONE, I HAD MY BODY PLACED INSIDE THIS CRYO-CHAMBER...
...YOU KNOW, FOR SAFEKEEPING.
DIDN'T WANT TO SPOIL LIKE A BAD BANANA OR ANYTHING.

"Hey, that's you!" OB said, pointing up at the window.

"Sure is, kid," Erasmus said to the turtle. "Something to behold."

"Why did you freeze your remains?" Kirby asked as he walked slowly around the cryogenic freezer, carefully examining the cooling apparatus.

"Besides not wanting to spoil?" Erasmus asked, floating after him. "Figured it was the thing to do if I ever wanted to come back."

Kirby stopped. "Come back?"

"Yeah," Erasmus said. "That's what you're going to help me do."

Again, Kirby felt the beginnings of annoyance blossoming at his core. He definitely didn't have time for this.

"No," the Frenchie said, shaking his blocky head. "The amount of time I would require to perfect reanimation would be detrimental to my true purpose and . . ."

"Slow down there, Kurtis," Erasmus interrupted. "I've already got all that worked out."

"Explain," Kirby commanded again.

The ghost flew from the vault and disappeared into the lab.

"Haunting my house for years, waiting for somebody to come along, somebody worthy enough to lend me a hand, I had to keep the old mind flexible or go wackadoodle, if you know what I mean," Erasmus called from somewhere in the laboratory.

"I most certainly do," Kirby agreed, impatiently waiting for the ghost to return.

The sound of a mess being made resounded about the lab.

Curiosity drove Kirby and OB from the vault to find Erasmus hovering above a bookcase, a stack of magazines strewn about the floor.

"Inside one of these magazines, I found the way I'm going to catch a bus back from the land of the dead," Erasmus said. He leafed through a magazine, then tossed it over his shoulder and reached for another one.

"I love the bus!" OB announced happily.

"This is how I'm gonna make my grand return," Erasmus said. "With your assistance, of course, oh Frenchie-friend-o-mine."

Kirby crossed his arms, watching as the ghost continued his mad search. "What could you possibly have read in one of these moldering periodicals that . . ."

"A-hah!" Erasmus exclaimed, staring at a particular magazine. "I forgot she was on the cover."

"She?" OB questioned. "Let's see."

Erasmus turned the cover to face them. It was an issue of *National Scientific*, and the photo was of a cow.

"Ain't she a beauty?"

"That's a cow," Kirby said.

"It is," Erasmus agreed with an eager nod. "But it's a cow with a spectacular difference!"

"Does she produce chocolate milk?" OB asked, excitedly dancing in place.

Both Kirby and Erasmus just stared.

"I'll be quiet," the box turtle said.

"What is this difference?" Kirby asked the scientist. "What makes this particular member of the bovine species so . . . special?"

Erasmus smiled. "This one's got a nuclear ticker."

"Excuse me?"

"That's right," Erasmus said, holding the magazine up close to his face. "She's got a nuclear heart."

He gave the picture on the cover a quick peck.

"And with your help, Klyde ol' pal, it's gonna belong to me."

BACK ON US ROUTE 50.
STILL THE LONELIEST ROAD IN AMERICA.

"Why did we have to bring your body with us?" OB asked. The turtle had turned around in his seat and was looking through the rear window at the trailer the Eldorado pulled behind it. "It's kinda, y'know, creepy."

"Yeah, even gives me the willies," Erasmus said, his ghostly body shivering. "But it was too risky leaving it back there."

"Even locked away in the vault?" OB wanted to know.

Erasmus considered the question, then totally dismissed it.

"Vaults ain't perfect, ya know. What if raccoons broke in, or there was a power failure . . . or raccoons caused a power failure? We could come home to a slimy puddle and some bones! I want my body where I can keep an eye on it," the ghost said, crossing his arms. "And besides, this way we can transfer the heart on the spot!"

It became momentarily quiet in the car, and Kirby reveled in the silence, the hum of the road beneath the car's tires putting him in a contemplative fugue state. If only it could stay that way until they reached their destination and . . .

"I can just feel that nuclear cow heart beating inside the old birdcage now," Erasmus announced happily, fingers tapping on his bare, ghostly chest. "Ba-thump! Ba-thump! Ba-thump!"

"Who's gonna operate?" OB wanted to know.

"I will perform the surgery," Kirby announced.

"That's right, he'll be doing the cutting—under my supervision, of course," Erasmus said. "He'll take the nuclear heart out of the heifer and put it to better use inside of me. It'll be glorious!"

"And the cow is at this Area 51 place?" OB asked.

"That's right, Area 51 or the Forbidden Toy Box, as some of my science bros used to call it," Erasmus answered wistfully.

"They have cows *and* toys there?"

Kirby felt his pulse quicken with the thought of the mysterious location. Long had Area 51 been a subject of fascination for him. A place of supposed secret knowledge too earthshaking to be seen by the normal human populace? He imagined that a future world conqueror might be able to find some items of use there.

"Oh yes," Kirby said, practically drooling in anticipation. "Toys the likes of which we have never seen."

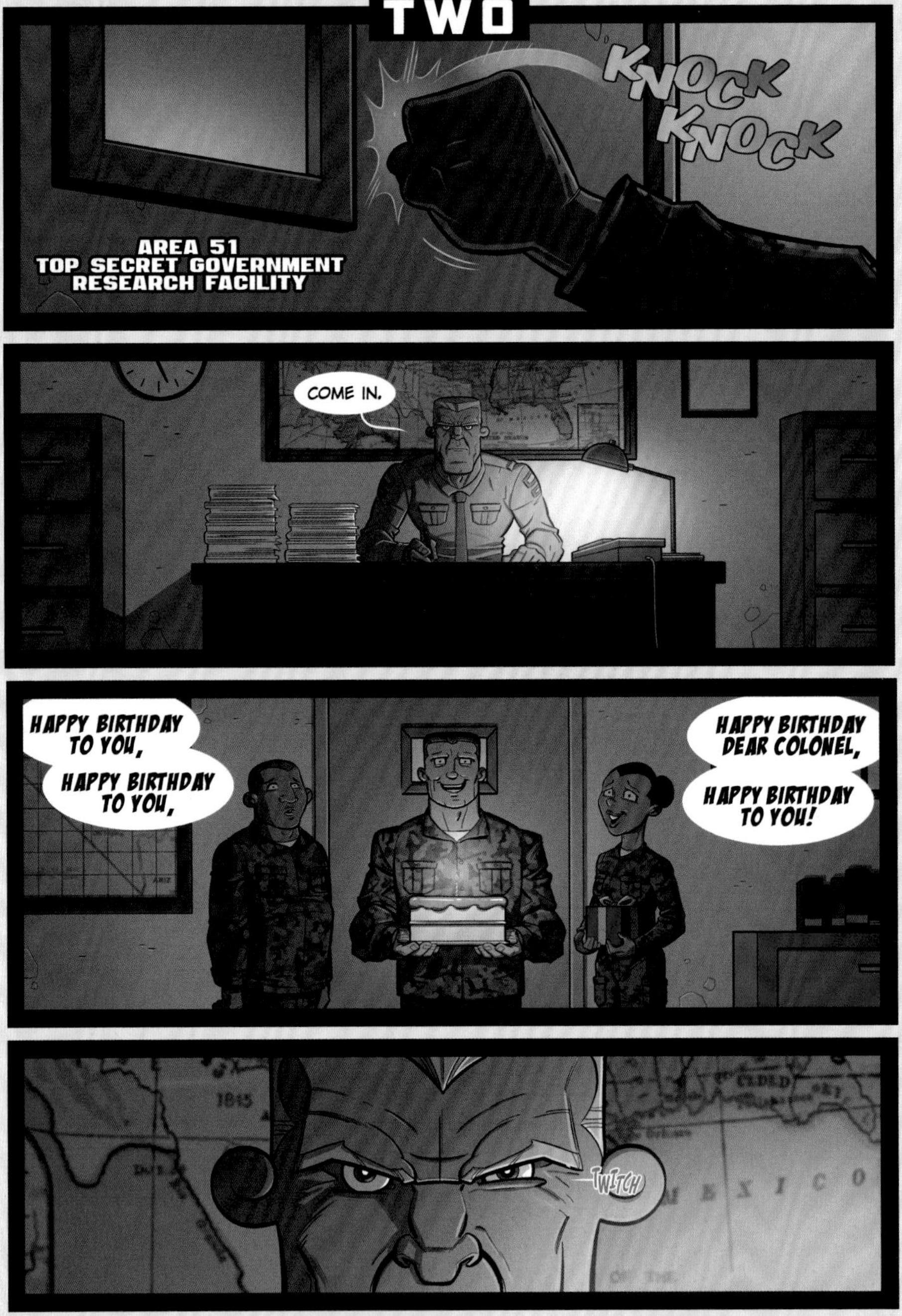
TWO
KNOCK KNOCK
AREA 51
TOP SECRET GOVERNMENT RESEARCH FACILITY
COME IN.
HAPPY BIRTHDAY TO YOU,
HAPPY BIRTHDAY TO YOU,
HAPPY BIRTHDAY DEAR COLONEL,
HAPPY BIRTHDAY TO YOU!
TWITCH

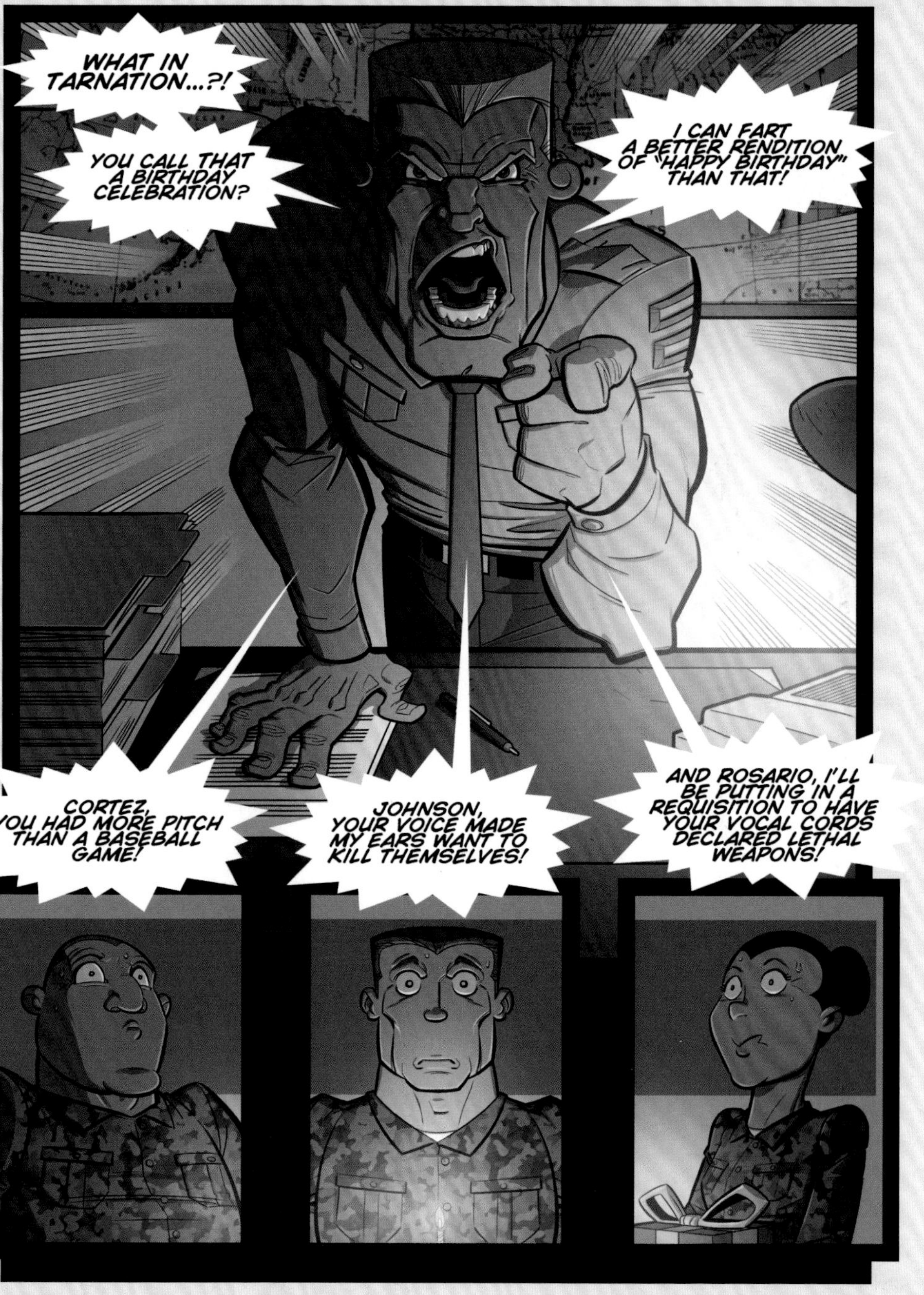
WHAT IN TARNATION...?!
YOU CALL THAT A BIRTHDAY CELEBRATION?
I CAN FART A BETTER RENDITION OF "HAPPY BIRTHDAY" THAN THAT!
CORTEZ, YOU HAD MORE PITCH THAN A BASEBALL GAME!
JOHNSON, YOUR VOICE MADE MY EARS WANT TO KILL THEMSELVES!
AND ROSARIO, I'LL BE PUTTING IN A REQUISITION TO HAVE YOUR VOCAL CORDS DECLARED LETHAL WEAPONS!

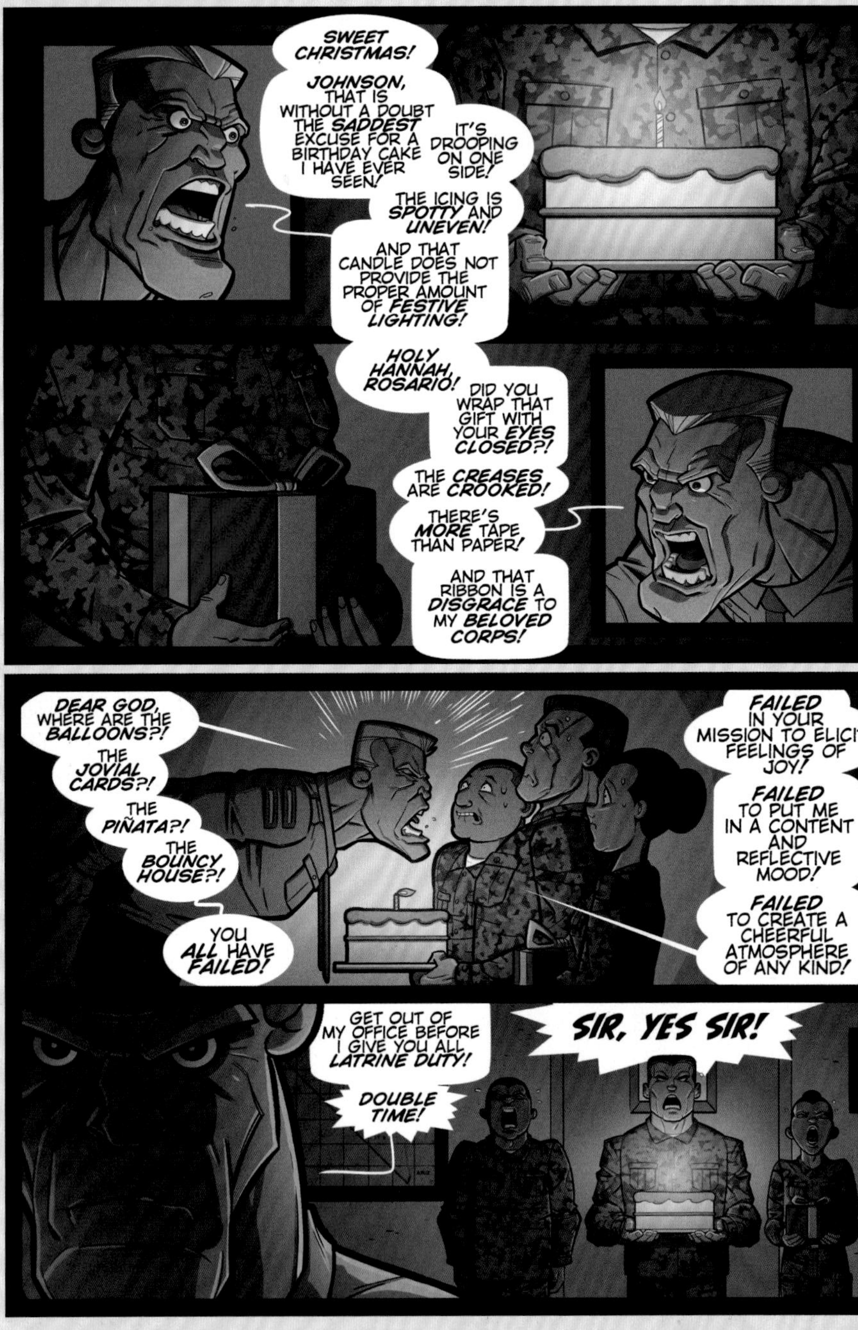
SWEET CHRISTMAS!
JOHNSON, THAT IS WITHOUT A DOUBT THE SADDEST EXCUSE FOR A BIRTHDAY CAKE I HAVE EVER SEEN!
IT'S DROOPING ON ONE SIDE!
THE ICING IS SPOTTY AND UNEVEN!
AND THAT CANDLE DOES NOT PROVIDE THE PROPER AMOUNT OF FESTIVE LIGHTING!
HOLY HANNAH, ROSARIO!
DID YOU WRAP THAT GIFT WITH YOUR EYES CLOSED?!
THE CREASES ARE CROOKED!
THERE'S MORE TAPE THAN PAPER!
AND THAT RIBBON IS A DISGRACE TO MY BELOVED CORPS!
DEAR GOD, WHERE ARE THE BALLOONS?!
THE JOVIAL CARDS?!
THE PIÑATA?!
THE BOUNCY HOUSE?!
YOU ALL HAVE FAILED!
FAILED IN YOUR MISSION TO ELICIT FEELINGS OF JOY!
FAILED TO PUT ME IN A CONTENT AND REFLECTIVE MOOD!
FAILED TO CREATE A CHEERFUL ATMOSPHERE OF ANY KIND!
GET OUT OF MY OFFICE BEFORE I GIVE YOU ALL LATRINE DUTY!
DOUBLE TIME!
SIR, YES SIR!

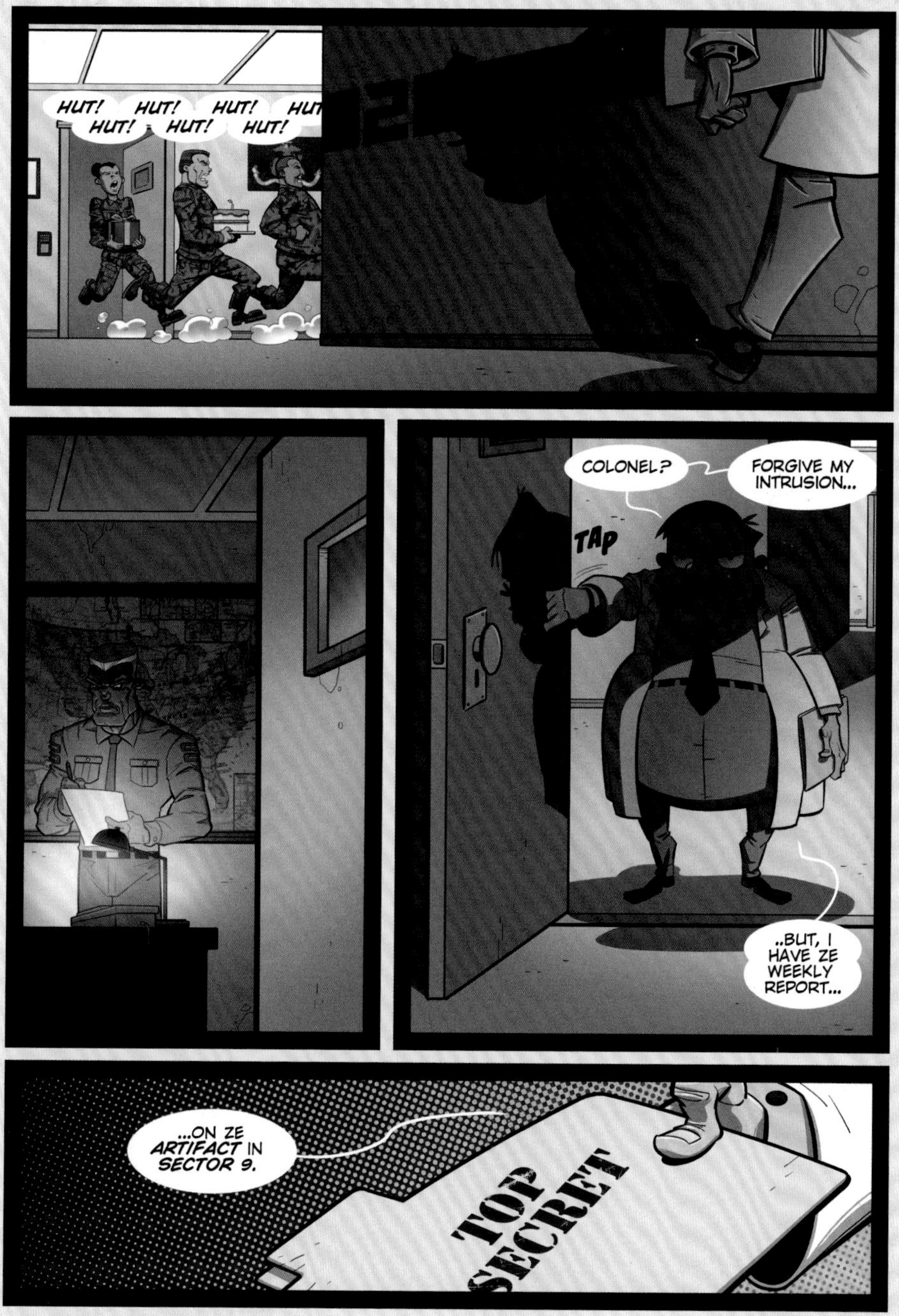
HUT! HUT! HUT! HUT! HUT! HUT! HUT
COLONEL?
FORGIVE MY INTRUSION...
TAp
..BUT, I HAVE ZE WEEKLY REPORT...
...ON ZE *ARTIFACT* IN SECTOR 9.
TOP SECRET

The scientist closed the door behind him, leaving the old soldier alone with silence and his work.

His work. Was that what this was? he wondered. Colonel Killshot looked down at the folders and paperwork on his desk and felt a bitter resentment begin to rise.

He was a soldier, a lifelong military man, highly decorated during Operation Desert Storm and the invasion of Iraq.

Now look at him, guarding useless artifacts and babysitting a bunch of nerdy scientists. He was bored beyond comprehension, but he really didn't have much of a choice. It was either this, or retirement.

His birthday today drove that point home all the more.

Killshot longed to return to action, but he knew that just wasn't in the cards for him these days.

The old soldier sat down heavily in his chair and moved the papers around on his desk, deciding what he would look at first.

"What have we here," the colonel grumbled, the title stamped on the cover of the top secret folder catching his eye. "Atomic Frenchie," he muttered, opening the file. "What the heck is that supposed to mean?"

And he began to read.

♥

The ghost of Erasmus Peckinpah floated about four inches above the Eldorado's back seat, hands clasped behind his head.

"This is one smooth machine, ain't it, fellas?" the ghost asked. "Cars today ain't got nothin' on the classics."

"I've never been in a car without my tank," OB said, referring to the aquarium that he lived in back at Tom and LeeAnne's house. "I think it's amazing."

Kirby did not care to comment. He liked the vehicle. It was serving its purpose well, especially with the upgrades he'd installed. Upgrades that he would need to uninstall once they returned from their mission.

The car had been a dream project for Tom, Kirby's "owner." The human tinkered with it every chance he had. The fact that the Frenchie had it up and running in a matter of hours was not for Tom to know. The Eldorado would be returned as Kirby had found it—a worthless ton of steel, plastic, rubber, and glass.

"Hey Kirb, are you sure Tom and LeeAnne aren't gonna miss us and the car?" OB asked.

"I assure you, they will not," the Frenchie said, recalling how he had ensured their absence would go unnoticed.

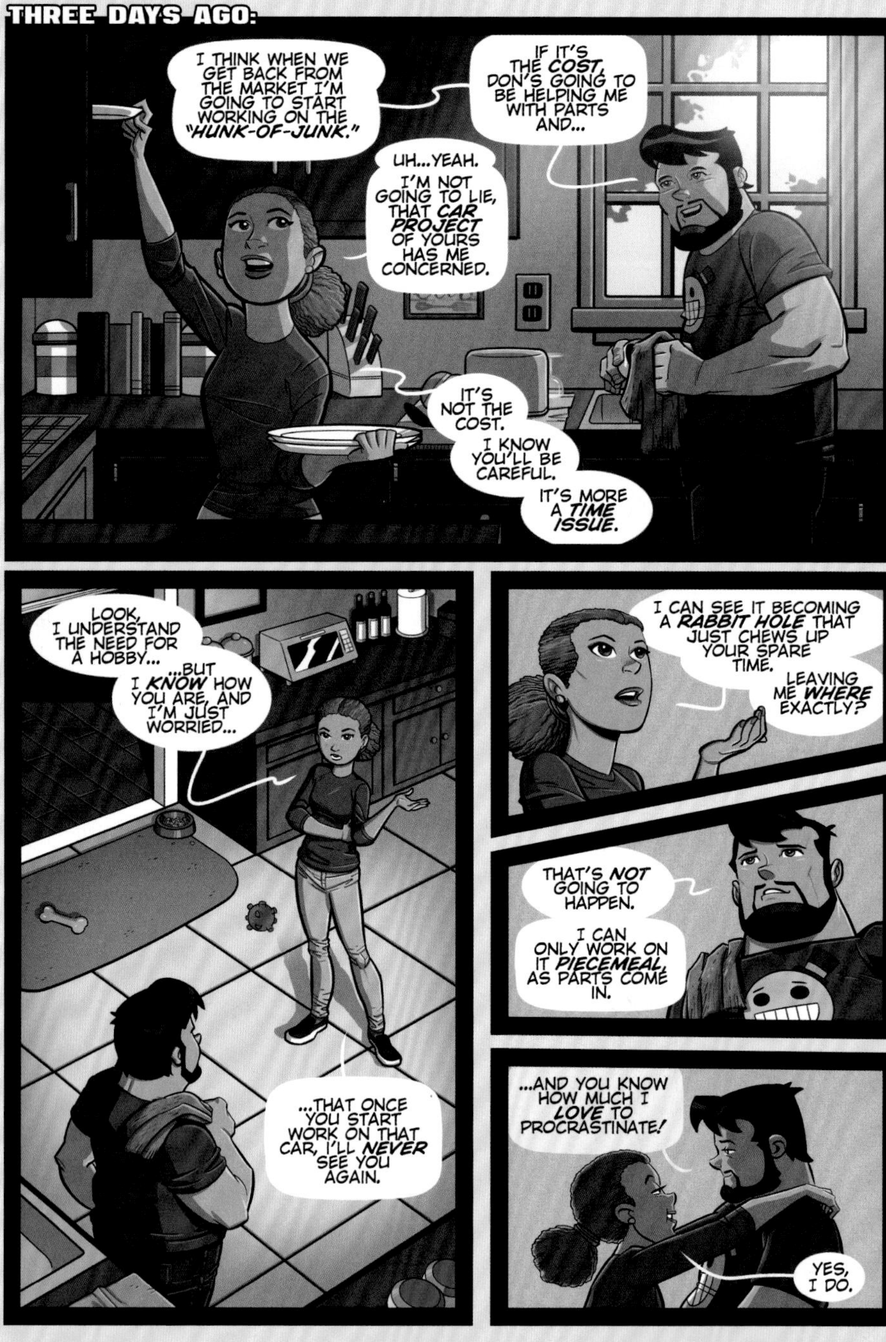
THREE DAYS AGO:
I THINK WHEN WE GET BACK FROM THE MARKET I'M GOING TO START WORKING ON THE "HUNK-OF-JUNK."
UH...YEAH.
I'M NOT GOING TO LIE, THAT CAR PROJECT OF YOURS HAS ME CONCERNED.
IF IT'S THE COST, DON'S GOING TO BE HELPING ME WITH PARTS AND...
IT'S NOT THE COST.
I KNOW YOU'LL BE CAREFUL.
IT'S MORE A TIME ISSUE.
LOOK, I UNDERSTAND THE NEED FOR A HOBBY...
...BUT I KNOW HOW YOU ARE, AND I'M JUST WORRIED...
...THAT ONCE YOU START WORK ON THAT CAR, I'LL NEVER SEE YOU AGAIN.
I CAN SEE IT BECOMING A RABBIT HOLE THAT JUST CHEWS UP YOUR SPARE TIME.
LEAVING ME WHERE EXACTLY?
THAT'S NOT GOING TO HAPPEN.
I CAN ONLY WORK ON IT PIECEMEAL, AS PARTS COME IN.
...AND YOU KNOW HOW MUCH I LOVE TO PROCRASTINATE!
YES, I DO.

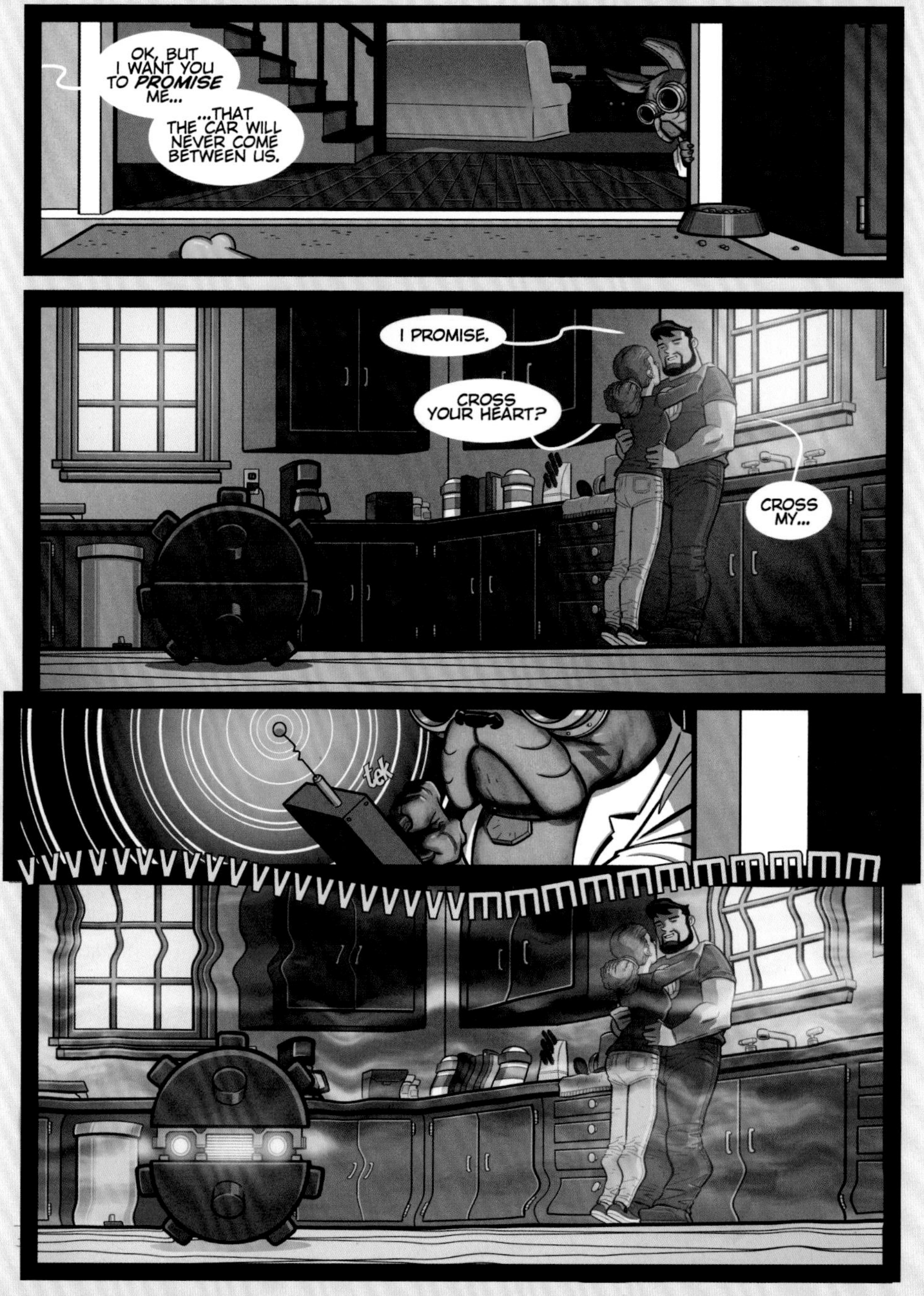
OK, BUT I WANT YOU TO PROMISE ME...
...THAT THE CAR WILL NEVER COME BETWEEN US.
I PROMISE.
CROSS YOUR HEART?
CROSS MY...
tek
VVVVVVVVVVVVVVVVVVVVVVVVVVVVVVVVMMMMMMMMMMMMMMMMM

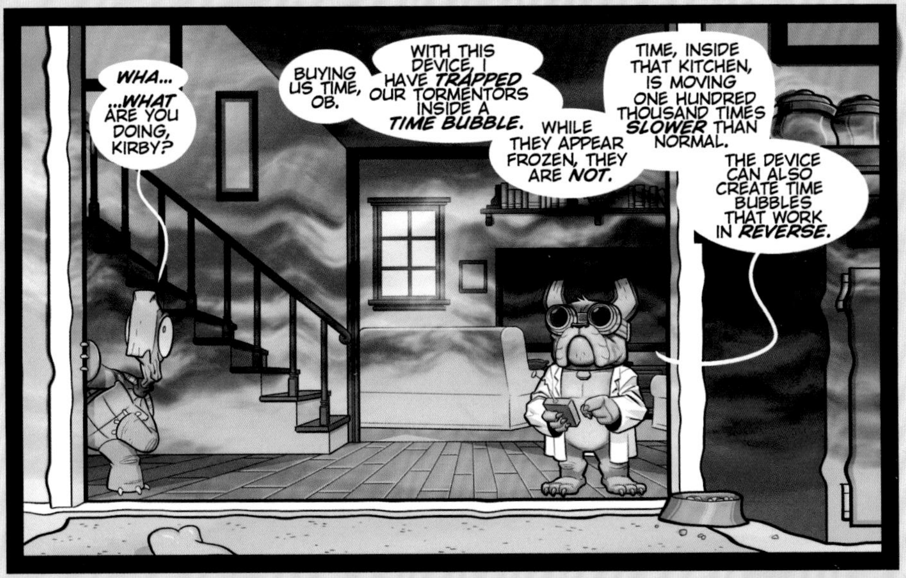
WHA... ...WHAT ARE YOU DOING, KIRBY?
BUYING US TIME, OB.
WITH THIS DEVICE, I HAVE TRAPPED OUR TORMENTORS INSIDE A TIME BUBBLE.
WHILE THEY APPEAR FROZEN, THEY ARE NOT.
TIME, INSIDE THAT KITCHEN, IS MOVING ONE HUNDRED THOUSAND TIMES SLOWER THAN NORMAL.
THE DEVICE CAN ALSO CREATE TIME BUBBLES THAT WORK IN REVERSE.

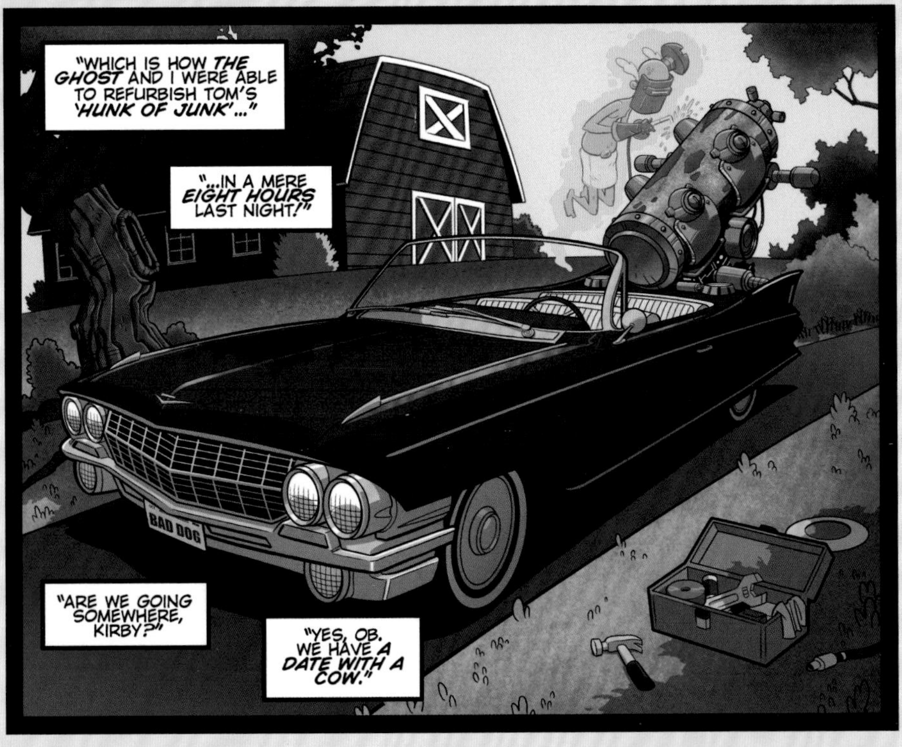
"WHICH IS HOW THE GHOST AND I WERE ABLE TO REFURBISH TOM'S 'HUNK OF JUNK'..."
"...IN A MERE EIGHT HOURS LAST NIGHT!"
BAD DOG
"ARE WE GOING SOMEWHERE, KIRBY?"
"YES, OB. WE HAVE A DATE WITH A COW."

"When we return, it will be as if no time has passed for them," Kirby explained.

"That's good," OB said, relaxing in the passenger seat. "I'd hate to have them worrying about us."

"Should be nothin' but smooth sailin' until we hit Area 51," Erasmus said from the back seat. "I might even take a little snooze until we . . ."

They were suddenly besieged by sound. Roaring motors surrounded them on all sides.

Kirby saw them reflected in the rearview and side mirrors and knew instantly what was happening.

They were under attack.

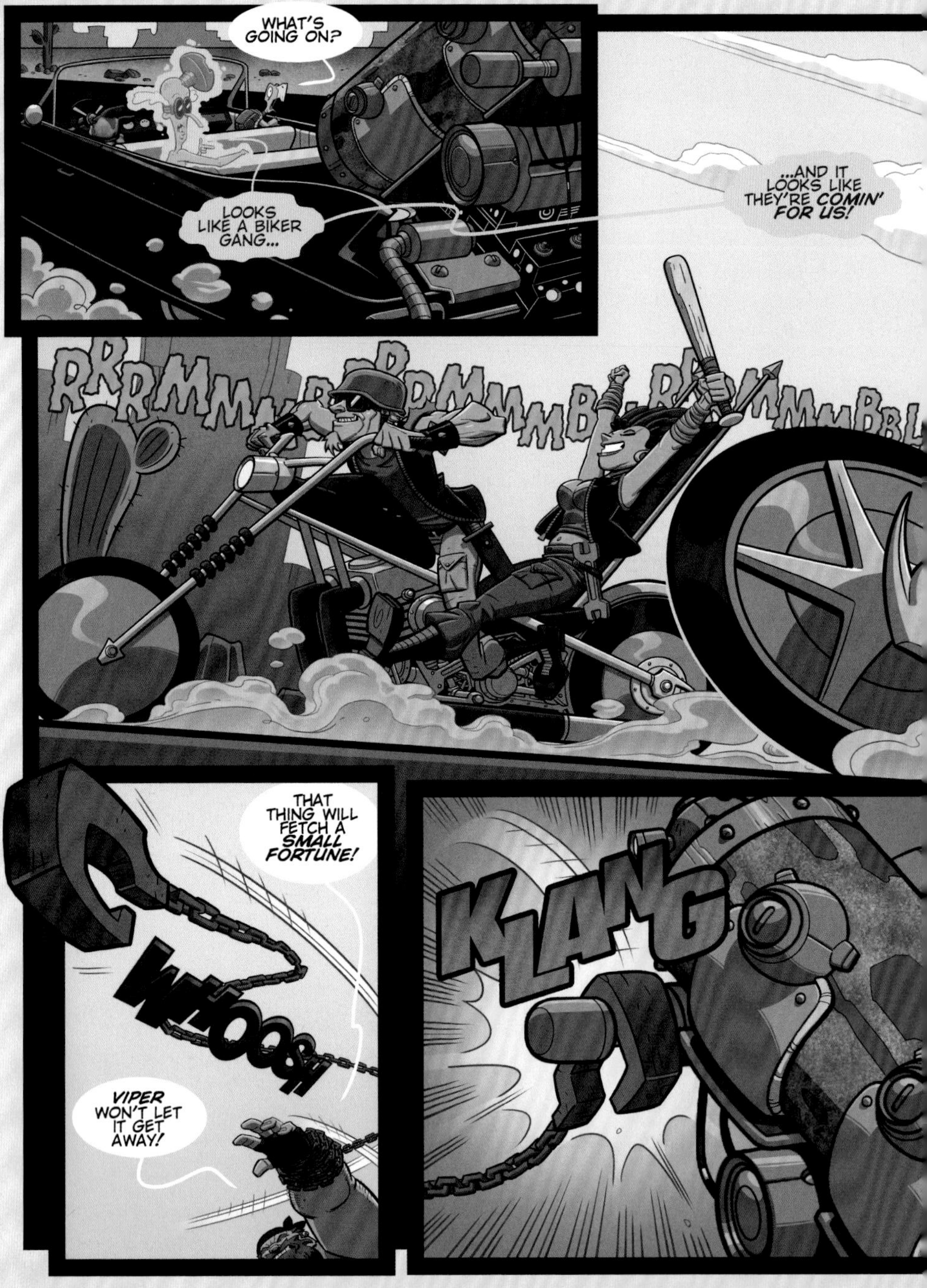

WHAT'S GOING ON?
LOOKS LIKE A BIKER GANG...
...AND IT LOOKS LIKE THEY'RE COMIN' FOR US!
RRRMMMBL RRMMMMBL RRMMMMBBL
THAT THING WILL FETCH A SMALL FORTUNE!
WHOOSH
VIPER WON'T LET IT GET AWAY!
KLANG

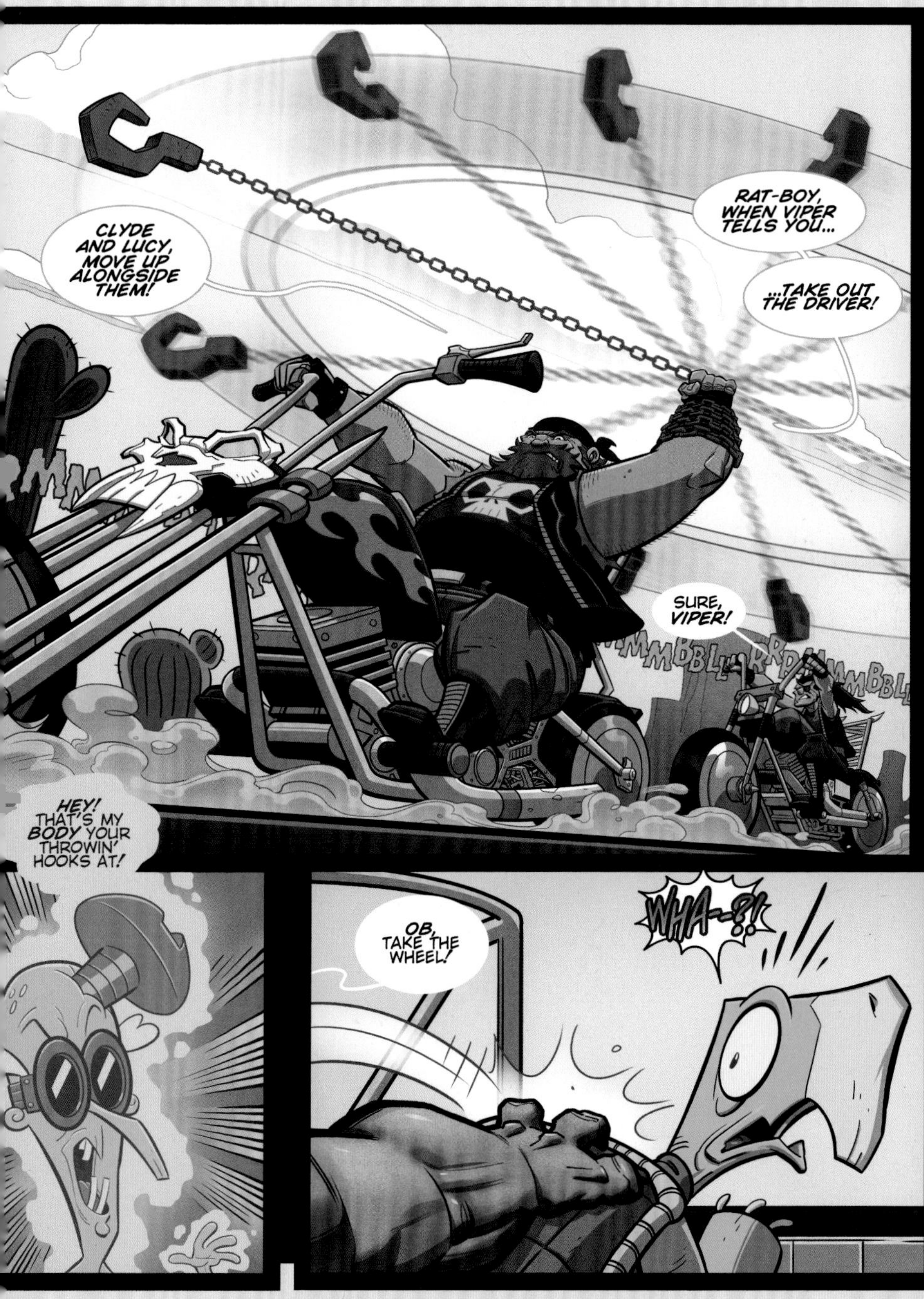
CLYDE AND LUCY, MOVE UP ALONGSIDE THEM!
RAT-BOY, WHEN VIPER TELLS YOU...
...TAKE OUT THE DRIVER!
SURE, VIPER!
HEY! THAT'S MY BODY YOUR THROWIN' HOOKS AT!
OB, TAKE THE WHEEL!
WHA--?!

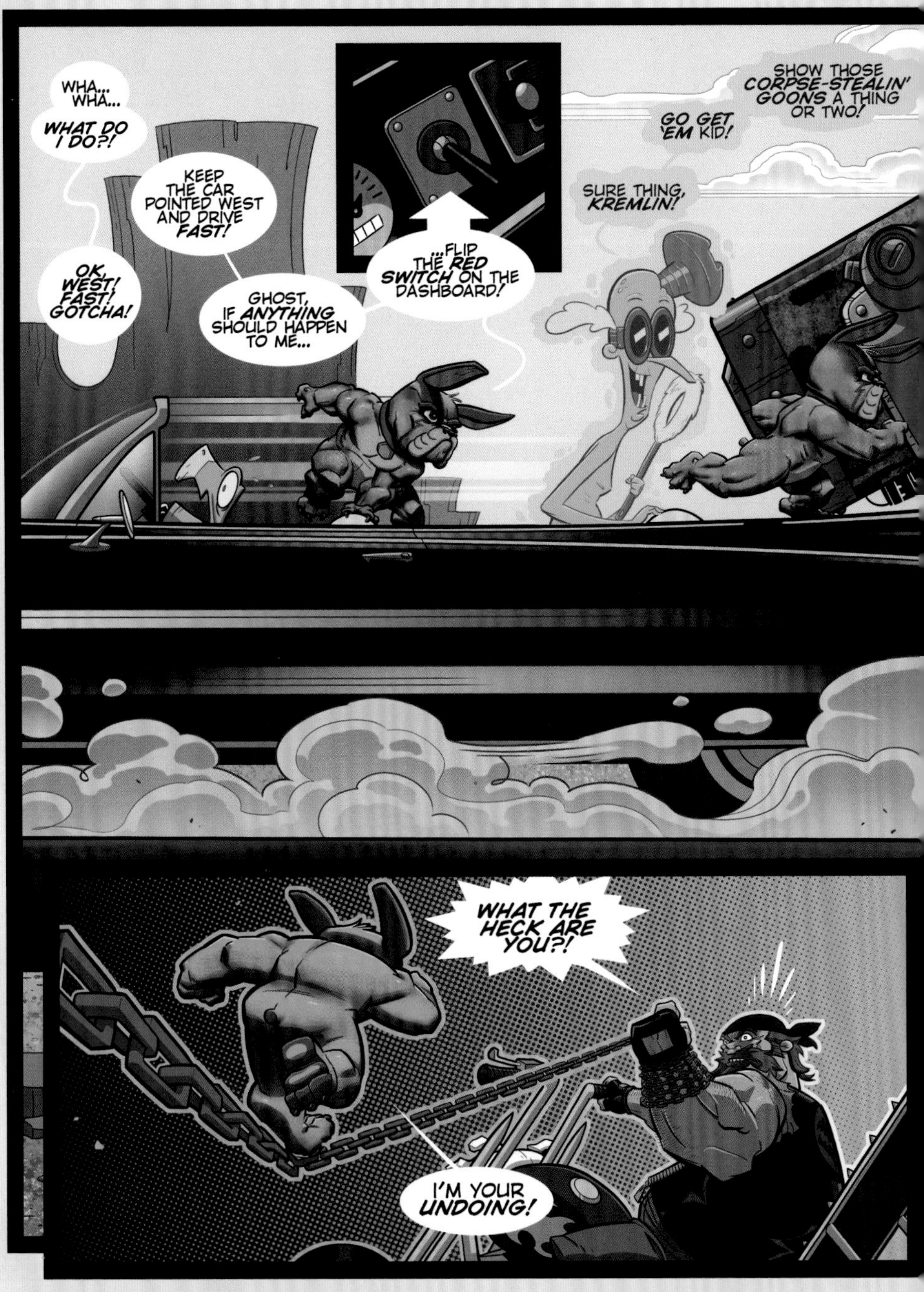
WHA... WHA...
WHAT DO I DO?!
KEEP THE CAR POINTED WEST AND DRIVE FAST!
OK, WEST! FAST! GOTCHA!
GHOST, IF ANYTHING SHOULD HAPPEN TO ME...
...FLIP THE RED SWITCH ON THE DASHBOARD!
GO GET 'EM KID!
SHOW THOSE CORPSE-STEALIN' GOONS A THING OR TWO!
SURE THING, KREMLIN!
WHAT THE HECK ARE YOU?!
I'M YOUR UNDOING!

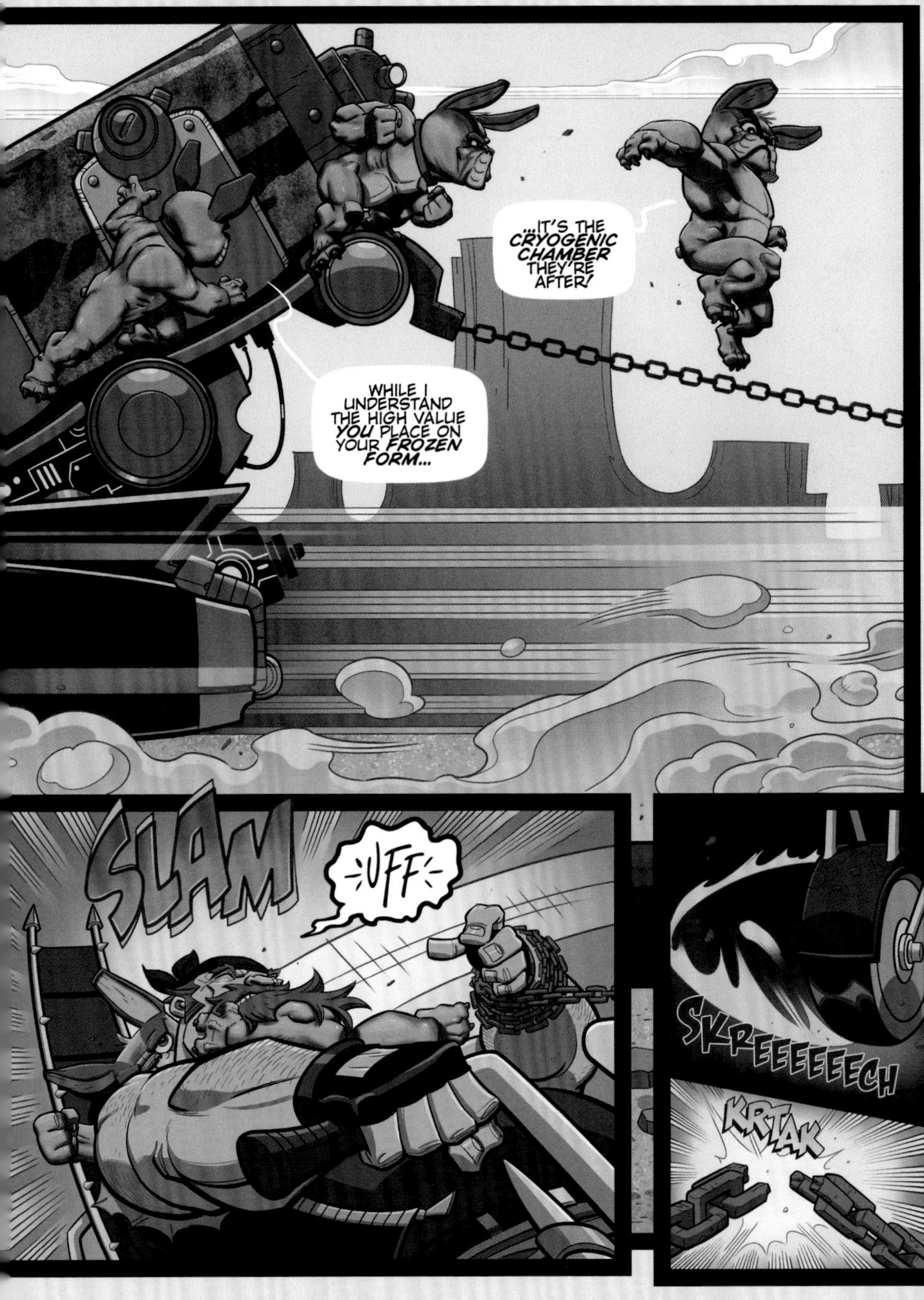
...IT'S THE CRYOGENIC CHAMBER THEY'RE AFTER!
WHILE I UNDERSTAND THE HIGH VALUE YOU PLACE ON YOUR FROZEN FORM...
SLAM
UFF
SKREEEEEEECH
KRTAK

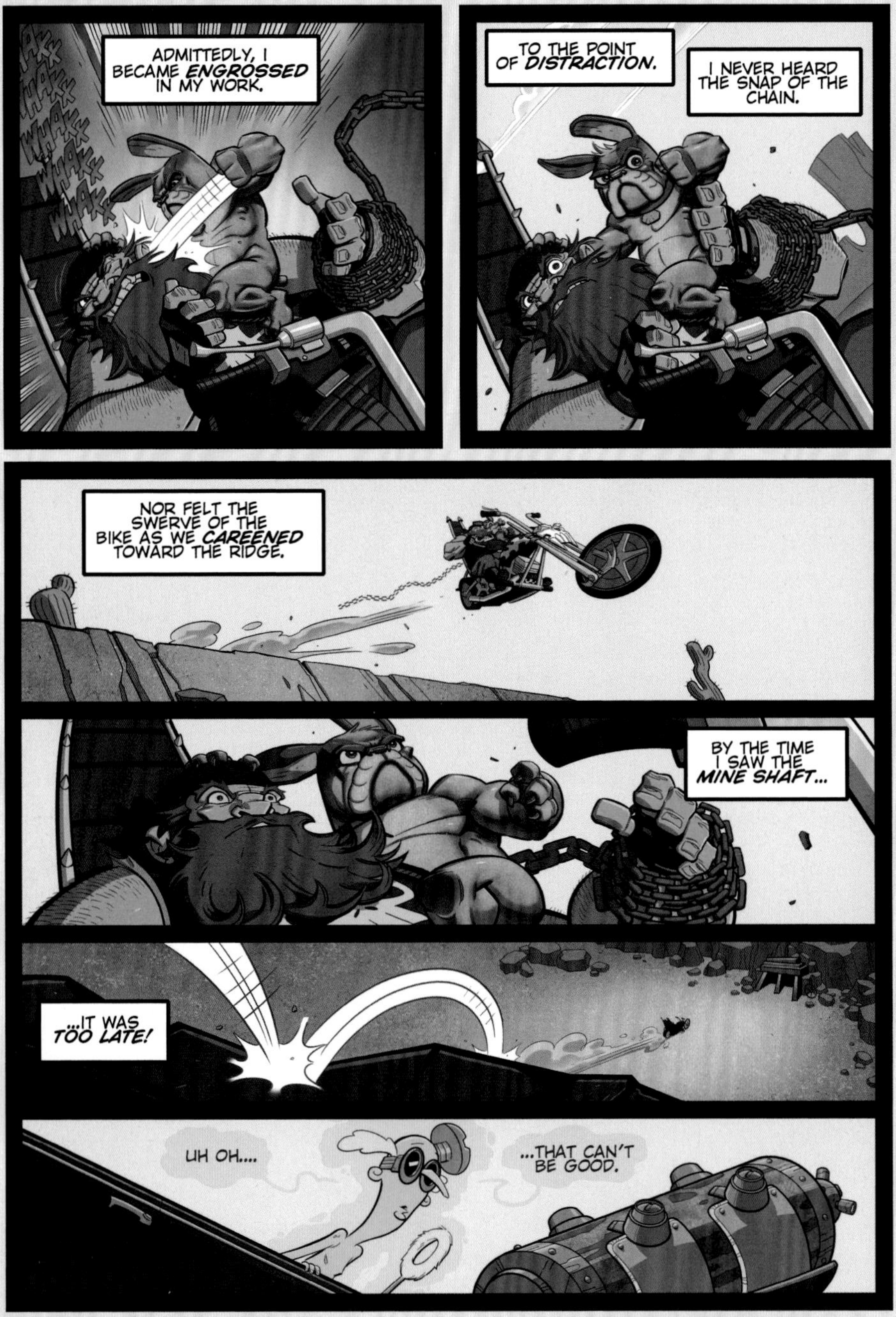
WHAKK WHAKK WHAKK WHAKK WHAKK
ADMITTEDLY, I BECAME ENGROSSED IN MY WORK.
TO THE POINT OF DISTRACTION.
I NEVER HEARD THE SNAP OF THE CHAIN.
NOR FELT THE SWERVE OF THE BIKE AS WE CAREENED TOWARD THE RIDGE.
BY THE TIME I SAW THE MINE SHAFT...
...IT WAS TOO LATE!
UH OH....
...THAT CAN'T BE GOOD.

At breakneck speed, the out-of-control motorcycle raced through the entrance to a long-abandoned mine.

"This should be interesting," Kirby muttered beneath his breath as Viper screamed in the sudden darkness.

And then they began to fall.

♥

"Holy moly, a mine shaft!" Erasmus shouted. He was watching Kirby and the biker disappear into the mine through the back window of the speeding Eldorado. "I haven't seen one of them since, well . . . ever!"

"What mine shaft?" OB screamed, still driving the car and trying to get away from the remaining bikers.

"Kostner was pretty specific about what we were supposed to do if he went off radar," Erasmus said, floating up into the front of the car with the turtle.

"I'm worried about the mine shaft!" OB screamed.

"Old news, shell-boy," Erasmus said, scrutinizing the red switch that Kirby had pointed out.

The biker gang was converging again, the roars of their motorcycles filling the car.

"They're trying to run us off the road!" OB danced nervously in the driver's seat, steering wheel clutched tightly in his tiny turtle claws.

"No sense putting it off any longer," Erasmus said, extending a crooked, ghostly finger toward the switch and giving it a . . .

Flick!

"Huh . . . nothing," Erasmus said, looking around the vehicle for signs of something—anything!

"Well, it better do something quick, because we're about to be . . ."

There was a sudden flash and a strange humming sound that even the ghost found bothersome.

"Ouch!" he squealed, sticking a finger inside one of his large ears and giving it a wiggle.

"Look!" OB squealed, stretching his turtle neck closer to the windshield.

The bikers were swerving uncontrollably, some crashing into each other, while others went off the road.

"What's gotten into them?" Erasmus asked. The sound still vibrating in the air made him wince as he watched the bikers, confusion spreading across their filthy faces, and then he heard the question.

"Where did it go?" one of the bikers shouted.

"I haven't the foggiest!" cried another. "It was here, and then *poof*!"

Erasmus began to cackle crazily.

"What's so funny?" OB asked, still trying to maneuver the old car away from the stupefied bikers.

"I know what that button did," the ghost of the mad scientist announced triumphantly. "And I have to say, it's something I wish I had come up with."

"What is it?"

"We're invisible, shell-boy," Erasmus said. "Kornel must've installed a cloaking device while he was making all the other repairs and upgrades."

The ghost looked out the back window and saw that the bikers were regrouping and riding off. No sense chasing after a car they could no longer see.

"They're leaving! We got away!"

OB steered the car over to the side of the lonely road and brought it to a stop.

"I'm gonna have a heart attack," the little turtle gasped.

"Just take deep breaths and stay calm," Erasmus told him. "No need to get yourself all worked up."

"What about Kirby?" OB asked between gulps of air. "Did you say he went down a mine shaft?" The turtle's breathing was becoming more labored, and tiny sparks of electricity began to dance around his head.

"Pull it together, kid!" Erasmus ordered, remembering that the last time the turtle was upset, he'd transformed into a bolt of lightning. "We don't need you changing into something that could wreck the car! Think of a cool mountain spring," he suggested. "Or how about a cold rock with a nice sunlamp! How's that?" he asked, not really sure exactly what a turtle would find relaxing.

"Too late! I think something's gonna happen!" OB announced. The sparks around his head began to form a swirling crown of crackling embers.

"Oh jeez!" Erasmus drifted away from the turtle. "Why do I think this is gonna hurt?"

OB opened the door and fell out onto the side of the road.

Erasmus braced himself for the inevitable.

The ghost waited.

If he could have held his breath, he would have.

But nothing happened.

"Hey!" he yelled. "You okay? Why didn't you explode or turn to dust or lava or something?"

When he didn't get an answer, Erasmus cautiously floated across the seat and out of the still open driver's side door to find OB lying in the sand. The turtle appeared to be snoring.

"Huh, that's an odd superpower!" Erasmus admonished, hands upon his hips. "And here I was thinking you were gonna blow like Vesuvius."

But then he noticed . . .

"Wait a second." He leaned closer to OB, examining the back of the turtle's neck. A feathered dart protruded from the leathery skin—a tranquilizer dart.

"Now where'd that come from?" the ghost muttered. He reached down to pluck the object from his friend's neck. "Usually stuff like this is shot from a . . ."

The desert was suddenly alive with activity, as what had looked like cacti and rocks revealed themselves to be heavily armed soldiers in disguise.

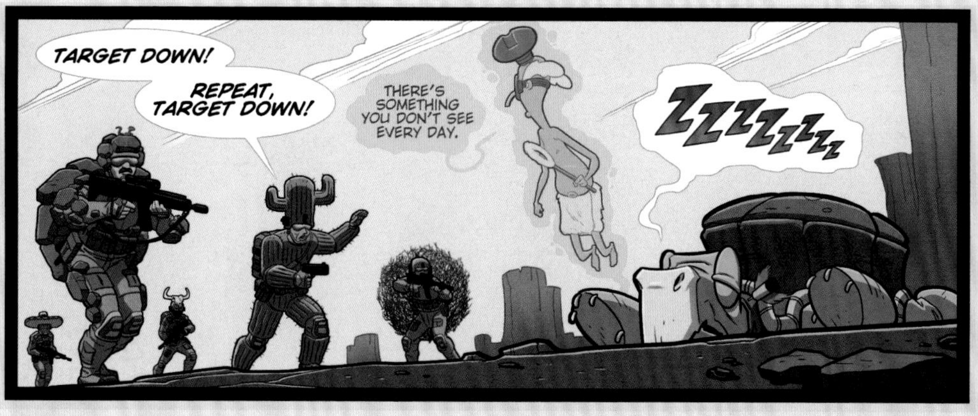
TARGET DOWN!
REPEAT, TARGET DOWN!
THERE'S SOMETHING YOU DON'T SEE EVERY DAY.
ZZZZZZZZ

They converged upon the sleeping turtle, aiming their weapons while one of their own knelt and scooped him into a pet carrier.

"Hey! Take him out of there at once!" Erasmus bellowed, hauling back a spindly arm and punching one of the soldiers in the helmet. His arm crumpled like an accordion, and the soldiers didn't even notice his presence.

The sound was sudden and loud, and for a moment Erasmus thought the bikers were back. But he quickly realized that the sound was much louder than motorcycle engines . . .

And it was coming from above.

He looked to the sky and saw a huge military helicopter hovering above them, a large mechanical claw descending from its belly.

"This cannot be good."

The mad scientist watched as the claw locked onto the Eldorado and began to lift it, and the cryo-chamber, up into the sky. Immediately, the soldiers returned to their camouflaged vehicles, pet carrier in tow, and followed the helicopter as it flew off.

"Oh yeah, not good at all," Erasmus said, slowly scrubbing his naked back with his ghostly brush as he attempted to figure out what he should do next.

THREE

Defying the laws of physics, the motorcycle remained perfectly balanced over the rocky ledge of a seemingly bottomless ravine.

HMMMM...
...PRECARIOUS, WOULDN'T YOU AGREE?

"Viper can't believe the situation you've put him in!" the biker yelled, spinning ever so slightly from his chain.

"The situation that *I've* put *you* in?" Kirby replied. "Exactly who attacked whom?"

"You couldn't just give us the refrigerator and let us be on our way! Oh, noooooooooooooooo! You had to fight back and make Viper look bad in front of his bros!"

"I'm sure you were doing a good job of that before I came on the scene," Kirby sniped.

"When Viper gets his hands on you, doggie, he's gonna make you wish you'd just pulled over and given us the fridge. Viper is gonna show you the true meaning of playing dead."

Kirby slowly tilted his body to one side and the bike began to tip.

Viper panicked. "Nice doggie! Nice! Stay still . . . please!"

"As you can see," said Kirby, "I hold your miserable life in my paws."

"Yeah, yeah, okay, okay! So . . . so what're you gonna do?"

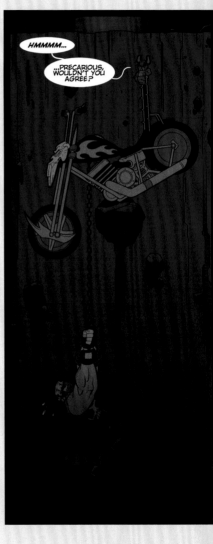

It was a good question, considering the current situation.

"Listen very closely," Kirby instructed. "There is only one way that we're getting out of this precarious predicament alive."

"Okay," the biker answered. "If Viper has to."

"Viper has to," Kirby said. "Now give me your belt."

"What?!"

"You heard me! Your belt, toss it up to me if you want to live."

Viper began to argue when the bike shifted suddenly, reminding him just how little choice he had in the matter. Carefully—oh so carefully—with one hand, he undid the buckle of his belt. Then slowly—oh so slowly—he pulled the leather belt through the loops of his jeans and out.

"Got it," he announced proudly.

"Toss it up to me," Kirby commanded, leaning slightly forward and extending his paw. "Carefully! Balance must be maintained."

Viper cautiously pulled his arm back and sent the belt soaring upward toward the Frenchie's waiting paw.

"Got it," Kirby said, snatching the leather belt from the air. "Now give me your pants."

"My pants? Why would you . . . ?"

"Do I stutter, ruffian?" Kirby asked with an air of petulance. "If they were not a necessity to our survival, I would not require them."

"Okay, okay, Viper just don't understand what . . ."

"Now."

"All right already, Viper is doing it," Viper grumbled.

Carefully—oh so very carefully—he undid the button of the front of his jeans, slowly slid the zipper down, and cautiously—oh so very cautiously—began to maneuver himself out of them.

"Viper did it!" the biker finally exclaimed with a laugh that sounded as if he were on the verge of losing his mind. "HAHAHAHA!"

"Toss them up to me," Kirby ordered.

Again, Viper did as the Frenchie told him.

"Okay?" he asked. "Viper's arm is getting pretty tired . . ."

"Your boots," Kirby interrupted.

"What about them?"

"I need them."

"Both of them?"

"Of course both of them," Kirby snarled. "What would I do with only one? Fool."

The sweat was pouring from Viper's body. Removing his boots was going to be a real challenge. He took a deep breath, rubbed the sweat from the tips of his free hand on the front of his filthy T-shirt, then slowly—oh so slowly—reached for his left boot.

"HAHAHAHAHAHAHAHA!" Viper laughed, as he held up the boot.

"I'm guessing you were successful," Kirby said. "Toss it up to me and take the other off. Quickly. We're running out of time."

Viper tossed first the left boot to Kirby, then followed a few minutes later with the other worn and dusty boot.

The Frenchie deftly caught them both. "Thank you, I have everything I need," the dog muttered.

"Now what?" Viper asked.

Without a word, Kirby carefully placed the boots side by side on the seat in front of him. Then he took the biker's jeans and rolled them tightly, shoving them into the opening of one boot.

"Hey! Viper wants to know what's next."

Kirby wrapped the belt around the boots and cinched it tight. Then he held the package out over the ledge.

"Are you watching?" he asked the biker. And with that, Kirby dropped the bundle of Viper's clothes into the darkness of the ravine below.

Viper watched incredulously as his clothing passed him on its way to the bottom. "Why did you . . . ?" he managed with a squeak.

He looked up to see the French bulldog casually waving bye-bye. The biker's eyes bulged large enough to explode from his thick skull, and he let out a shriek that echoed throughout the chamber.

"Why you . . . pug-faced . . . rat dog!" were the only words that Kirby caught before the biker was on the move.

In a feat of incredible dexterity, Viper hauled himself up the chain and over the side of the ledge with murder in his bloodshot eyes. "Viper kill!" he roared.

Kirby took that as his signal to move and leapt from the bike, throwing its balance wildly off.

Viper landed upon the cycle as it slid over the side. The biker's expression going from insanity to *uh-oh* in an instant . . .

Priceless.

The bike disappeared over the edge, and Viper was about to as well when Kirby acted.

The muscular bulldog grabbed hold of the chain that had come loose of the cycle, wrapped it about his wrist, and planted his feet.

Viper was a porker for sure, and Kirby felt his feet slide across the rocky earth toward the cliff's edge, but eventually he came to a stop.

"Here we are again," Kirby said to Viper, who was back to square one, dangling over the abyss.

"Pull Viper up!" the biker screamed.

"Funny thing about that," Kirby said. "I thought we had an understanding, and yet you attacked me."

"You threw Viper's clothes over the cliff."

"That was incentive for you to save yourself," Kirby said.

"Oh," Viper answered.

"Pug-faced rat dog?" Kirby asked.

"Excuse me?"

"You called me a pug-faced rat dog."

"Yeah, guess Viper did," the biker said. "Viper was mad . . . didn't mean it. Sorry. Ah, could you pull Viper up now?"

"Hmmm, I'm afraid I must disagree," Kirby said. "I don't believe you were mad. I believe there is something inherently wrong with you."

"Viper is . . ." Viper started to explain.

"You attacked my friends and me, tried to steal my property, and then insulted me. That sounds an awful lot like bullying to me. I believe you are a big fat bully. Are you a big fat bully?"

"Grrrrrrrrr," Viper growled.

Kirby let a bit of the chain slip from his grasp.

"Yeah, yeah, Viper is!" the biker screamed.

"What? You are what?" Kirby taunted, peering over the side of the cliff at the red-faced biker looking up at him.

"Viper . . . Viper is a big fat bully!"

"And?"

"Uh . . . and a mean person . . . and Viper don't smell too good?"

"No," Kirby said, letting more of the chain go.

"Ahhh! What? What is Viper?"

"A teapot," Kirby said. "A little teapot to be precise."

"A teapot?"

Kirby nodded.

"Short and stout?"

"There you go," Kirby said with a nod. "I believe you know the song."

Viper glowered. If looks could kill, Kirby would have been dead 20 times over, but the biker was not gifted with such a power.

Kirby let the chain go even farther.

"Here is my handle, here is my spout!" Viper sang horribly. "When I get steamed up, hear my shout! Tip me over and pour me out! Okay? Happy now! Can you pull Viper up . . . please?"

Kirby considered the request.

"I guess," the Frenchie answered, and complied, hauling the biker up enough that the captive could use his stockinged feet to climb up over the edge.

"That wasn't so bad, was it?" Kirby asked, patting the top of the biker's bald head.

"Gonna," Viper gasped, "gonna . . . kill you!"

"Oh, we're back to that again?" Kirby was seriously considering pushing Viper back over when . . .

"Do you hear that?" the Frenchie asked, cocking one of his bat-like ears.

"Hear what?" Viper was slowly crawling to his feet.

What sounded like laugher echoed eerily throughout the cavern.

"That," Kirby said, turning in the direction of the cackling sounds of amusement.

In the distance, a section of the cavern had begun to brighten with an eerie blue glow.

"What the heck is that?" Viper asked, fear in his voice.

A ghostly figure drifted through the air toward them, laughing insanely as it drew closer.

“Is that a gho . . . gho . . .?” Viper began, but wasn’t able to finish, his naked knees knocking in terror.

“It is,” Kirby acknowledged, observing its long, pointed nose, its circular glasses, and the pickax sticking out from the top of its skull. “A ghostly prospector to be precise!”

OB dreamed of sugar beets.

The little turtle had never had the vegetable, but he had read about them once in a magazine and thought they sounded wonderful.

Sugar beets. Even the name sounded happy to him. Sugar beets.

The turtle giggled as the sugar beets danced around his head. He never knew that they could fly, but he shouldn’t have been surprised. Sugar beets were wonderful.

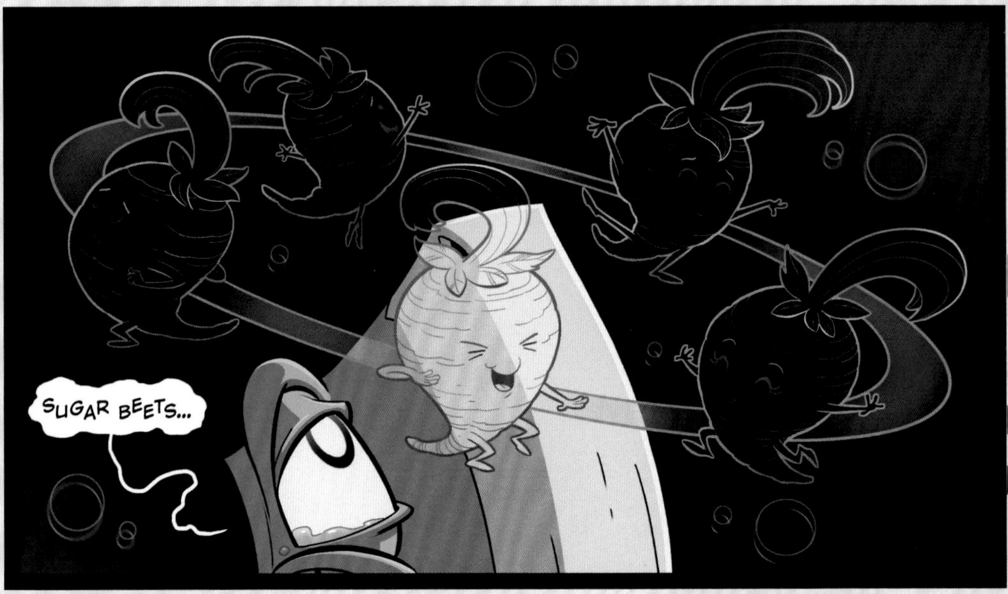
SUGAR BEETS...

"What's he smiling about?" asked one of the dancing beets. Its voice was much gruffer than OB would have imagined for a sugar beet.

"How can you tell he iz smiling?" asked another sugar beet.

"Look at his beak," answered the gruff one. "It's kinda bent upward. That's a smile for sure."

"I don't know, maybe it iz gas," offered the other.

"Naw, that's a smile."

"I vonder what for?"

"No clue."

"Tee-hee," giggled OB. "I'm smiling 'cause you guys are so awesome!"

"Is he talking about us?" asked Gruffy.

"I zink he is," answered the other.

"I think we should wake him up."

"Let me find ze antidote to ze sleep dart und . . ."

The sudden, thunderous bang caused OB to scream, his eyes flying open, the real world chasing away his dream of weightless, dancing sugar beets.

He saw where he was and felt instantly afraid.

The gruff army man banged again on the top of the plastic cage containing OB while a man in a lab coat looked on.

"Well zat certainly seemed to do ze trick," the lab coat man said.

"Thought it would," said the army guy.

OB could see, through the clear plastic walls of the cage, that he was in some sort of laboratory, though not half as cool as the one back in Strasburg where he lived. As he looked around, he saw the old Eldorado and a group of guys in white lab coats standing around it writing notes on clipboards.

The turtle gasped when he saw another group unhitching the cryo-chamber with Erasmus's body still inside. They placed the chamber on a gurney.

At first OB was afraid that his ghost friend's body might start to thaw, but then he remembered that Kirby had attached something called a cold fusion reactor so the chamber would stay frozen no matter the outside temperature.

Phew, the turtle thought, watching as the gurney was wheeled past him. What a relief.

"Who built that?" the army guy with the gruff voice asked, snapping OB's attention to him.

"My friend Kirby, sir."

"Your friend Kirby built it," the army guy said. "Does this Kirby have a last name?"

OB thought a minute. "Nope," he said, quickly shaking his head. "Just Kirby."

"Let me try, Colonel Killshot," said the lab coat man.

"Give it your best, Dr. Oddfellow. I don't have all day."

Oddfellow came forward, his wide face very close to the plastic side of OB's cage.

"Hello zhere, little fellow," the doctor said. OB could tell that he was just pretending to be nice. There was something about the man that gave the turtle the willies.

"Hello," OB replied to be polite.

"Zhat cryogenic freezing chamber zhat just passed." The man pointed in the direction the gurney had gone.

"Yes," answered OB.

"Zhere was a cold fusion reactor attached to it," the man said. He smiled, and OB found it so disturbing that he thought bugs were going to fall from the man's mouth. "Und you say someone name Kirby built it?"

"Yep, he did," OB said, nodding his turtle head.

"Und who is this . . . Kirby?" Dr. Oddfellow questioned.

"Why he's my best friend in the whole world," OB said, and then found himself becoming very sad, remembering he had no idea what had happened to his Frenchie friend.

"We're wasting time here," Colonel Killshot barked. "He's stalling, and I have no time for games. I say we use the extraction chair ASAP."

"Oh!" Dr. Oddfellow said excitedly. "It has been some time since we have used ze Brain Drain!"

"Brain Drain?" OB asked and gulped.

There was a flurry of activity at the back of the lab as two white-coated scientists wheeled a scary-looking chair closer.

"Get the little guy out of there and strap him in . . ." the colonel began. But he was interrupted as a soldier rushed into the lab.

"Sir, you're needed in Sector 9, sir!" he said, standing at attention and saluting his commanding officer. "Sir, it's urgent, sir!"

"Oh, horse nuggets," Colonel Killshot grumbled. He turned toward the door. "Pull everything that you can from the turtle's brainpan and give me a full report sooner rather than later," he barked as he marched out with his soldier.

"Vill do," Oddfellow called after the man, turning his attention back to OB.

"Okay zhen, little fellow," the doctor said, displaying that horrible excuse for a smile again. "Looks like it is just you and me now."

Gulp.

Something told OB that he might be in some trouble, and he wished he was dancing with sugar beets again.

The ghostly prospector was laughing so hard he was almost choking.

"That's the funniest durned situation I've seen in a dog's age. I should pay you two a penny each fer the entertainment!"

"So glad we could amuse you," Kirby said with a slight bow.

"Viper isn't around for anybody's amusement," the biker grumbled, angered by the words but still afraid of the floating apparition.

The ghost cocked his head as he drifted forward, studying Kirby.

"Now wait a durned minute," he said, lifting his glasses to study the Frenchie more closely.

"Yer a dog!" the ghostly prospector proclaimed, drifting backward through the air.

"I see we can't pull the wool over your eyes," Kirby said sarcastically.

The ghost surged toward them, and Viper let out a high-pitched shriek as he covered his face. Kirby stood unmoving.

"You gettin' smart with me, dog?" the prospector asked menacingly.

Kirby got up in the ghost's face. "What if I was?"

The two glowered at one another as Viper continued to cower in fear.

The prospector suddenly let out a whoop of laughter, grabbing his ghostly belly as it jiggled with hysteria.

"I like yer style, puppy dog!"

"Kirby," the Frenchie said.

"What'chu say?" the ghost asked him.

"My name is Kirby."

The ghost put his hands on his hips. "All right then, Kirby, my name is Jedidiah!" He stuck out his ghost hand for the Frenchie to shake.

"Jedidiah Peckinpah!"

"You don't say," Kirby said, taking the prospector's cold, ethereal hand in his.

"I does say," Jedidiah said proudly. "I does say too that I'm the best durned prospector in these here United States!"

A familiar voice called out from somewhere in the cave, catching Kirby's and the ghost's attention.

"Hello? Kurtland? Are you in here?"

"I wonder who that could be?" the Frenchie asked, already knowing.

Erasmus Peckinpah drifted into the cave, his own eerie glow lighting the way.

"Oh no!" Viper cried out, dropping to the ground and covering his head. "Another one!"

Erasmus floated closer. "Is this a party?" the ghostly mad scientist asked. "Thanks for inviting me!"

"Who in tarnation is this?" Jedidiah demanded.

Kirby looked from Erasmus to the phantom prospector.

"Excuse me?" Erasmus said, hands upon his hips. "Would somebody care to explain what's going on here?"

"Jedidiah Peckinpah, meet Erasmus J. Peckinpah," Kirby said.

The ghostly prospector floated closer to Erasmus. "You tryin' to tell me that this is kin?" Jedidiah asked the Frenchie.

"I am indeed."

Jedidiah scrutinized Erasmus with a cautious eye, moving in real close to inspect every inch of the mad scientist.

"Not too close there, Festus!" Erasmus said, attempting to push the other ghost away.

"Nope, I can't see it," Jedidiah said with a shake of his head. "There ain't no way in heck that this here is a Peckinpah!"

"Excuse me?" Erasmus exclaimed again. "And what exactly is that supposed to mean?"

"Come on, I'll show ya," Jedidiah told him.

And the two ghosts disappeared.

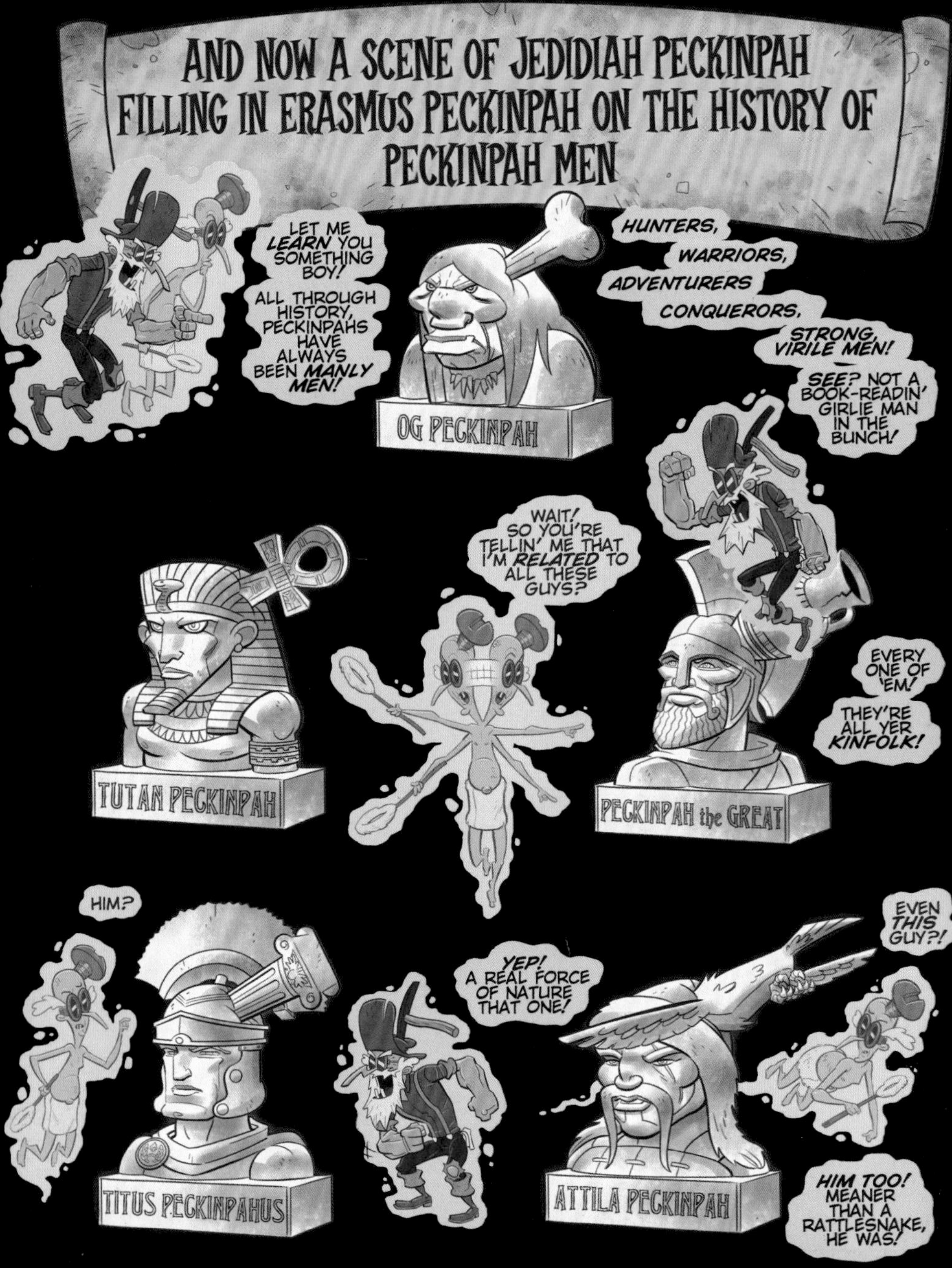
AND NOW A SCENE OF JEDIDIAH PECKINPAH FILLING IN ERASMUS PECKINPAH ON THE HISTORY OF PECKINPAH MEN
LET ME LEARN YOU SOMETHING BOY!
ALL THROUGH HISTORY, PECKINPAHS HAVE ALWAYS BEEN MANLY MEN!
OG PECKINPAH
HUNTERS,
WARRIORS,
ADVENTURERS
CONQUERORS,
STRONG, VIRILE MEN!
SEE? NOT A BOOK-READIN' GIRLIE MAN IN THE BUNCH!
WAIT! SO YOU'RE TELLIN' ME THAT I'M RELATED TO ALL THESE GUYS?
TUTAN PECKINPAH
EVERY ONE OF 'EM!
THEY'RE ALL YER KINFOLK!
PECKINPAH the GREAT
HIM?
YEP! A REAL FORCE OF NATURE THAT ONE!
TITUS PECKINPAHUS
EVEN THIS GUY?!
HIM TOO! MEANER THAN A RATTLESNAKE, HE WAS!
ATTILA PECKINPAH

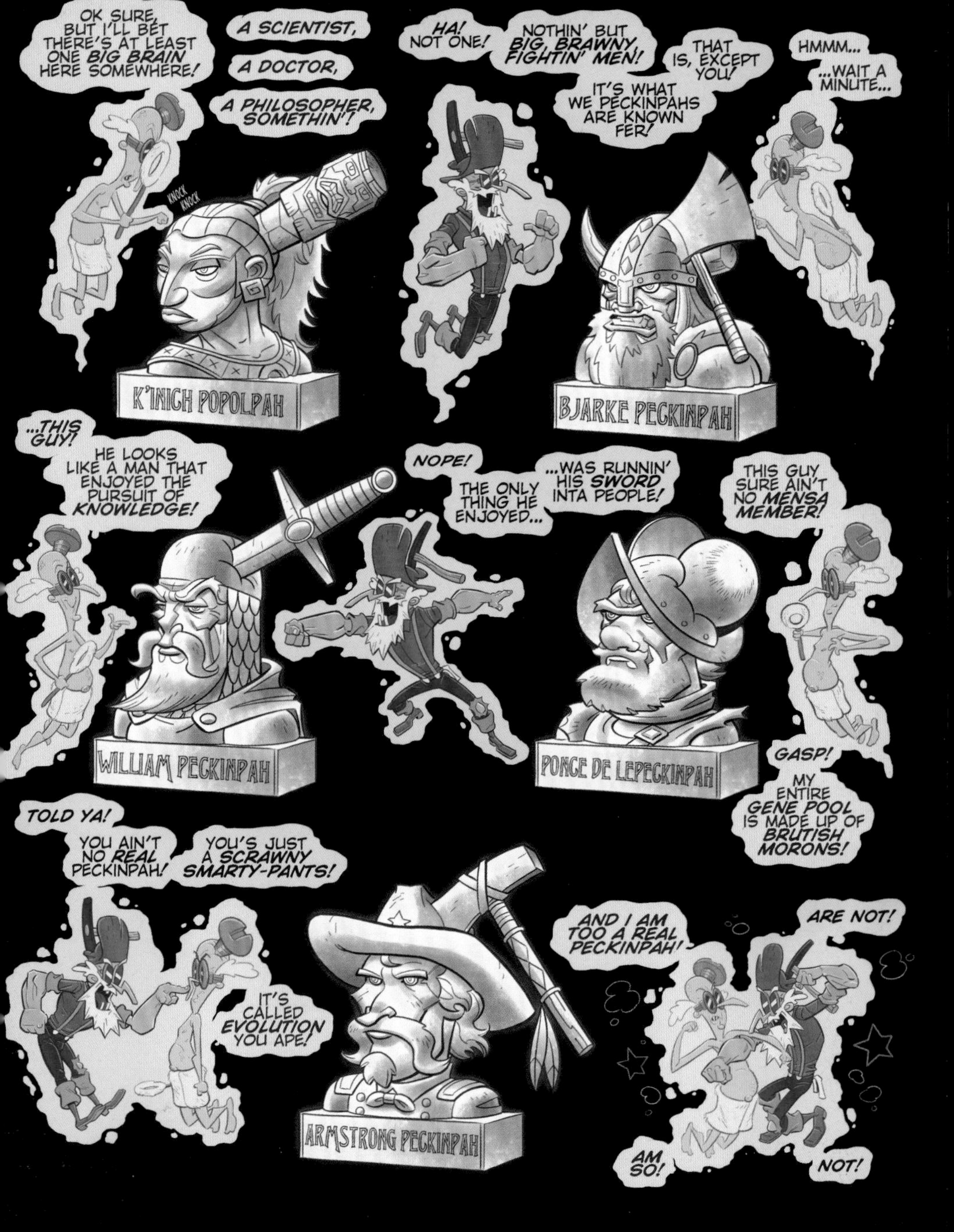

OK SURE, BUT I'LL BET THERE'S AT LEAST ONE BIG BRAIN HERE SOMEWHERE!
A SCIENTIST,
A DOCTOR,
A PHILOSOPHER, SOMETHIN'!
KNOCK KNOCK
HA! NOT ONE!
NOTHIN' BUT BIG, BRAWNY, FIGHTIN' MEN!
IT'S WHAT WE PECKINPAHS ARE KNOWN FER!
THAT IS, EXCEPT YOU!
HMMM...
...WAIT A MINUTE...
K'INICH POPOLPAH
BJARKE PECKINPAH
...THIS GUY!
HE LOOKS LIKE A MAN THAT ENJOYED THE PURSUIT OF KNOWLEDGE!
NOPE!
THE ONLY THING HE ENJOYED...
...WAS RUNNIN' HIS SWORD INTA PEOPLE!
THIS GUY SURE AIN'T NO MENSA MEMBER!
WILLIAM PECKINPAH
PONCE DE LEPECKINPAH
GASP!
MY ENTIRE GENE POOL IS MADE UP OF BRUTISH MORONS!
TOLD YA!
YOU AIN'T NO REAL PECKINPAH!
YOU'S JUST A SCRAWNY SMARTY-PANTS!
IT'S CALLED EVOLUTION YOU APE!
ARMSTRONG PECKINPAH
AND I AM TOO A REAL PECKINPAH!
ARE NOT!
AM SO!
NOT!

The Peckinpah ghosts appeared in the midst of battle.

"Look at you!" Jedidiah bellowed, swinging a fist at Erasmus. "With your girly arms, head screw, fancy towel, and scrub brush! I'd sooner change my name then think'a you as a Peckinpah!"

Erasmus ducked beneath the punch. "Listen, you muscle-bound illiterate," he warned. "I'd welcome being adopted if it meant that I didn't have to share a family tree with the likes of someone who makes a Neanderthal look like a Rhodes scholar!"

"What'chu call me, you lily-livered . . ."

Viper curled into a tight little ball on the ground, covering his head in mortal terror.

"Make the ghosts go away!" he wailed. "Viper is scared!"

Kirby forced himself between the specters.

"Gentlemen," the Frenchie said, looking at Erasmus, and then Jedidiah. "Please. Civility if you will."

"I'll show him the civil side of the back of my hand," Jedidiah said, raising his arm.

"Oh yeah?" crowed Erasmus. "I'll feed you a knuckle sandwich you'll be digesting for a month!"

"Listen to you with your fancy book talk! That ain't no towel you's wearin', that's a dress!"

"Why I oughta . . ." Erasmus began.

But Kirby had had enough. "Peckinpahs, if you please!" he barked, silencing the pair.

They stared at him now, instead of each other.

"There are matters of far greater importance to be addressed than this useless schoolyard banter."

"Oh yeah," Erasmus said. "About those greater matters."

"Go on," Kirby said, preparing himself for life's latest curveball.

"The Eldorado, OB, and the cryo-chamber with my body have been taken. I think it was the army . . . or I guess it could've been a special branch of the armed forces stationed at Area 51," he added thoughtfully.

"The deuce you say!" Kirby spat.

"Yeah, came out of nowhere and snatched them all up," Erasmus continued. "I tried to stop them but . . ."

"But you was probably too busy hidin' and cryin' fer your mama," Jedidiah finished for him with a laugh.

"That's it!" Erasmus cried, drawing back a spectral fist.

"Enough," Kirby snapped, his voice filled with a frightening authority. "I require complete and utter silence if I am to solve this conundrum."

Jedidiah laughed uproariously.

"What? This ain't no problem you can solve with yer brain, doggie!" the ghostly prospector proclaimed. "This is a problem you gotta solve with yer arms! These arms!"

Jedidiah showed off his impressive muscles, making them dance as he flexed. "And this pick!"

He then pulled the ghostly pickaxe from his ghostly skull.

"Now stand back. I don't want you girls gettin' hurt!"

And with those final words, the ghost of Jedidiah Peckinpah began to dig.

FOUR

OB watched in horror as Oddfellow approached with the shiny metal helmet.

Two of Oddfellow's scientists had taken the little turtle from the clear plastic carrier and strapped him into the chair.

"That's not gonna fit on this melon," OB tried to joke. "Think you're gonna have to try another size."

"No worries," Oddfellow replied. "One size fits all." He placed the helmet atop the turtle's tiny head. The little turtle began to breathe harder, terror making his little reptile heart beat faster.

"This isn't gonna hurt, is it?" OB asked nervously.

"Ja, it iz," the creepy scientist said as he tightened the strap beneath OB's chin. "A great deal, I am afraid."

"Look, this isn't necessary," the turtle pleaded. "You don't have to empty my head—and to tell you the truth, there isn't all that much in there anyway!"

"Mmmm," the scientist responded, checking the wire connections that trailed from the helmet to the mechanisms on the back of the chair.

"I'll make this super easy for you," OB said. "I had nothing to do with makin' the reactor thingy on the car! That's Kirby's invention 100 percent!"

"Ah yes, Kirby," Oddfellow repeated, tugging on the connections to make sure they were properly attached to the back of the helmet.

The scientist then turned toward the console to which the cables from the chair were connected. He fiddled with a few of the knobs, flipped some switches, and studied a paper printout trailing from a slit at the top of the machine.

"Your best friend in ze whole wide . . ." Oddfellow started, but stopped cold when he saw the small, muscular figure standing beside the chair. It was a dog but unlike any dog the scientist had ever seen. There was something about the way he stood and a great intensity in his brown eyes. Calling this powerful figure a dog was akin to calling a nuclear device a stick of dynamite.

"The turtle exaggerates," Kirby stated coldly as Oddfellow gasped. "I have no friends."

Kirby sprang, the tight Frenchie muscles in his legs propelling him into the air and toward the scientist. The man had no time to react before the Frenchie grabbed hold of his clothing and head-butted him unconscious.

Kirby rode the stupefied scientist to the floor and leapt from the man's doughy body to quickly assess the situation.

He watched Viper grab the other two scientists as they scrambled for the exit. The biker knocked their heads together and let them fall limply to the floor, then turned toward Kirby.

"Viper is helping only as long as it takes for him to get the heck out of here, dog," he said with a snarl.

The Frenchie caught movement from the corner of his eye and spun around to find an armed soldier aiming his weapon. Kirby's mind raced—was he fast enough to propel himself across the room before the man could fire his weapon?

But before he could test himself, Jedidiah passed through the wall next to the soldier. The ghost of the prospector loomed before the startled military man. Kirby watched as Jedidiah's face grew long and terrifying, his tongue wiggling about his elongated mouth like a python doing the samba. The soldier let out a wild shriek of panic and turned to run away, only to crash into another wall, knocking himself out cold.

The prospector cackled insanely, giving Kirby the thumbs up as he hovered over the stunned soldier.

"Am I glad to see you!" OB exclaimed as Kirby set about releasing the turtle from the chair.

"Erasmus and me didn't . . . wait a sec, have you seen Erasmus?" the turtle asked, suddenly concerned.

As if summoned by some magical spell, the ghost of the mad scientist flew up through the floor, fists cocked, ready for combat. The ghost of the scientist floated there, spinning in the air, spectral fists lashing out at invisible foes.

"Let me at 'em!" the spook roared. "Give me what's left and I'll make mincemeat out of them!"

"Ahem," Kirby cleared his throat.

Erasmus looked around the lab. "Oh. Looks like you have the situation well in hand."

"No thanks to you," Jedidiah snarled, spitting a wad of glowing ectoplasm onto the floor.

"Manners!" Erasmus screamed.

"Take your manners and stuff 'em under yer towel," Jedidiah said, wiping a dribble of ghostly spit from his lips.

Erasmus flew at his ancestor, his face twisted in anger. "I've had just about enough you!" the scientist ghost growled.

Jedidiah was ready, his ethereal fingers flexing. "Bring it on, egghead. I'll beat ya so bad you'll think ya died twice!"

"Gentlemen," Kirby barked. "And I use the term loosely. Please refrain from spectral fisticuffs at least until our mission is complete."

Kirby picked OB up from the chair and placed him on the floor.

"How did you get here without a car?" OB asked.

"Our newest ghostly compatriot has a unique talent that I put to use," Kirby said absently, his curious eyes scanning the lab.

His Frenchie gaze landed upon a section of the laboratory floor and the hole from which they'd emerged from below. As he surmised, the ghostly prospector and his pickax had provided them with the quickest route to the military base. It certainly was a feat to behold.

Kirby recalled the prospector's actions, impressed by what the ghost could do.

Jedidiah Peckinpah hit the ground with incredible force, sparks leaping up into the air as the first layer of rock began to crumble. The pick fell again and again, rock giving way and becoming rubble. Before long, a hole began to form, the sharp point of the prospecting tool biting into random rock and dirt. The hole was turning into a tunnel, a winding passage beneath the earth taking the ghost and his new compatriots exactly where they needed to go.

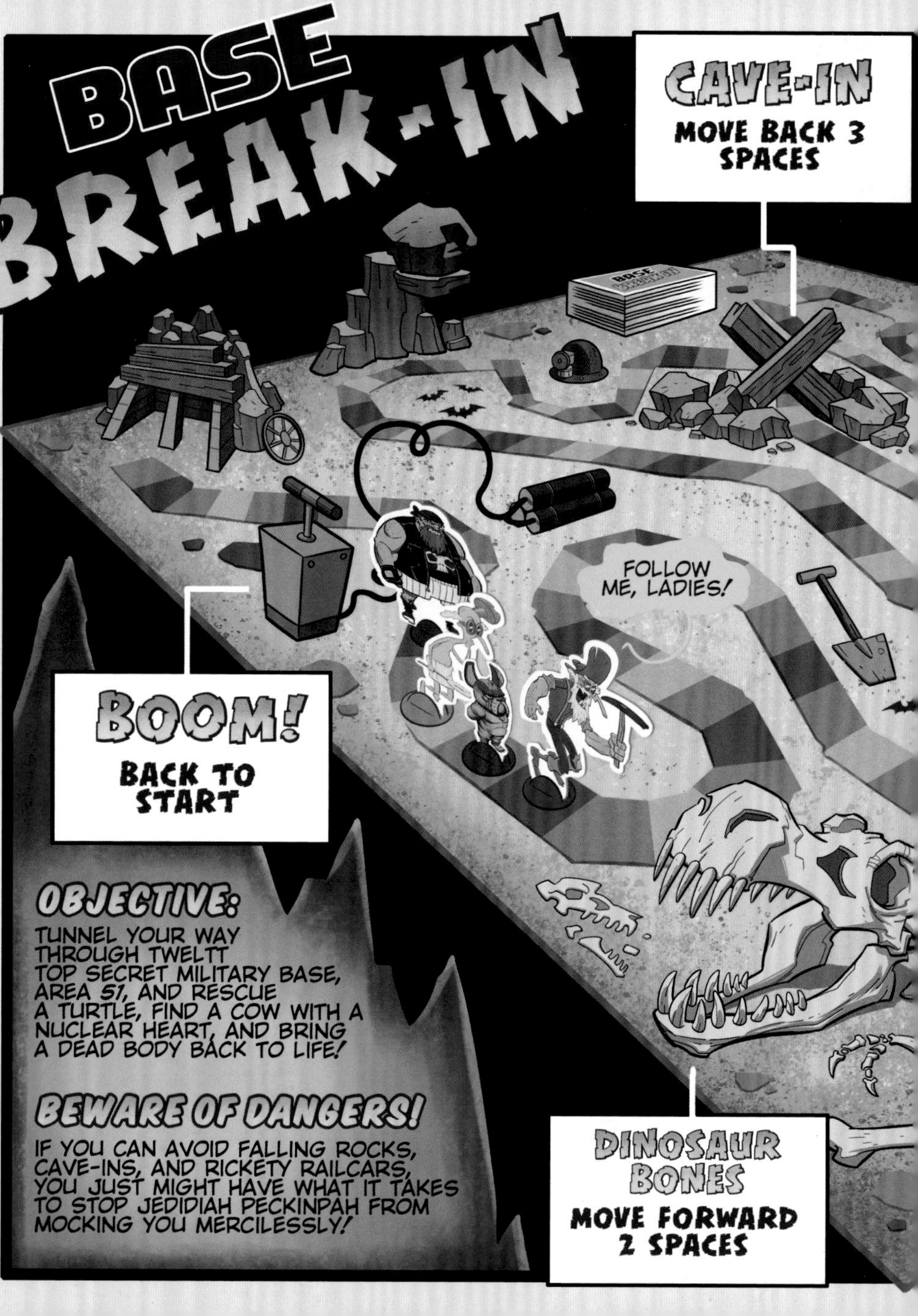
BASE BREAK-IN
CAVE-IN
MOVE BACK 3 SPACES
BASE BREAK-IN
FOLLOW ME, LADIES!
BOOM!
BACK TO START
OBJECTIVE:
TUNNEL YOUR WAY THROUGH TWELTT TOP SECRET MILITARY BASE, AREA 51, AND RESCUE A TURTLE, FIND A COW WITH A NUCLEAR HEART, AND BRING A DEAD BODY BACK TO LIFE!
BEWARE OF DANGERS!
IF YOU CAN AVOID FALLING ROCKS, CAVE-INS, AND RICKETY RAILCARS, YOU JUST MIGHT HAVE WHAT IT TAKES TO STOP JEDIDIAH PECKINPAH FROM MOCKING YOU MERCILESSLY!
DINOSAUR BONES
MOVE FORWARD 2 SPACES

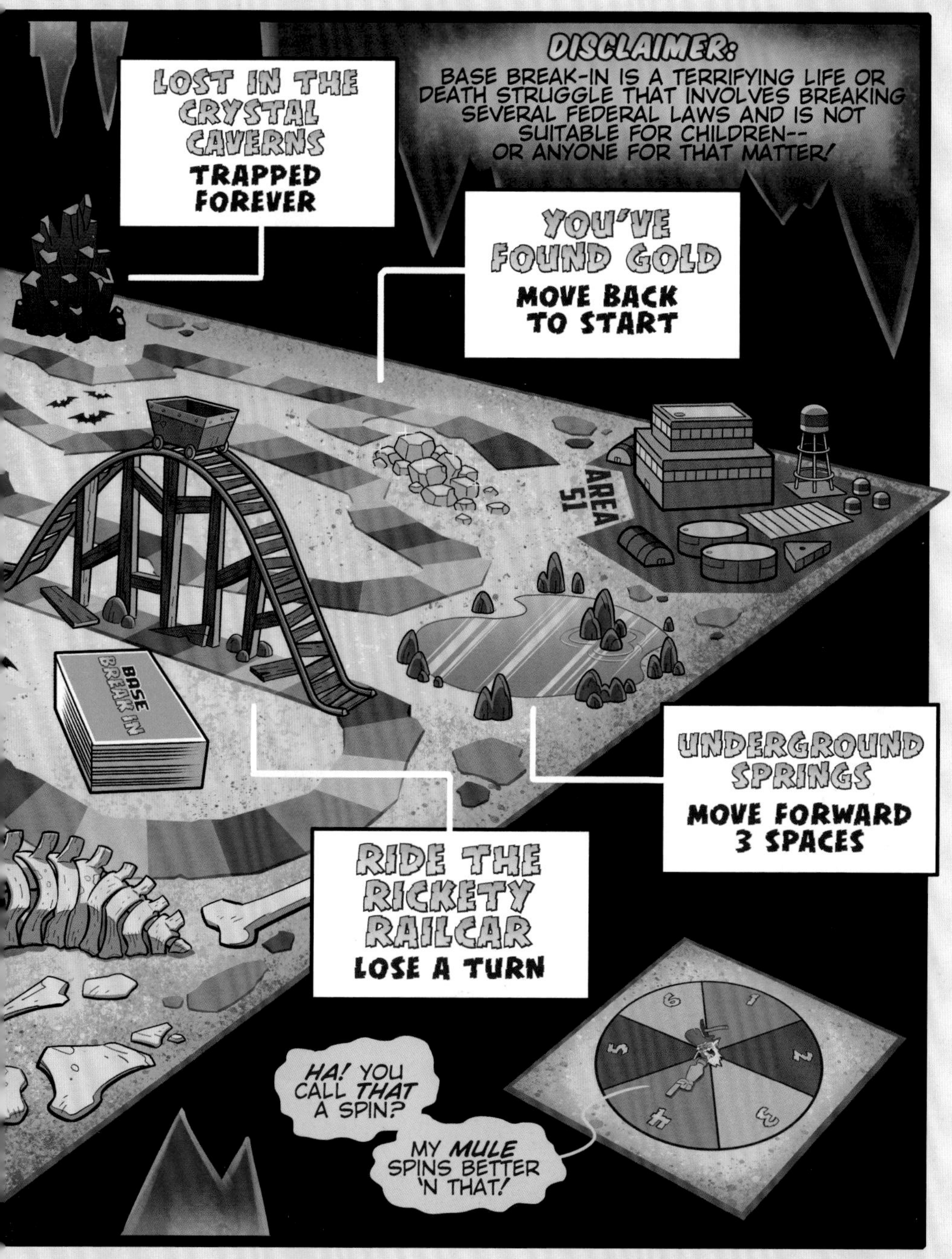
DISCLAIMER:
BASE BREAK-IN IS A TERRIFYING LIFE OR DEATH STRUGGLE THAT INVOLVES BREAKING SEVERAL FEDERAL LAWS AND IS NOT SUITABLE FOR CHILDREN-- OR ANYONE FOR THAT MATTER!
LOST IN THE CRYSTAL CAVERNS TRAPPED FOREVER
YOU'VE FOUND GOLD MOVE BACK TO START
AREA 51
BASE BREAK IN
UNDERGROUND SPRINGS MOVE FORWARD 3 SPACES
RIDE THE RICKETY RAILCAR LOSE A TURN
1
2
3
4
5
6
HA! YOU CALL THAT A SPIN?
MY MULE SPINS BETTER 'N THAT!

Kirby's keen eyes landed on the Eldorado parked in the room's corner, then noticed the cryo-chamber minus the reactor.

"The fusion reactor is missing," he announced. "We must speed up our time-table. Without the reactor, Erasmus's body will quickly thaw."

Erasmus hovered above the cryo-chamber, hands on his hips. "Yeah, I'm not lookin' too good," he said. "And that's sayin' somethin' when you're staring at a dead guy."

"What are we gonna do, Kirby?" OB asked.

"We have to find the cow with the nuclear heart at once," the Frenchie said. Immediately, he turned his attention to the chair that OB had been strapped to and the machines connected to it. "This appears to be a crude version of a brain-extractor."

"Yeah, they were gonna suck information right out of my noggin!" the turtle announced.

"I doubt they would have found much," Kirby said wryly.

"That's what I said!" OB announced proudly.

Kirby shook his head as he checked the calibrations on the machine. "Viper!" he barked.

The biker jumped, his face like a deer caught in the headlights of an 18-wheeler.

Kirby marched toward the moaning form of Dr. Oddfellow still lying on the floor of the lab. "Help me get this man into the chair."

"Can't believe Viper is doing this," the pantsless biker grumbled as he joined the Frenchie, quickly lifting the husky scientist and plopping him onto the seat. "Viper should be out hijacking trucks for flat-screen TVs and waffle irons."

Oddfellow groaned, his eyes flickering as Kirby strapped the scientist down.

"Vhat . . . vhat are you doing?" the scientist slurred.

"I need information, and I need it quickly." The Frenchie leapt up onto the scientist's lap to place the helmet atop his head and tighten the chin strap.

"I hear that hurts," OB said, watching wide-eyed from the floor.

"Quite a bit, I'd imagine," Kirby said, jumping down and turning to the control panel. "Shall we begin?" he suggested as he began to flip the switches.

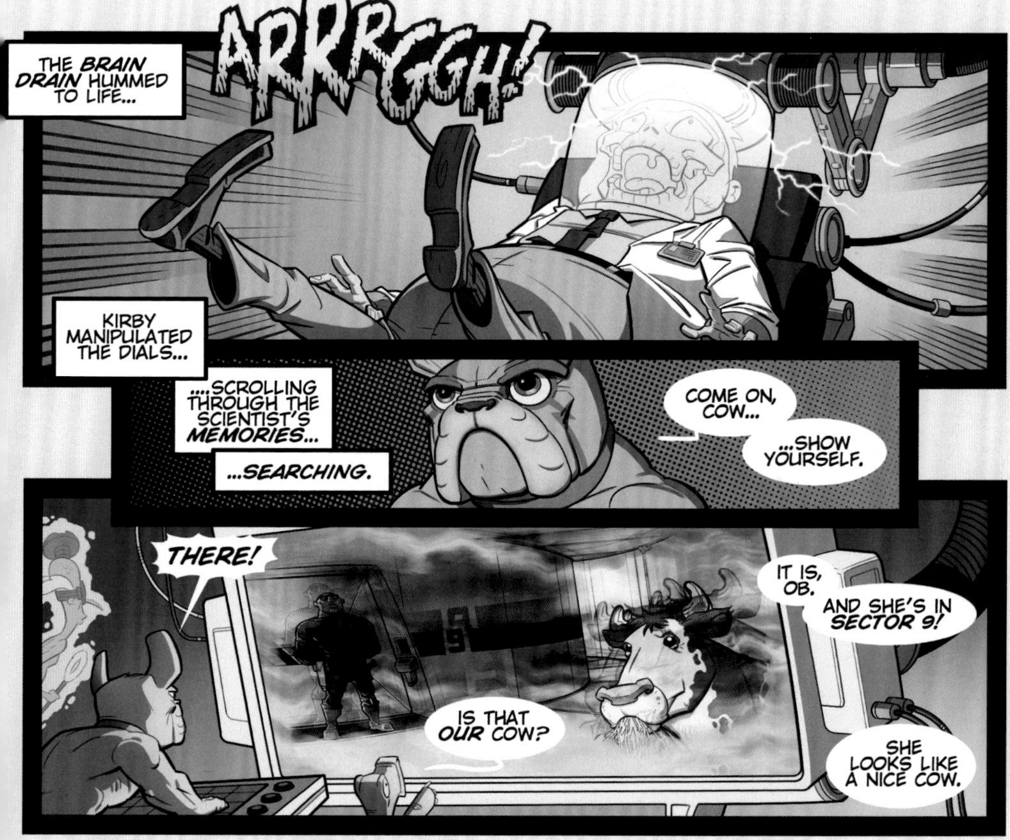

THE BRAIN DRAIN HUMMED TO LIFE...
ARRRGGH!
KIRBY MANIPULATED THE DIALS...
...SCROLLING THROUGH THE SCIENTIST'S MEMORIES...
...SEARCHING.
COME ON, COW...
...SHOW YOURSELF.
THERE!
IS THAT OUR COW?
IT IS, OB.
AND SHE'S IN SECTOR 9!
SHE LOOKS LIKE A NICE COW.

The video memory showed a black-and-white cow eating hay in a stall. Her body was attached to various diagnostic devices, and scientists wearing white lab coats jotted notes on clipboards as they reviewed the various readouts.

"She's cute," OB said with a giggle.

Kirby looked at the turtle sternly.

"What?" OB asked. "I can't help it if she's a looker!"

Again Kirby shook his head in disgust as he began to carefully the study the images. "There," he said when the image shifted to another part of the laboratory. "Sector 9. That is where the cow is being held."

"Well let's get goin' then!" Erasmus cheered. "I can feel that nuclear-powered ticker thumping in my chest already."

Jedidiah floated over to the monitor. "So these pictures are from Porky here's head?" he asked, gesturing toward Oddfellow strapped to the chair.

"They are," Kirby said, turning the dials and switches to get as much information about Sector 9 as he could.

"See anything about gold in there?" Jedidiah asked the Frenchie.

"Gold?" Kirby questioned. "No, why?"

"It's what I live for!" the ghostly prospector proclaimed.

"You're not alive," Kirby reminded him.

"Figure of speech!" the prospector shrugged. "I've been searching for gold for over a hunnert and fifty years, and I ain't restin' in peace till I find me some!"

"Well there is none here," Kirby said, annoyed by the ghost's interruption.

"Says you, puppy dog," Jedidiah said, sniffing the air with his pronounced proboscis. "But I think my supernaturally enhanced sniffer might've found me a vein close by."

"Sure you aren't smellin' yourself?" Erasmus asked, waving a hand beneath his own pronounced nose. "Even dead you stink like roadkill."

The prospector's ghost snarled.

"If I wasn't on the trail of a potential fortune I'd make you eat that scrub brush," Jedidiah said before turning away and diving through the floor.

"Goodbye to bad rubbish," Erasmus said, returning his attention to the monitors. "So, let's get goin', Kenny!"

"It isn't going to be that easy," Kirby said, his atomically enhanced brain already working on the problems he'd discovered.

"Why not?" Erasmus asked. "We just waltz into Sector 9 there and . . ."

"One does not *waltz* into Sector 9," Kirby informed him. "I've been reviewing Oddfellow's memories, and I've found that Sector 9 is the most top-secret level on the base. Only people with Level 1 security clearance can get in. A new pass is issued to each holder daily, and a fingerprint-recognition scan is located outside the door along with an armed guard."

"Is that all?" Erasmus asked with sarcasm. "I'll never get my cow heart!" the ghost exclaimed, throwing his spindly arms into the air.

Oddfellow gurgled loudly from his seat. It appeared that he had not weathered the extraction well.

"Here is our key," the Frenchie said. He hopped up into the man's lap, grabbing his fat face in his paws.

"Wake up, Doctor!" Kirby commanded. He slapped the doctor's cheeks. A trail of spit dribbled from the man's slack mouth to stain the front of his shirt . . .

And the identification card that dangled there from a chain.

"Hmmm," Kirby said, looking at the plastic identification card. He scratched his hairy chin.

"What'chu thinking, Kirb?" OB asked.

"I'm thinking we have all we need right here," Kirby announced.

"Hot dog!" OB jumped up and down excitedly. "Do tell!"

"Yeah, how we gettin' past security central there?" Erasmus asked.

"This security clearance will suffice," Kirby said, showing them the laminated pass. "But we'll have to take him with us for the fingerprints."

Viper walked over to give the doctor a look. "Viper doesn't think he's going anywhere on his own," the pantsless biker said.

"Exactly," Kirby said. "Which is where Erasmus's talents are needed."

"Me?" Erasmus asked. "And what talent exactly are you looking for? I've got many."

"You're an apparition," Kirby said. "Have you ever taken possession of a living body?"

Erasmus considered the question.

"Negatory to that," the ghost said. "Above my spectral pay grade I'm afraid."

"Drat." Kirby pounded a fist into the center of his other paw.

"Hey! How about this?" Erasmus suggested. His ghostly form began to fade away. "I can turn invisible!"

At first Kirby prepared to berate the ghost for wasting time when he suddenly understood.

"Invisible," Kirby repeated, and he began to nod, the idea forming inside his head. "Yes, that just might work."

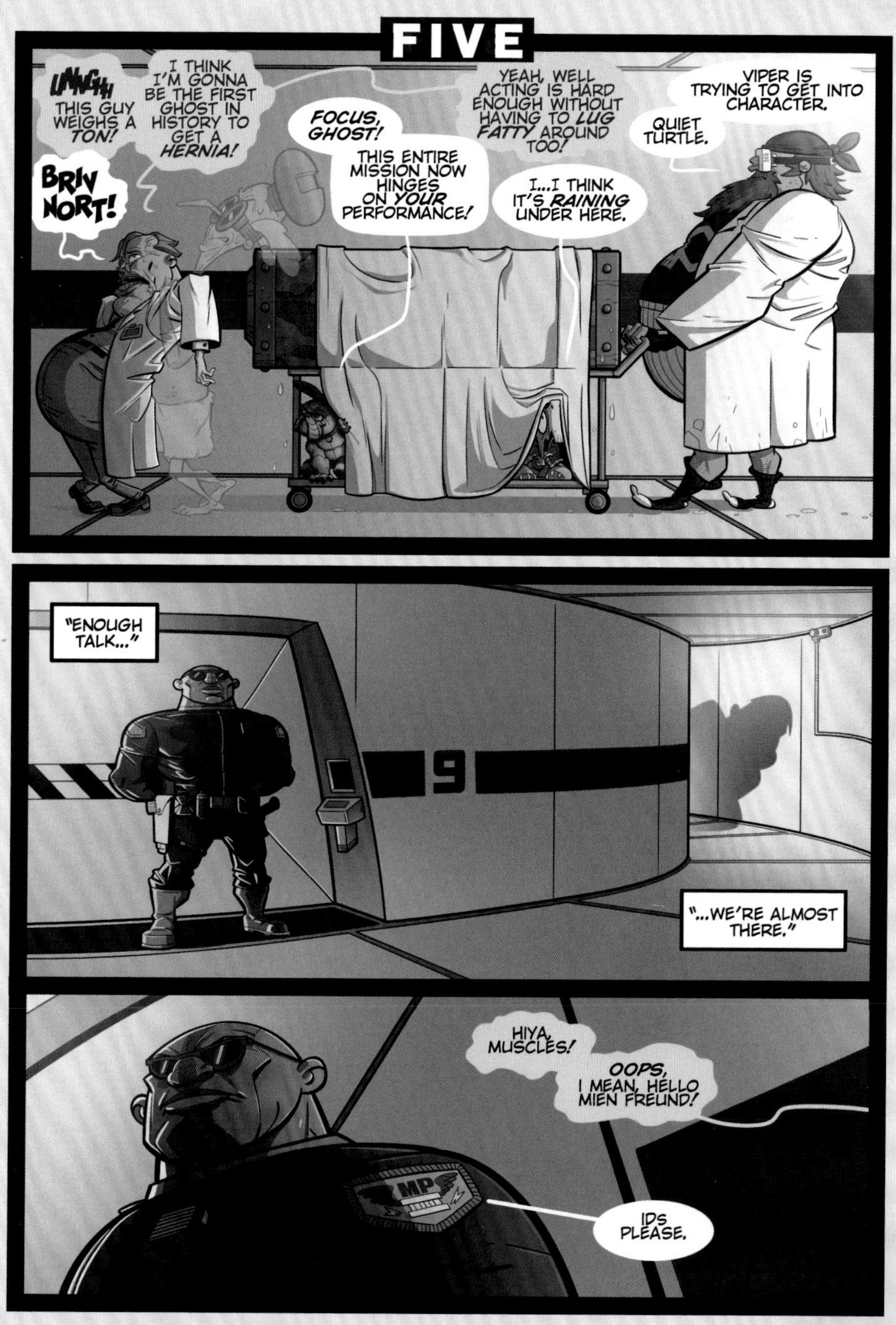
FIVE
UNNGHH
THIS GUY WEIGHS A TON!
I THINK I'M GONNA BE THE FIRST GHOST IN HISTORY TO GET A HERNIA!
BRIV NORT!
FOCUS, GHOST!
THIS ENTIRE MISSION NOW HINGES ON YOUR PERFORMANCE!
YEAH, WELL ACTING IS HARD ENOUGH WITHOUT HAVING TO LUG FATTY AROUND TOO!
I...I THINK IT'S RAINING UNDER HERE.
VIPER IS TRYING TO GET INTO CHARACTER.
QUIET TURTLE.
"ENOUGH TALK..."
"...WE'RE ALMOST THERE."
HIYA, MUSCLES!
OOPS, I MEAN, HELLO MIEN FREUND!
IDs PLEASE.

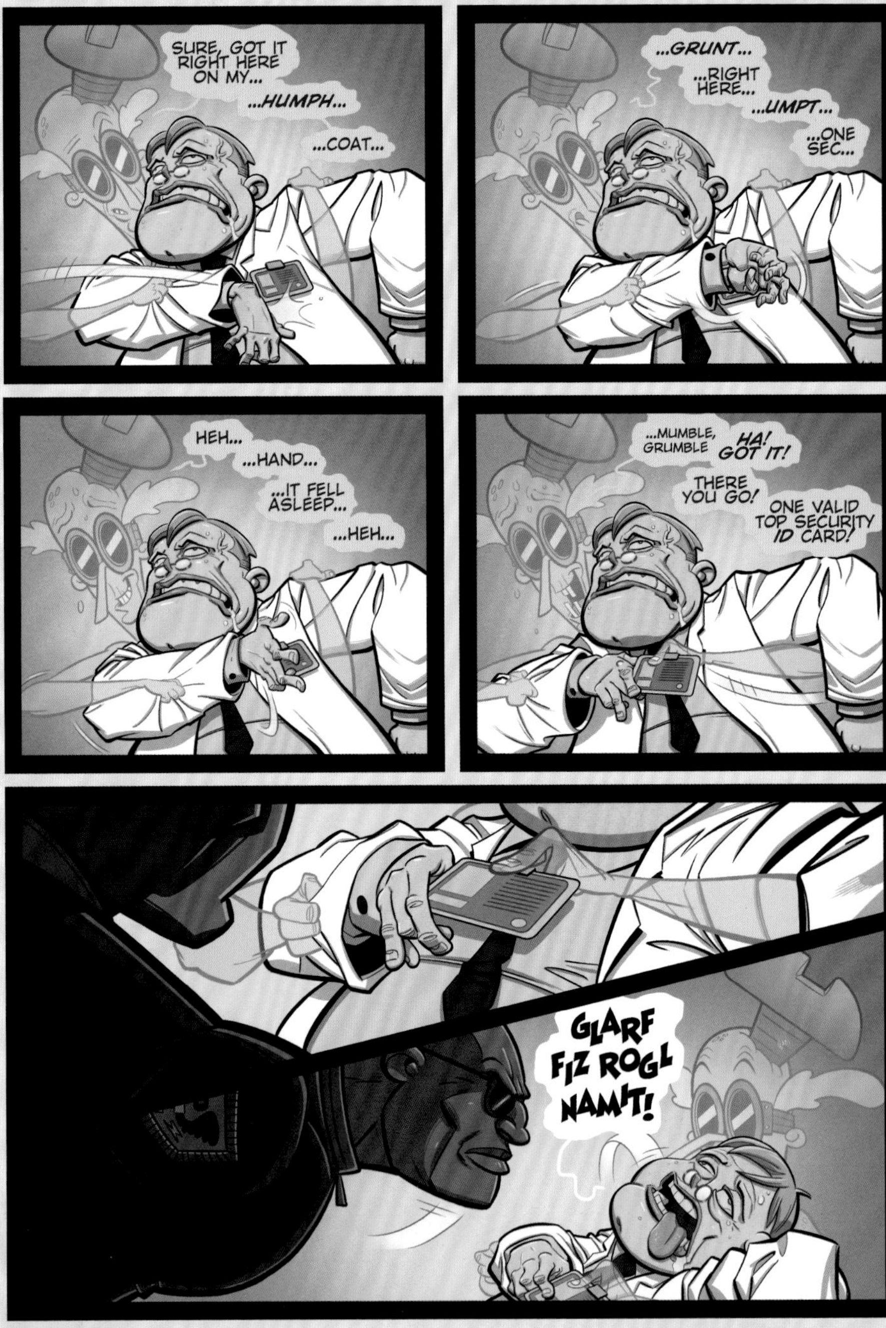
SURE, GOT IT RIGHT HERE ON MY...
...HUMPH...
...COAT...
...GRUNT...
...RIGHT HERE...
...UMPT...
...ONE SEC...
HEH...
...HAND...
...IT FELL ASLEEP...
...HEH...
...MUMBLE, GRUMBLE
HA! GOT IT!
THERE YOU GO!
ONE VALID TOP SECURITY ID CARD!
GLARF FIZ ROGL NAMIT!

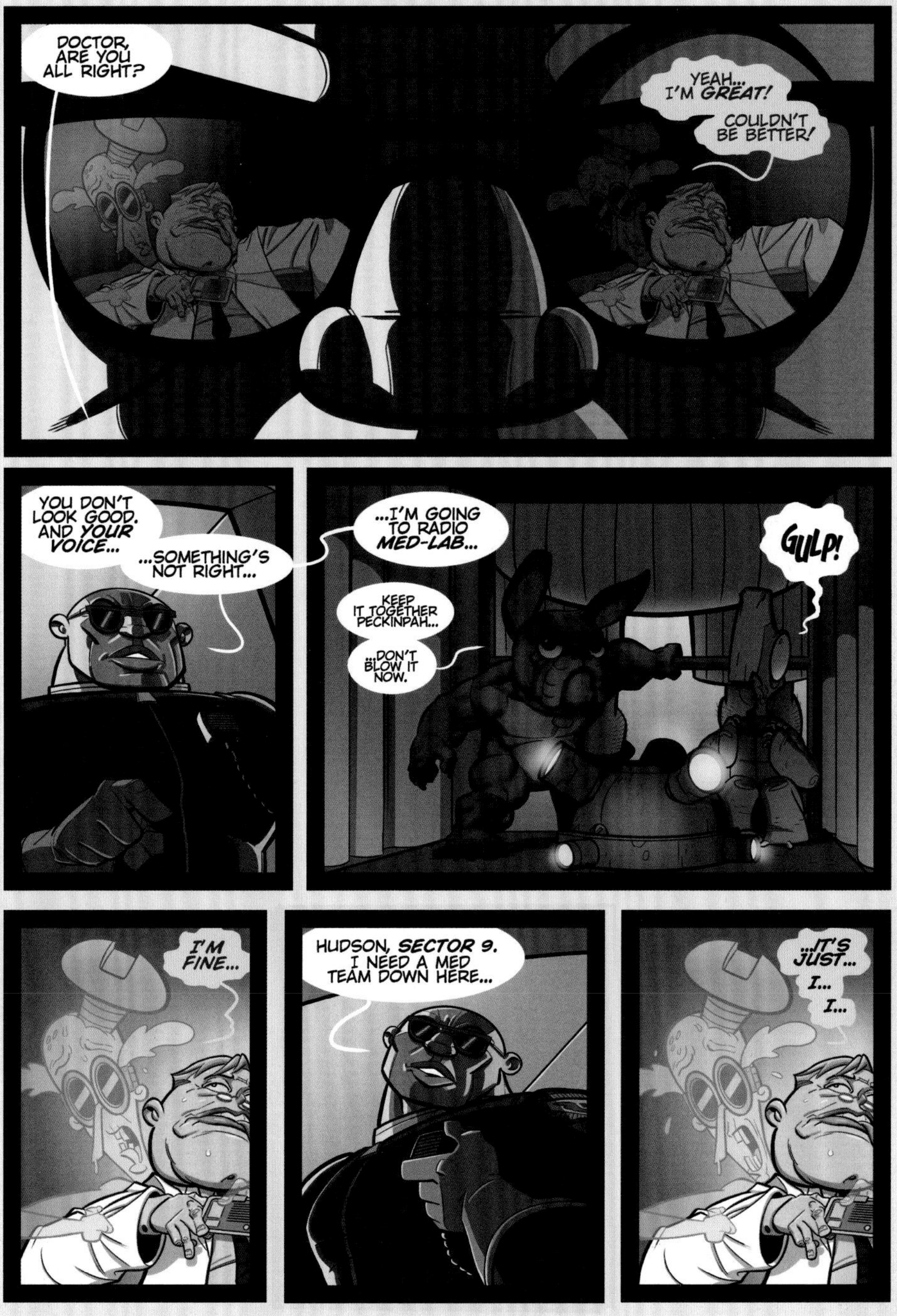
DOCTOR, ARE YOU ALL RIGHT?
YEAH... I'M GREAT!
COULDN'T BE BETTER!
YOU DON'T LOOK GOOD. AND YOUR VOICE...
...SOMETHING'S NOT RIGHT...
...I'M GOING TO RADIO MED-LAB...
GULP!
KEEP IT TOGETHER PECKINPAH...
...DON'T BLOW IT NOW.
I'M FINE...
HUDSON, SECTOR 9. I NEED A MED TEAM DOWN HERE...
...IT'S JUST...
I...
I...

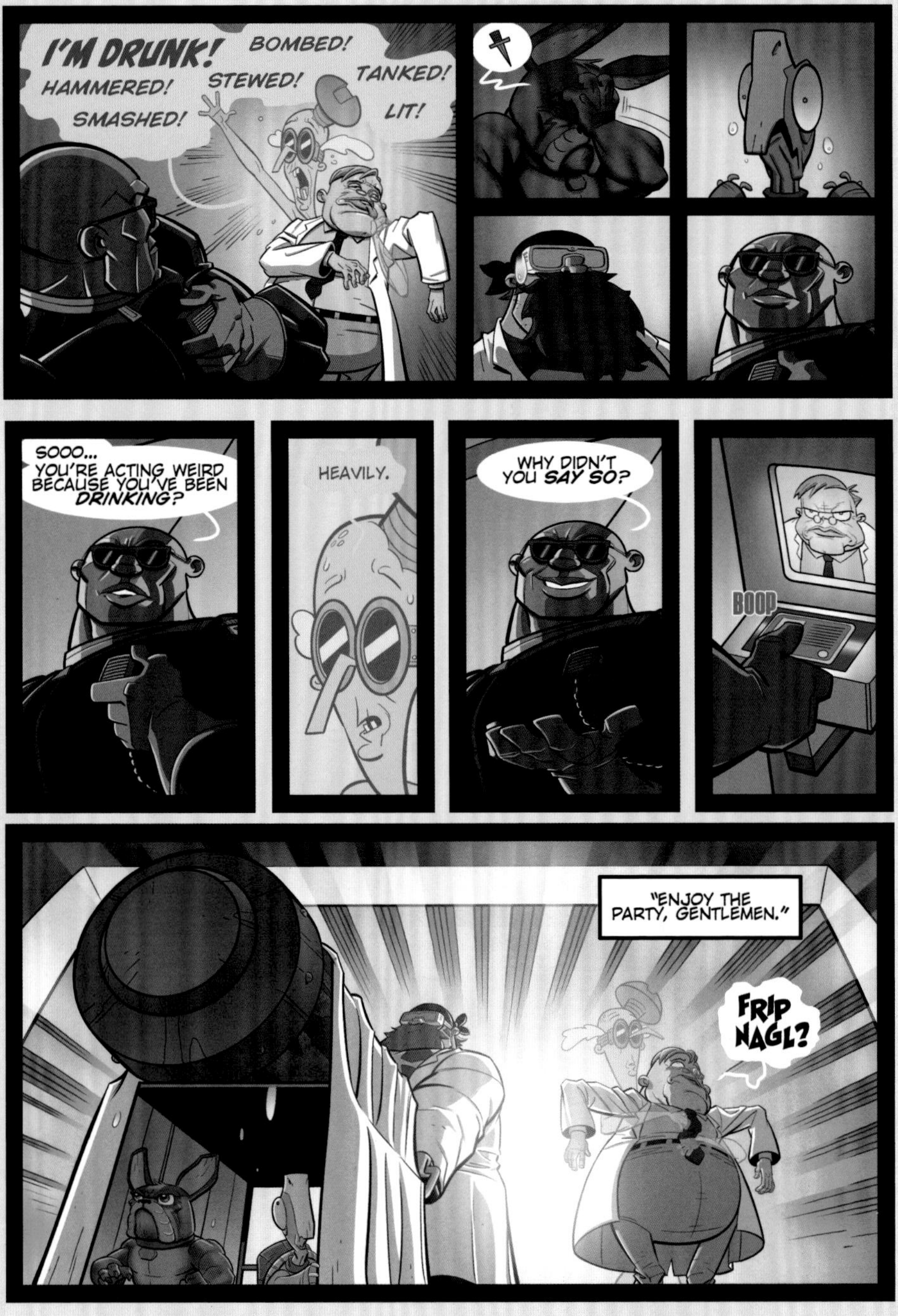
I'M DRUNK!
BOMBED!
HAMMERED!
STEWED!
TANKED!
SMASHED!
LIT!
SOOO... YOU'RE ACTING WEIRD BECAUSE YOU'VE BEEN DRINKING?
HEAVILY.
WHY DIDN'T YOU SAY SO?
BOOP
"ENJOY THE PARTY, GENTLEMEN."
FRIP NAGL?

Kirby gasped, not believing his eyes, but they did not lie.

"Oddfellow!" a lab coat–wearing scientist shouted as he headed for the group. "You old son of a gun! Get your flabby PhD-enhanced butt in here!" He grabbed Oddfellow's limp arm and dragged him farther into the lab.

"Does that man have a lampshade on his head?" OB asked. He had stretched his long neck out from under the sheet to see what was going on.

"I believe he does," Kirby acknowledged, observing not scientific experimentation but a party that could best be described as . . .

Totally.

Out of.

Control.

🦇

"Wow, this is some party!" OB said happily, tapping his foot to the disco music. "Wonder who it's for?"

Viper was wheeling the gurney beneath them through an archway made of red, white, and blue balloons and into a hangar the size of a football field. A DJ was set up in the center of the space, and a banner hanging from the ceiling read "Happy Birthday, Colonel Killshot."

"Somebody named Killshot," Kirby answered his turtle compatriot. "Colonel Killshot."

"I feel bad I didn't get him anything," OB said, eyes darting around the room to find soldiers juggling hand grenades while riding unicycles, a pin-the-tail-on-the-communist game in full swing, a nuclear bomb–shaped piñata hanging from the long gun barrel of a tank.

"Not to worry," Kirby said. "If all goes according to plan, *we* will be the ones leaving with a present today. Viper," he hissed as they passed a gaggle of soldiers wielding an arsenal of Silly String, water balloons, and flash grenades, squealing with excitement like preteens at a K-pop concert. "Head right, and stay close to the wall. We're looking for a laboratory off of the main floor."

Viper wheeled the gurney closer to the wall. A choir of younger soldiers was singing a wonderfully melodious version of "Happy Birthday." They stood by an ice sculpture of a bald eagle and a table bearing a huge cake decorated to look like the American flag and easily capable of feeding a third world nation.

OB suddenly gasped, and Kirby quickly followed the box turtle's gaze, anticipating yet another threat to their plan. Instead, he saw an inflated structure filled with lab-coated scientists and fatigue-wearing soldiers joyously bouncing around.

"A bouncy house!" the turtle squealed. "I've always wanted to go inside one of them."

Kirby glared at the turtle, but then something beyond the foolish bouncy house caught his attention. Whatever it was, it was huge and covered with multiple tarps. He felt the fur at the back of his neck rise. His Frenchie sense told him that something of great importance was concealed there. He made a mental note to peek at the hidden object before they left Sector 9.

"Sir, happy birthday, sir!" a voice boomed.

Viper wheeled the gurney past an older man talking with three soldiers. The stars on the man's uniform indicated he was a colonel.

"Well done, soldiers!" Colonel Killshot barked at the men standing in front of him. "A classic example of misdirection. By you three creating a false narrative earlier, I lowered my guard, leaving myself open for a surprise attack. Sun Tzu would be proud."

"Sir, thank you, sir," the three soldiers roared in unison, the expressions on their faces telling Kirby they were quite proud to have been noticed by their superior.

Kirby shifted his position beneath the gurney and his hand fell into something wet.

A puddle.

Kirby looked at OB.

"It wasn't me," OB declared defiantly.

The Frenchie knew the source of the moisture at once, and it wasn't good. The cryo-chamber containing Erasmus's body was warming more quickly than expected.

"We haven't much time," Kirby muttered. And then he caught sight of a metal door with a slit for a window not too far from their position—a door the Frenchie had last seen in Dr. Oddfellow's video memories.

"Viper, that door just ahead of us, quickly."

The gurney had barely reached the door before Kirby was slipping from beneath the sheet, OB at his tail.

"Open it," the Frenchie ordered Viper, who glared at the dog through his safety goggles.

"Do I stutter?" Kirby asked impatiently.

Viper snarled, pointing a sausage-sized finger at the Frenchie.

"Yes, yes. Now do as I say and open the door before someone sees us."

The biker grumbled beneath his breath as he angrily poked the large red button on the side of the door.

The door rolled open with a hiss.

"Yeee-hawww!" cried a shirtless soldier astride a cow. He was waving a cowboy hat in the air above his head while two other soldiers also wearing cowboy hats cheered him on.

The brown-and-white cow appeared to be completely oblivious of the soldier sitting atop her as she stood in her stall, calmly munching on a pile of hay.

"What the . . . ?" Viper began.

But Kirby had already stepped farther into the room, ignoring the nonsense before him and assessing the location. The room, though now used to house the cow, had originally been designed as a surgical theater, with three rows of stadium-style seating lining the rounded walls and a large wall cabinet just to the left of the entrance.

Yes, it would do just nicely.

"Get rid of these cow-riding imbeciles," Kirby ordered over his shoulder as he marched to the cabinet and began pulling open drawers and doors.

The biker glared but strode toward the cow and the soldiers.

"Howdy, Doc," the soldier acknowledged Viper as he slid off the cow's back to the floor, landing upon wobbly legs. "I believe the next ride has your name on it!"

The other soldiers laughed as if it was the funniest thing they had ever heard.

Viper was about to tell the soldiers to beat it when . . .

The air before them shimmered like a heat wave, and suddenly Erasmus appeared.

"Oh!" said the mad scientist, clapping his hands with glee. "Can I be next? Pleeeeeeeeeeeeeeeeeeeeeeeeeeease!"

The soldiers' mouths dropped open and their eyes bulged, then almost as one, they turned and ran for the exit, tripping over one another as each fought to get out the door first.

"Nicely done," Kirby said. He'd found a drawer of surgical instruments and was admiring a particularly sharp-looking scalpel.

"Now quickly. We must prepare for surgery."

SIX

Oddfellow sat slumped in a chair in the corner of the room, gradually regaining some of his faculties.

A trickle of drool ran from the corner of his mouth, down his chin, and onto his starched white shirt. He lifted a limp hand, attempting to wipe away the spit trickle, but only served to slap himself in the face.

As his vision gradually cleared, the scientist's view of the vast warehouse coming into focus, he saw that a party was going on full swing.

But there was no time for such festivities, his addled brain sluggishly recalled.

There were intruders within the facility.

Oddfellow searched the festive crowd, looking for a sign of the interlopers, but he did not see them.

Where? Where had they gone?

The memory was suddenly there, tender like a fresh bruise. They had used the extraction device—the brain-drain—on him, searching for something.

Searching for a cow.

Yes, that was it, he recalled, struggling to stand up from where he sat.

He saw that the lights were lit within the former operating theater across the warehouse, where the cow specimen was being kept.

Oddfellow smiled, a new stream of drool running down his face, as he lurched forward.

Drunkenly, he stumbled toward the operating room.

Kirby leaned forward so that OB could tie his surgical mask. The Frenchie was wearing an oversized surgeon's gown, and rubber gloves covered his paws.

"Once I begin the removal of the nuclear heart, nothing must interrupt me. Understood?" Kirby asked, his voice slightly muffled by the mask across his muzzle.

"Why can't the turtle assist you?" Viper asked. He too was wearing a surgical gown and rubber gloves, with a mask across his face. "Viper doesn't think . . ."

"Exactly," Kirby interrupted. "Viper doesn't need to think. Viper just needs to follow orders."

Kirby could see the anger flash in the biker's eyes.

"Shall we proceed?" the Frenchie asked, holding his rubber gloved paws aloft.

Kirby climbed to the top step on a metal stool that had been positioned beside the cow, which continued to chew its mouthfuls of hay.

"Viper, anesthetize the cow, exactly as I showed you."

"Hey, wait a minute!" OB called up from the bottom step of the stool.

Kirby glared at the turtle from atop his perch. "What is it?"

"If . . . if you take out her heart, won't the cow . . . y'know, die?"

"Of course she will," Kirby replied without an ounce of regret. He picked up a black sharpie from a table filled with instruments and began to draw a dotted line where he planned to make his incision on the cow's side.

"But . . . but . . . ," OB stammered.

"Sorry, kid," Erasmus said. "Sometimes to make an omelet you got to break a few eggs." He rubbed his hands together eagerly. "And I say, let's make some breakfast!"

"However, should these people, at the end of their party, find a dead cow and missing nuclear-powered heart, our gooses would be cooked," Kirby said.

"So you're not gonna kill her?" OB asked hopefully.

"No," Kirby said with a shake of his head. He pointed to the cryo-chamber now atop the gurney. "Bring that over here," the Frenchie commanded.

Viper strolled over to the gurney and wheeled it closer.

From the top of the step stool, Kirby bent over, flipped the clips that kept the cryo-chamber closed, and lifted the lid. A freezing fog flowed up from the case as Erasmus's body was exposed to room temperature.

"That is why I am going to replace it with . . . ," the Frenchie began, reaching into the chamber and rummaging around Erasmus's body until he found the object of his search.

"This!" Kirby proclaimed.

"Whoa!" OB said. "Is that what I think it is?"

"It is," Kirby answered. "A mechanical heart. I cobbled it together with bits and pieces I found lying about the lab in Strasburg before we departed."

Erasmus floated in closer for a look.

"And it works?" the ghost asked.

"What do you think?" Kirby replied, offended that his genius would be questioned.

The ghost stroked his pointed chin as he studied the pulsing, mechanical organ.

"So if that actually works," he suggested. "Then why couldn't we have put that inside . . ." Erasmus pointed to his bare chest.

"This heart is specifically designed and calibrated for the bovine species," Kirby explained. "And not what is required to reanimate one who has been dead as long as you."

"Aha, we're gonna need a touch of the nuclear for that," the ghost said, eagerly rubbing his hands together.

"Precisely," Kirby said as he turned back to the table where his surgical instruments awaited him. His rubber-gloved paw hovered over the selection as he considered which tool he would start with.

"Viper, the anesthesia if you will."

Viper did as he was told, placing a rubber mask over the cow's face—a mask attached to a hose attached to a large metal tank.

"Let's begin," Kirby said, bringing the scalpel toward the cow's marked flesh.

OB held his breath, eyes widening as he watched the surgical blade.

Erasmus floated in the air, looking on while shoving ectoplasmic popcorn from a bag into his gaping mouth.

The scalpel's point was just about to touch the cow's flesh when . . .

The door to the operating theater slid open, revealing a lone, ominous figure.

"Eeek!" OB cried.

"Oh, for the love'a Mike!" Erasmus said through a mouth of popped kernels.

"You!" Kirby said, his disdain for the man standing there obvious, yet muffled, through the surgical mask.

"Owwwwwzzzzoooooggahhhhhhhhhhhhhh!" Oddfellow bellowed.

The scientist lurched into the operating room screaming, murder in his glassy, bulging eyes. "Gaaaaaaaaaaaaaaaaaaaaaahhhhh! Gaaaaaaaaaaaaaaaahhhhh!"

⬤

"Quiet, please!" Private Fitzgerald yelled above the pulsing disco music. "Quiet!"

He motioned to the DJ, who turned the music down to a barely audible *thump, thump, thump*.

Private Rosario produced a bag, and Private Johnson rummaged around inside it before pulling out a beautifully wrapped package. He handed the package to Private Fitzgerald as Colonel Killshot looked on.

"What's going on here, privates?" the colonel asked as soldiers and scientists alike began to gather around them.

Fitzgerald cleared his throat before speaking, obviously emotional. "First off, we'd like to thank everyone who came to this extravaganza to celebrate the birth of one of the greatest military minds this world has ever seen."

Everyone began to clap wildly.

"Get on with it, private," the colonel growled. "I've got some more partying to do, and this is just slowing things down."

"Of course, sir," Fitzgerald said. "Rosario, Johnson, and I racked our brains trying to find something appropriate, and we decided on this."

Fitzgerald tentatively handed the package off to the colonel.

"Hope you like it."

The colonel gave it a shake and listened to it. "Not a bomb is it?" he asked.

The three privates began to laugh uproariously, and the laughter spread to all others present.

"That's enough of that!" the colonel yelled, plunging the room into silence. "Nothing worse than a room full of suck-ups," he grumbled as he tore away the wrapping paper to reveal a book. He stared at the cover.

"It's a first edition," Johnson offered.

"*The Only Good Commie Is a Dead Commie*," Colonel Killshot read. "*The Love Poetry of John Wayne.*"

The colonel began to flip through the pages.

"I'd always heard that he was a sensitive soul," Killshot said.

"Happy birthday, sir!" Fitzgerald said, saluting his commanding officer. Everyone in the vast room followed suit.

Killshot looked around, seeing it all, and even began to feel the pangs of something that just might have been emotion.

"At ease, everyone," he commanded, and all did as he asked.

"I'd like to thank everyone who took the time from their busy schedules to . . ."

The sound was awful.

"GHHHHAAAAAAAAAAAAAAAAAAAAAA!"

The sound of something in terrible torment.

"What in the name of all that's holy is that?" Colonel Killshot asked, looking about the vast enclosure.

The crowd was looking as well, and all eyes turned to an open door at end of the room.

"OOOOHHHHHHGGGGAAAAAHHH!" came the terrifying sound again.

"Well, not sure what all the caterwauling is about," the colonel said, marching toward the door. "But I'm about to find out!"

"Viper, if you would be so kind as to remove the brain-addled doctor from the room," Kirby said. "I'm attempting heart surgery here."

Oddfellow twitched and moaned as he came farther into the room, pointing a twisted finger at them.

The biker intercepted the man and was just about to grab his arm when . . .

"What in the name of San Juan Hill is going on in here?" Colonel Killshot roared from the doorway behind Oddfellow.

The scientist spun toward the colonel, gurgling loudly and gesticulating wildly.

"Calm yourself, Dr. Oddfellow," the colonel said, brushing past him and into the room. "I can see for myself."

"Uh-oh," OB said, hiding behind Kirby's stool.

"You there!" the colonel barked, pointing at Kirby atop his perch and marching closer.

Kirby lowered the scalpel.

"What can I do for you, colonel?" the Frenchie asked from behind his surgical mask, already formulating a plan that would include pouncing on the officer and the three soldiers accompanying him and rendering them unconscious with the cow's anesthesia.

But even Kirby was surprised when the colonel stopped, stood at attention, and saluted the Frenchie.

"I salute you, sir!" the colonel said.

"You do?"

"I do," he said. "I admire the work ethic of you and all you fellas here." The colonel saluted Kirby's entire team.

OB politely saluted back.

"Here we are having a grand old time outside, while you all are in here, giving it your all, forsaking fun and frivolity for the sake of your duty!"

"Why, of course," Kirby agreed, quickly recovering. "I'm a slave to my work ethic."

"Viper too!" Viper said and giggled like a nervous child.

Kirby glared at the biker.

Oddfellow lurched over, frantically pointing first at Kirby, then to the cow. "AAAAGGGAAHHHHHHHHBLLURP!"

"And I agree," said the colonel. "It is an outrage!"

"ZOOOP?" Oddfellow questioned.

"Exactly," the commanding officer said. "These hard-working gents are missing out! Johnson!"

"Yes, sir!" Johnson said, snapping to attention.

"Go and find these fine gentlemen some cake!"

"Yes, sir, sir!" Johnson bolted for the door, followed by Fitzgerald and Queenan, who were not about to be overlooked.

"GAHHHHHHH!" Oddfellow wailed, desperate to find his words again, but having no success.

"It is an amazing thing to find such dedicated professionals, I agree," the colonel said, gripping Oddfellow by the arm and escorting him toward the door. "Carry on, fellas," he called over his shoulder. "I thank you and so does the US of A!"

"ZAAAAAAAAAAAAAAGGGH!" Oddfellow squawked, struggling to free himself from the colonel's grasp.

"Sure there's dancing," the colonel told him. "I'll even show you how to turkey trot," he offered as he pulled the scientist through the door.

The door closed behind them with a snakelike hiss.

"Well, that was close!" Erasmus said, his ghostly form appearing in the air. "Not sure how much more of this I can take!" He began to fan himself with his ectoplasmic scrub brush. "What now?"

"Now?" Kirby questioned. "Isn't it obvious?

"We operate."

SEVEN

Standing atop his step stool, Kirby prepared for the reason they had left the safety of Strasburg, Massachusetts, and traveled hundreds of miles: to perform complex open-heart surgery on a cow with a nuclear-powered heart and return a former mad scientist to life.

All in a day's work.

"Expose the corpse," Kirby commanded, pointing to the cryo-chamber.

"Kinda harsh, don't you think, Kent?" Erasmus asked as Viper began to loosen the shirt covering the body's chest.

Kirby glared at the ghost before turning his attention to the cow. "Until this nuclear heart is removed and placed inside the corpse's scrawny chest cavity, and it returns to living, that's all it is."

"Well, I guess when you put it that way," Erasmus agreed with a shrug.

"Is the cow properly anesthetized?" Kirby ask, scalpel hovering by the cow's side.

"She's asleep!" OB called up. The little turtle was standing down by the cow's face, gently patting her head and telling her that everything was going to be all right.

"Then we begin." Kirby acknowledged the turtle with a curt nod, then leaned forward and put the scalpel to work.

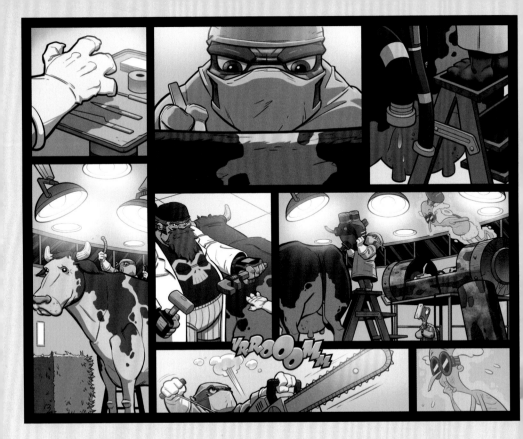

Kirby stared into the open chest cavity of Erasmus's body, mentally reviewing the next steps of his complicated plan.

He had safely installed the mechanical heart of his own design into the cow and deftly severed the nuclear-powered heart from the cow's circulatory system. Now he was ready to give the large heart a new home within the chest of Erasmus J. Peckinpah.

And once life was restored to the mad scientist's corpse, and they returned home from their mission victorious, Kirby would have access to countless plans that would bring him that much closer to his dream of planetwide dominance.

The nuclear-powered heart thrummed in his paws as he carefully lowered it into Erasmus's waiting body and . . .

The heart would not fit.

"Oh, snap!" Erasmus said floating over for a closer look. "Looks like a pretty tight fit."

"More like a no fit," Kirby said, placing the heart at his feet and peering into the open maw of Erasmus's chest. "In our haste to complete this transplant, we neglected to take into account how much larger a cow's heart is than a human's."

"I knew I was forgettin' something," Erasmus said, rubbing his chin thoughtfully as he floated above the cryo-chamber. "So what do you think?"

Kirby's atomically enhanced brain kicked into high gear, multiple scenarios flashing through his mind before the most appropriate one dropped into place.

"You'll wear it on your back," he announced.

"I'll what?" Erasmus asked incredulously.

"You'll wear it on your back like a backpack," Kirby explained, gently setting the heart beside the corpse and jumping from the stool.

OB began to laugh. "You'll be like me!" the turtle announced, turning around to show off his shell.

Erasmus thought about this for a moment and then shrugged. "Whatever, I'll always be one of the most brilliant minds on the planet even if I am wearing a nuclear-powered heart on my back."

Kirby ignored them as he searched the theater's supply cabinet. He found some old tubing in a drawer, held it up, and studied it for a few moments before carrying it back and up the step stool and dropping it unceremoniously on the corpse's legs.

"Out with the old." With that he reached in and expertly removed the dead heart from the corpse's chest.

Kirby looked to Viper, who had been leaning against the rail that separated the stadium seating from the floor of the theater, daydreaming. "Dispose of this, Viper," Kirby ordered, tossing the dead heart at the biker.

Viper screamed, the old heart rebounding off his chest before he caught it, bouncing the heart in his hands like a hot potato before dumping it unceremoniously into a nearby trashcan with a resounding clatter.

"Oh please," Kirby said with disdain. He turned back to the cryo-chamber and began working the tubes and wiring to connect the nuclear heart to Erasmus's internal workings.

"That should do it," he said finally, twisting the end of a wire and wrapping it around a screw on the side of the nuclear heart. "I'll use the straps in the cryo-chamber to make a sling for your back," Kirby told the ghost of the scientist.

"That's great," Erasmus said. "And once we get home, we can work on miniaturizing the heart so we can put it *inside* my chest where it belongs."

"After you give me your secrets," Kirby reminded him.

"Of course after the secrets," Erasmus agreed. "A deal's a deal."

"It certainly is." Kirby checked and rechecked all the connections between the tubing and the nuclear-powered heart, then closed up the corpse's chest using a stapler.

Everything seemed ready to go.

"Defibrillator!" Kirby barked.

Viper and OB jumped into action, wheeling the heart-shocking contraption over to the Frenchie. Kirby turned the machine on, hearing the high-pitched, mechanical whine grow as the electrical charge to the paddles intensified.

"Clear!" he yelled, placing the paddles against Erasmus's corpse and releasing the charge.

He pulled the paddles back, waited for the charge to build again, and . . .

"Clear!" he repeated, zapping the body again.

The corpse flopped a bit as the electricity coursed through it but otherwise remained still.

Frustrated, Kirby gave it another try, charging the paddles and filling the body with another blast of life-returning voltage.

"I don't understand this," he announced, as he again checked and rechecked the connections. And again, everything appeared to be fine. The nuclear-powered heart was working fine, but Erasmus's body did not live.

Something was greatly amiss.

"I was afraid of that," the ghost of Erasmus Peckinpah said sadly as he gazed down at his flaccid flesh-and-blood form.

"Afraid of what?" Kirby asked, his ire on the rise.

"Well, there's something I meant to tell you," the ghost began nervously.

"And that is?" Kirby demanded, glaring at the spirit hovering above him.

"Well, uh . . . there was this thing . . . uh, and . . ."

Kirby's pointed ears caught a strange noise when Viper suddenly called out.

"What the heck's going on with that?" The biker was pointing to Erasmus's lifeless body.

For a moment Kirby believed that he had been successful and the body lived, but he quickly realized that wasn't it at all. Something was going on with the large screw protruding from the mad scientist's skull.

It was glowing an unearthly blue.

The screw began to pulse, emitting a loud, ear tickling hum.

"Huh," the ghostly Erasmus said thoughtfully, floating a bit closer. "I don't remember it ever doing that before."

Kirby squinted his Frenchie eyes as he studied the strange item protruding from the body's skull.

"Fascinating," Kirby said. "What I always assumed was a large screw could very well be . . ."

The Frenchie reached out a careful paw and was about to touch the pulsing object when . . .

"AAAAH!" Viper cried out.

They all looked at the large man as he backed up, pointing toward the door.

A light very much like the blue light emanating from the screw was streaming in from the horizontal window above the door, only far brighter.

"What the deuce is going on here?" Kirby muttered to himself as he stroked his furry chin. Deciding that answers must be revealed, he leapt down from his stool, heading toward the door.

"You might not want to go out there!" OB called out nervously.

"And why would that be the case?" Kirby asked, reaching for the door. "On the other side of this door is the unknown—waiting to be broken and tamed by a superior will."

The Frenchie opened the door and was bathed in an unearthly light.

"Oh," Kirby said, eyes widening. "This could be interesting."

The party within the gigantic lab had come to a complete stop, with everybody staring in one specific direction.

Kirby and the others all gazed to the far end of the vast room, toward the large object covered in multiple tarps.

But it wasn't sitting anymore.

The hidden object, still draped in tarps, now hovered above the laboratory floor; pulsating blue light escaping from between gaps in the canvas covers.

"What is it, K?"

Kirby looked down to see that OB had followed him to the door. "I don't know," the Frenchie replied, feeling the hackles on his back beneath the surgical gown he still wore begin to rise. "And isn't that wonderful."

The object reached a certain point in the air and began to vibrate, and the tarps fell away to reveal . . .

"Hey, that looks just like . . . ," OB began.

"The screw in Erasmus's head!" Kirby finished.

But it was so much more than just a screw.

Kirby was about to go back inside the lab to observe what might be happening with the smaller version of the artifact when the strangest of things occurred.

It was as if gravity had been abruptly canceled for anything and anywhere near the strange craft. Kirby watched as the tarps drifted up into the air like ghosts on a Halloween night, followed by the ice sculpture and the bouncy house.

"Wow, look at that!" OB said.

"Yes, look at it," Kirby agreed, ducking back into the surgical theater.

The instruments that he'd used had begun to float, as Viper looked on in terror. The ghostly Erasmus drifted close by, fascinated by the screw in his body's head.

"I think this thing is glowing brighter!" the ghost said, pointing to the protruding object.

And the ghost was right. It was glowing brighter, as was the enormous facsimile drifting above the laboratory floor outside, the two objects reacting in unison.

"Hey, Kobe?" Erasmus called out, snagging Kirby's attention once more. "You might want to take a look at this!"

The ghost drifted back, away from his body, as Kirby came forward to see what had so alarmed the ghost.

"Isn't that a thing," Kirby said, eyes widening with wonder, as he watched the screw in Erasmus's head . . .

Slowly.

Begin.

To turn.

This was it. The moment he'd been waiting for—wishing for.

Now was the time for Colonel Killshot to command his troops as they should be commanded. This was a time of action, which he'd missed so greatly, and he would not let it slip away.

"Ninth Division!" he yelled at the top of his lungs. "Lock and load!"

His eyes darted around the floor like an expert chess player studying the board for his next move. "Gunther, Cray, and Walters, man that tank! Lekman, take off your boots in the bouncy house—that thing's rented!"

The soldiers followed his commands without hesitation; they too had been waiting for a moment such as this.

Killshot studied his glowing opponent, moving closer to the hovering artifact but not close enough to lose gravity.

"What are you?" the colonel muttered beneath his breath, removing the sidearm from the holster at his side—just in case.

Suddenly, there was movement at the base of the screw-shaped artifact, and Killshot tensed, ready for anything.

Or so he believed.

A seam had appeared at the base, and the seam turned into a rectangle, and the rectangle turned into a small door.

And the door was opening, and a small ramp to the ground came down.

There was movement at the door, and Colonel Killshot had to squint to get a good look as something emerged and started down the ramp.

"What in the name of H. G. Wells?!" Killshot exclaimed.

They were three of the strangest things he'd ever seen: no bigger than a foot tall, with tentacles, slithering down to the base of the ramp. Their coloring featured varying degrees of green, and they each had one large eye in the center of what could only be called a head.

Killshot noticed that the one in the middle was wearing what looked to be a crown and figured that was most likely the leader.

"Communications team!" the colonel roared. "Front and center!"

Five scientists dressed in skintight black suits came running over looking elated.

"On my mark, commence communication!" the colonel ordered.

Killshot raised his arm, eyeing the scientists, and then brought his arm down.

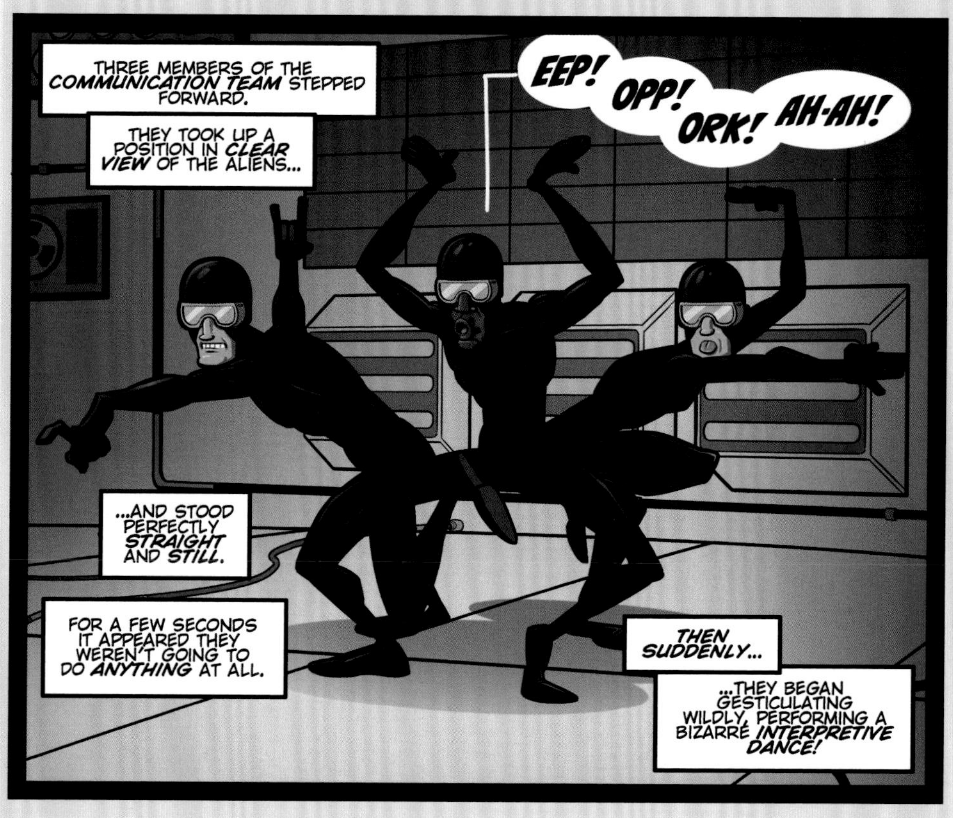

THREE MEMBERS OF THE COMMUNICATION TEAM STEPPED FORWARD.
THEY TOOK UP A POSITION IN CLEAR VIEW OF THE ALIENS...
EEP! OPP! ORK! AH-AH!
...AND STOOD PERFECTLY STRAIGHT AND STILL.
FOR A FEW SECONDS IT APPEARED THEY WEREN'T GOING TO DO ANYTHING AT ALL.
THEN SUDDENLY...
...THEY BEGAN GESTICULATING WILDLY, PERFORMING A BIZARRE INTERPRETIVE DANCE!

The aliens did not respond, instead looking at each other with their large single eyes, before looking back to the three, strangely garbed scientists gathered before them.

The first attempt a failure, the next of the scientists came forward, multiple props in hand, and quickly set the stage for his attempt.

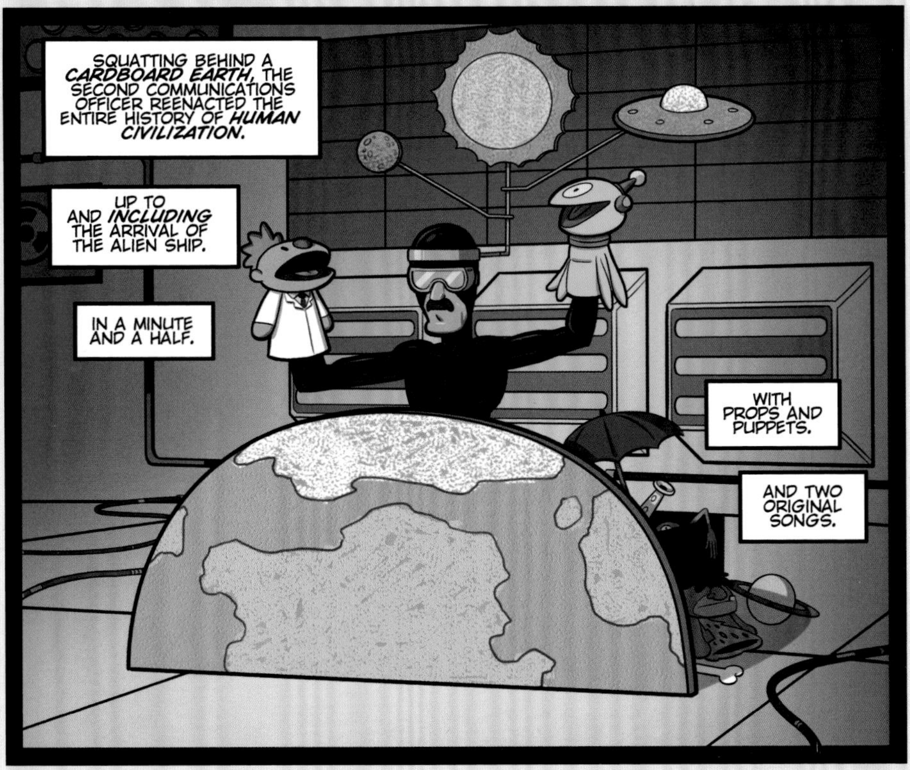
SQUATTING BEHIND A *CARDBOARD EARTH*, THE SECOND COMMUNICATIONS OFFICER REENACTED THE ENTIRE HISTORY OF *HUMAN CIVILIZATION.*
UP TO AND *INCLUDING* THE ARRIVAL OF THE ALIEN SHIP.
IN A MINUTE AND A HALF.
WITH PROPS AND PUPPETS.
AND TWO ORIGINAL SONGS.

The aliens, surprisingly, did not respond to this attempt to communicate either. It was up to the last member of the communications team to succeed.

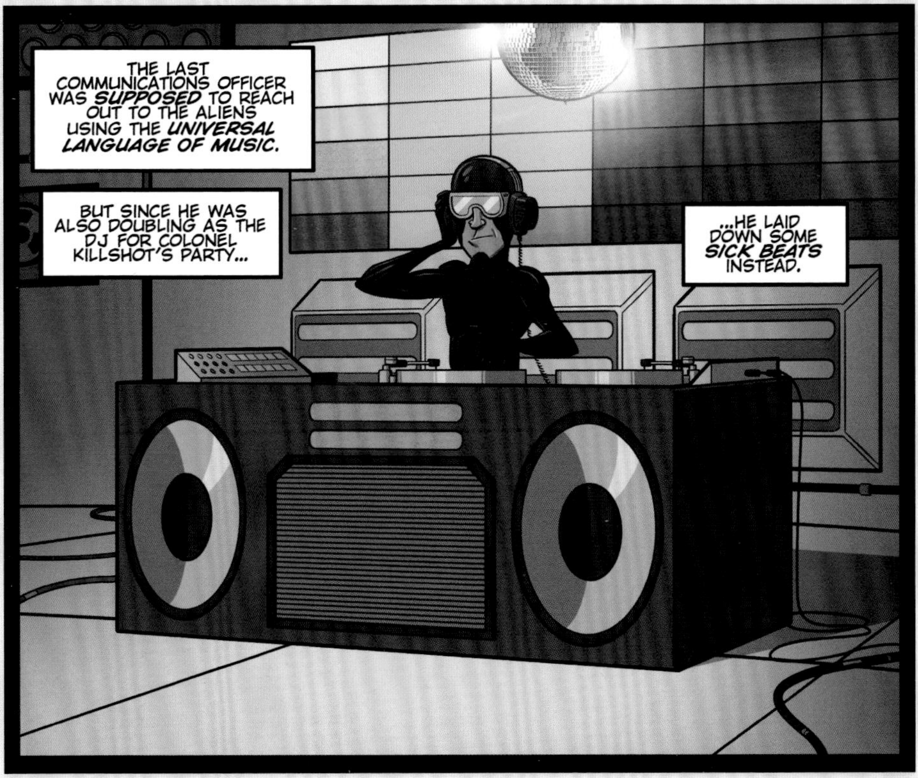
THE LAST COMMUNICATIONS OFFICER WAS SUPPOSED TO REACH OUT TO THE ALIENS USING THE UNIVERSAL LANGUAGE OF MUSIC.
BUT SINCE HE WAS ALSO DOUBLING AS THE DJ FOR COLONEL KILLSHOT'S PARTY...
...HE LAID DOWN SOME SICK BEATS INSTEAD.

The alien wearing the crown rolled his single eye before clearing his throat. It appeared that he was preparing to speak.

"People of Earth!" he proclaimed, perfectly understandable with his voice somehow amplified. "I am the Supreme Leader and I command you to chill! My ambassadors and I mean you no harm. We are here not to destroy your base. We do not have a death ray. We do not want to conquer your planet."

"Well, that's good to know," said one of the communication team members.

Killshot strode a little closer to the aliens.

"Then what do you want?" he asked them.

But before they could respond, another voice filled the empty air in reply.

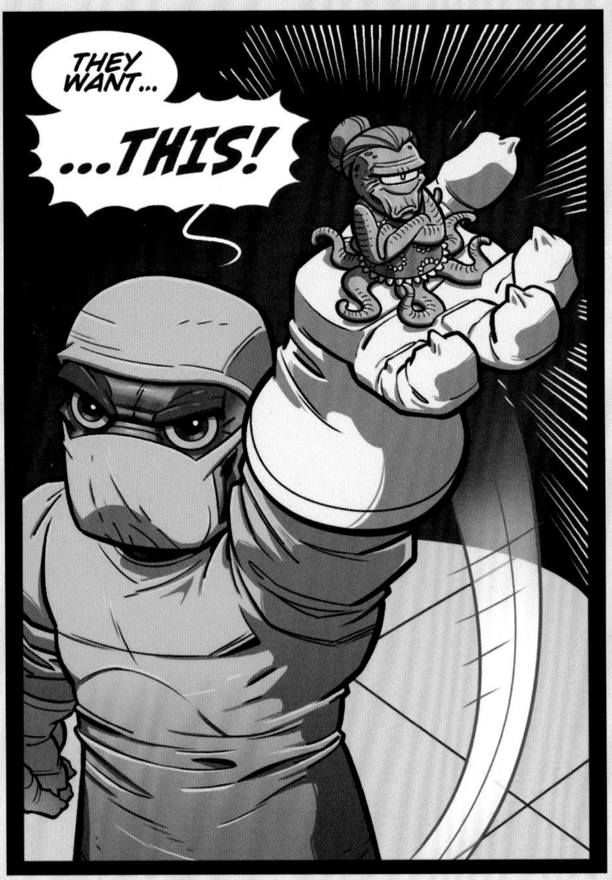
THEY WANT...
...THIS!

Kirby felt the eyes of the colonel scrutinizing him.

"And what do we have here," Colonel Killshot asked, referring as much to Kirby as to what the Frenchie was holding in his paw.

"I believe this is their queen," Kirby said.

"Their queen?" the alien standing in his palm asked, glaring at the Frenchie with her large, single eye. "Do I look like some royal snoot to you, moron? I'm their mother!"

Killshot gasped at the revelation.

"Mother, would you please just . . . ," the Supreme Leader began.

"Geez," said the ambassador alien to the right of the leader.

"I knew she was gonna do this," said the one to the left.

The crowned alien pulled himself together and began to address those in the laboratory again. "You see, she's very old," he started to explain. "She got confused and accidentally wandered into one of our emergency pods. We were concerned for her health and safety and . . ."

"Accidentally?" the mother shrieked at her sons. "I couldn't wait to get off that ship! It was no accident, it was an escape, I tell you!"

"Escape from who?" OB asked as he peeked out from behind Kirby.

The alien mom looked down from Kirby's paw at the tiny turtle. "Who?" she repeated. "Them!" She pointed multiple quivering tentacles at her three children. "You have no idea what it was like!"

The three alien sons looked down dejectedly as their mother continued to rip them up one side, and down the other.

"You see, I'm a procreator," she announced. "And proud of it! My special job is to make babies—23,241 babies a pop, to be precise. And as a red-eye," the alien mom pointed to the singular, scarlet orb behind the lens in the center of her face. "As a red-eye, I only make boy babies."

She paused for effect, making sure that they were all listening to her.

"Do you have any idea what it's like to live in a confined space with 23,241 teenage boys?"

The Supreme Leader cleared his throat nervously.

"Mother, perhaps you should . . ."

"The farting, the belching, the filth!" the alien mother bellowed. "Getting them to shower was like pulling teeth! You would think I was asking them to drink poison! And don't get me started on brushing their teeth!"

She buried her face in her tentacles.

"Ugh," she said. "Did I mention that one whole wing of the ship was filled with nothing but dirty dishes? Oh, and they wear the same clothes for days . . . sometimes weeks!"

"Mother, I think we have heard . . . ," the Leader tried to interject, but his mother was having none of that, bulldozing over his words with gusto.

"They're completely disgusting and I couldn't stand it anymore. I took one of the travel pods and headed to Earth. I was aiming for Hawaii, but something went wrong and I wound up on some tiny, barren island instead."

OB poked Kirby's leg. "She thinks Erasmus's skull was a barren island," the turtle said, putting a claw over his beak to hold back his laughter.

"Silence, terrapin," Kirby commanded. "It is neither the time nor the place."

Killshot clapped his hands together, getting everyone's attention.

"Okay then," the colonel said. "Seems like we've got ourselves a little domestic squabble here that needs to . . ."

"Domestic squabble?" the alien mother squawked. "I'll give you domestic squabble! Do you think that they're really concerned for my health and safety?"

She waited for Killshot to respond.

"Well, as their mother, I would imagine that they certainly must . . . ," he offered finally.

"HA!" the mother laughed. "Tell them the real reason you want me back! Go on, tell them!"

The Supreme Leader adjusted his golden crown with a tentacle while his brothers looked around sheepishly.

"Heh, you're our mother, Mother," he said. "Of course we want you back. We miss you terribly. After all, it's our duty to . . ."

Mom stomped a tentacle. "If you don't fess up, I'm coming over there and . . ."

"Okay! Okay!" the alien ambassador on the left cried out. "Because our spacecraft . . . our mothership . . . it isn't a mothership without a mother!"

"Boom!" Mom screamed. "Thank you so much for being honest. They only care about driving around in their precious mommyship!"

"It's mothership, Mother," the alien son on the far right said. "Mothership."

"Don't really care what it is," the alien mother grumbled.

"Mommyship," OB said with a giggle.

The three aliens heard the turtle's mocking laughter.

"No one drives regular ships anymore!" one of the ambassador sons tried to explain.

"Right," said the other.

"All the cool kids are driving motherships!" the Supreme Leader added, his brothers nodding vigorously in agreement.

"Oh, you mean those same cool kids who shower regularly and pick up after themselves?"

The three aliens seemed to wilt in shame.

"Oh, Ma," they cried in unison.

The mother put her tentacles where her hips would have been if she weren't a cephalopod and looked around the room.

"I ain't getting back on that ship, and I ain't getting any younger," she said. "So if someone could point me toward Hawaii, I'll let you apes get back to your shindig."

As if in reply, there was a deafening roar so intense that it shook the facility to its very foundation.

"What in the name of Krakatoa is that?!" Colonel Killshot cried, looking around.

Alarms had begun to wail and the room continued to tremble.

"Uh-oh," said one of the sons, looking toward the ceiling.

"Him," said the Supreme Leader with disdain, shaking his head disapprovingly.

Kirby could not help himself, the mystery demanding to be addressed. "Whom?"

"Our brother," said the ambassador on the right.

"Yeah," said the other on the far right. "Number 11,029. Carl."

"Carl?" Kirby repeated, as the alien mother turned to look at him.

"My brother's name was Carl," the mother alien said.

Kirby's eyes then widened in awe as the roof of the facility began to crumble, but instead of raining rubble, the pieces of concrete and steel drifted upward into the sky. Weightless.

All eyes were on the enormous gaping hole and the even larger, far more menacing spacecraft that hovered there.

"I thought I grounded him!" said the mother.

EIGHT

The music coming from the enormous spacecraft was most definitely heavy metal; screeching electric guitars and pounding drums caused the very air to vibrate.

The spacecraft above them was impressive, far showier than the smaller ship that hovered within the lab. Bright orange flames decorated its sides, and a grinning, one-eyed skull was painted on the front. Kirby guessed that the artwork was supposed to be intimidating, but he found it all a bit . . . juvenile.

And then came the voice, booming above the sound of the blaring metal music.

"People of Earth! Definitely don't chill! I mean you grave harm to the max! I am here to destroy you and your base and maybe the planet if I feel like it! I have a death ray and I'm not afraid to use it!"

Mother sighed, shaking her head. "There's always one," she muttered with shame.

"Oh, and Mom?" boomed the alien. "If you would please get in my ship, that would be awesome too. See? I asked nicely and used my polite words just like you always told me to!"

The mother alien reacted angrily. "Not on your life!" she screamed up at the floating spaceship. "You were always a brat and you're still a brat!"

The blaring speakers playing metal went quiet for a moment before Carl spoke again. He seemed kind of upset.

"Wow, Mom, that was kinda mean." There was another pause before . . . "Oh well, suit yourself!"

And with those words, the bottom of the spacecraft began to open slowly, and a terrible-looking device began to descend from within.

"The minute he doesn't get what he wants, out comes the death ray. Where did I go wrong?" the troubled alien mother asked Kirby and the colonel.

But Kirby did not hear the question, for two of the mother alien's words reverberated inside his atomically enhanced brain.

Death ray.

"That doesn't look like anything that would be used for something nice," OB said nervously, looking up to the ship.

The spacecraft lowered as the death ray began to hum, and at once the gravity within the lab further destabilized. All manner of lab equipment and advanced military weapons began to float up into the air.

"I would have to agree," Kirby said thoughtfully.

"We're under attack!" Colonel Killshot roared to the soldiers around him. "Fire!"

Kirby watched as the colonel and his troops pointed their pistols at the enormous craft above them and opened fire with everything they had. But the gravity fluctuations made the bullets useless, as the rounds left their weapons and then floated harmlessly in the air.

"Uh, Kensington?" said a voice from behind the Frenchie.

Kirby whirled to see the most bizarre of sights: Erasmus and Viper astride the cryo-chamber, holding Erasmus's thawed body. It appeared as though they were trying to push it back down to Earth but weren't having much success.

"Viper could use a little help here, dog!" the biker said as he grunted, forcing his full weight upon the chamber to little effect.

But the ghost and the biker were the least of Kirby's concerns, and he turned his attentions back to the mother alien still in his paw.

"You," Kirby said to her, walking back toward the operating theater.

"Yes?" she questioned, eyeing the Frenchie with her single orb.

"I must put you somewhere safe."

Inside the operating room he found a jar of cotton balls and emptied them onto the floor.

"You'll be safe in here," Kirby told her, dropping her inside the jar.

"I'd rather be in Hawaii!" her screeching voice cut off as he screwed the lid back on the jar.

"Don't let anything happen to her," Kirby said, handing the jar to OB, who had followed him.

The turtle looked inside the jar at the alien and smiled. "She's awfully cute!" he said.

The mother alien responded, whipping her tentacles at the turtle's face. "I'll give you cute!"

Kirby left the alien mother in OB's care and raced back into the main room of the enormous laboratory. Removing his surgical garb, he prepared for his next course of action.

He had a death ray to disable.

Dr. Oddfellow finally had total control of his faculties, just as all heck was breaking loose in the lab.

He'd seen the strange little dog take the alien mother into the operating room and exit without her.

Curious, the doctor thought, walking to the best of his ability toward the open door and into the operating theater once more. Carefully, he peered around the corner to see the turtle holding a jar.

A jar that held the prize he most desperately sought.

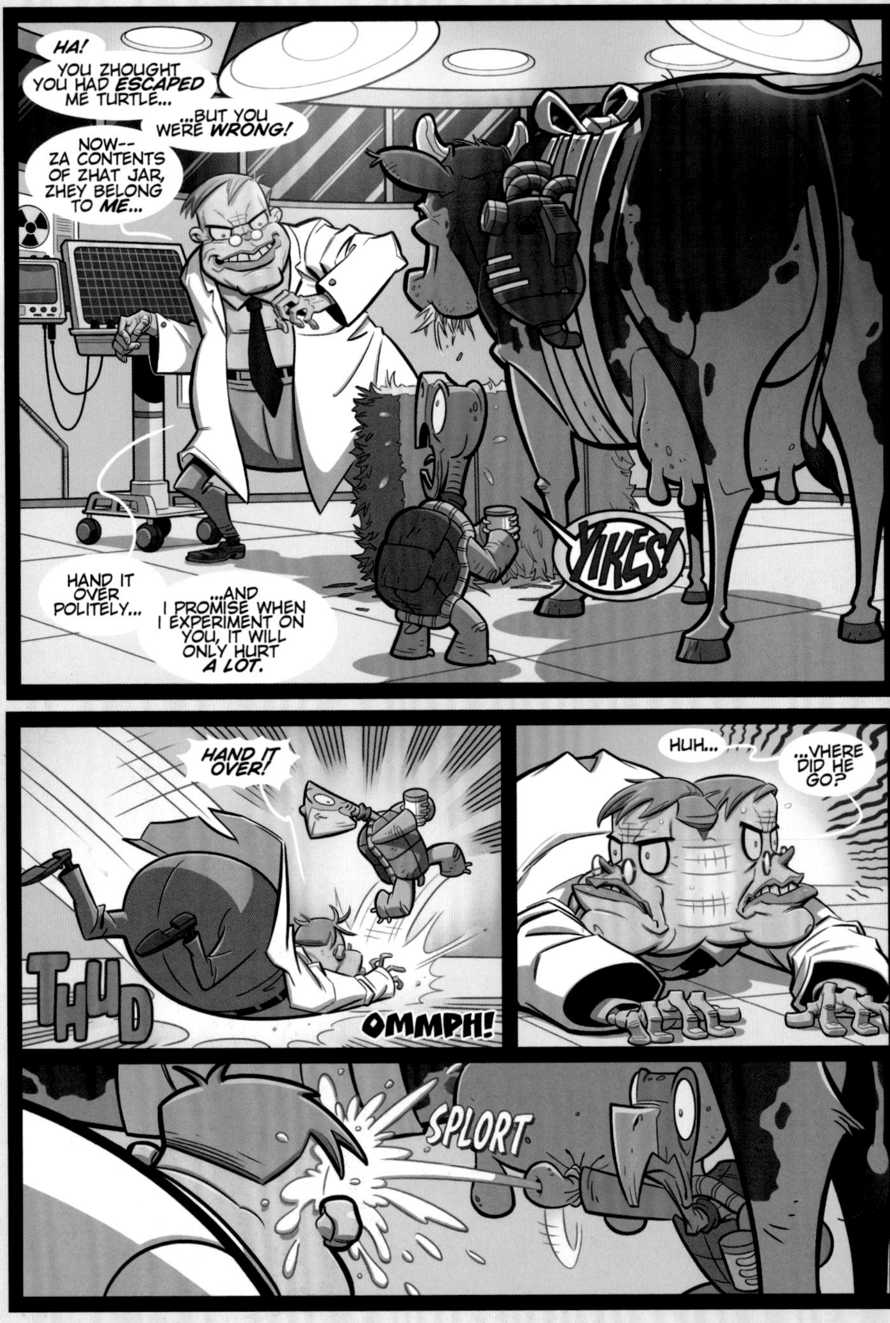
HA!
YOU ZHOUGHT YOU HAD ESCAPED ME TURTLE...
...BUT YOU WERE WRONG!
NOW-- ZA CONTENTS OF ZHAT JAR, ZHEY BELONG TO ME...
YIKES!
HAND IT OVER POLITELY...
...AND I PROMISE WHEN I EXPERIMENT ON YOU, IT WILL ONLY HURT A LOT.
HAND IT OVER!
THUD
OMMPH!
HUH...
...VHERE DID HE GO?
SPLORT

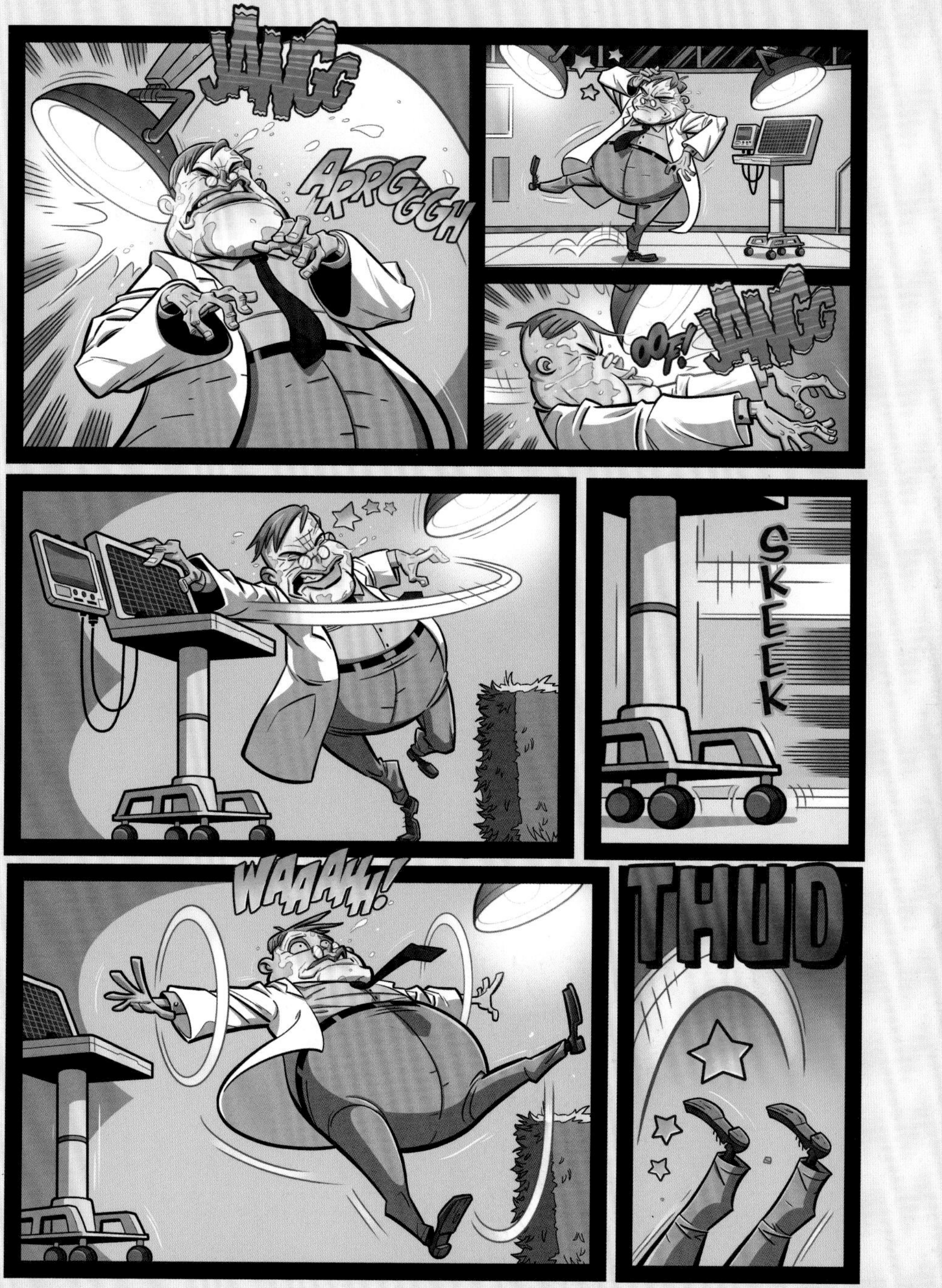

JANGG
ARRGGGH
OOF!
JANGG
SKEEK
WAAAHH!
THUD

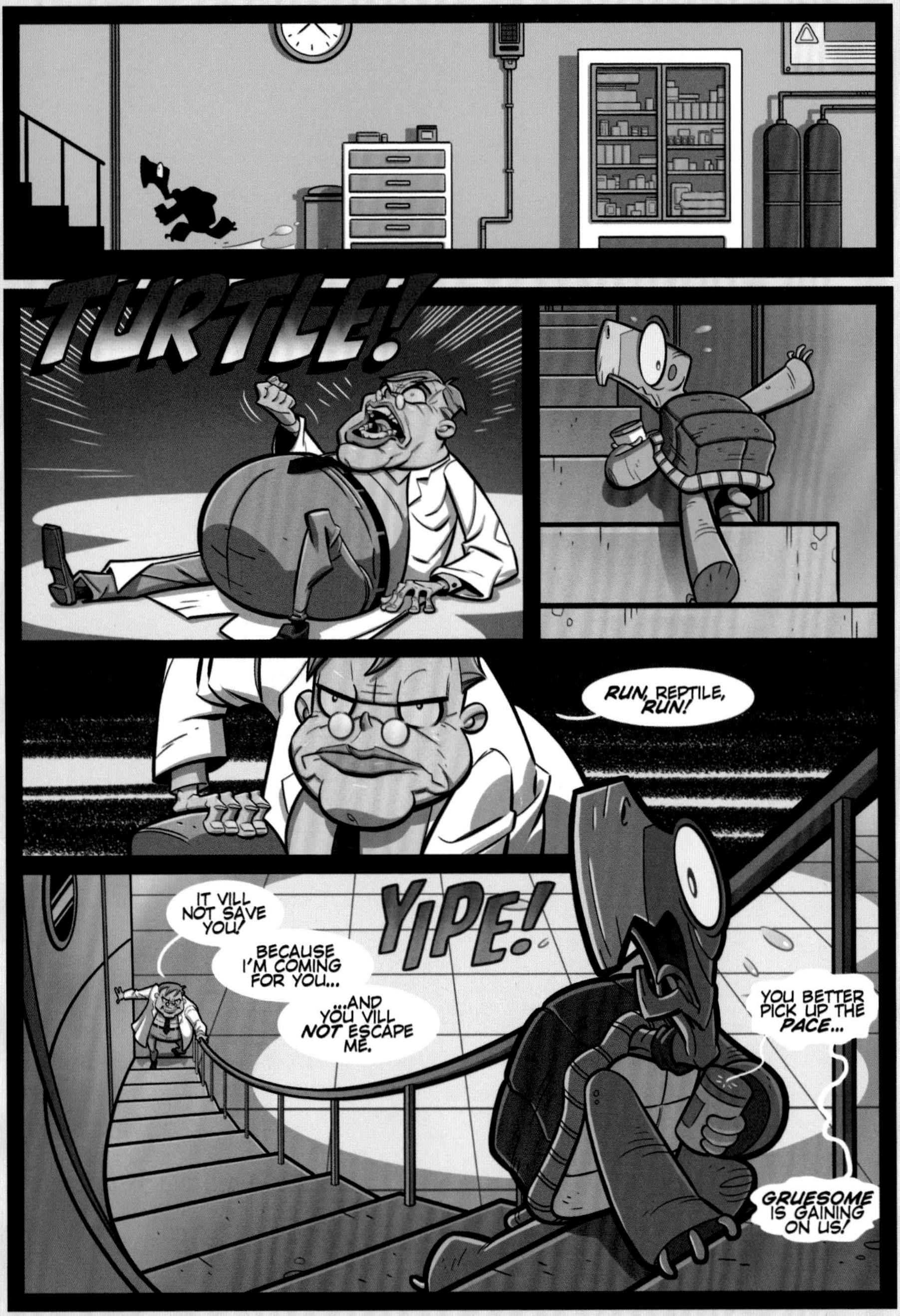
TURTLE!
RUN, REPTILE, RUN!
IT VILL NOT SAVE YOU!
BECAUSE I'M COMING FOR YOU...
...AND YOU VILL NOT ESCAPE ME.
YIPE!
YOU BETTER PICK UP THE PACE...
GRUESOME IS GAINING ON US!

Standing in the center of the main room, Kirby gazed up at the enormous craft, the fearsome weapon protruding from its belly, humming and crackling.

He knew what he must do.

He had to somehow disarm the alien death ray, and perhaps memorize the specs of the otherworldly weapon—after all, one never knew when one might need a death ray.

But how to get aboard that craft?!

And then, like a bolt of lightning, an idea struck him.

The gravity . . .

The gravity was still in flux, and the air was filled with all manner of rubble—rubble large enough to act as a makeshift staircase.

Yes, that just might work, Kirby thought, singling out a floating piece of ceiling as it drifted by.

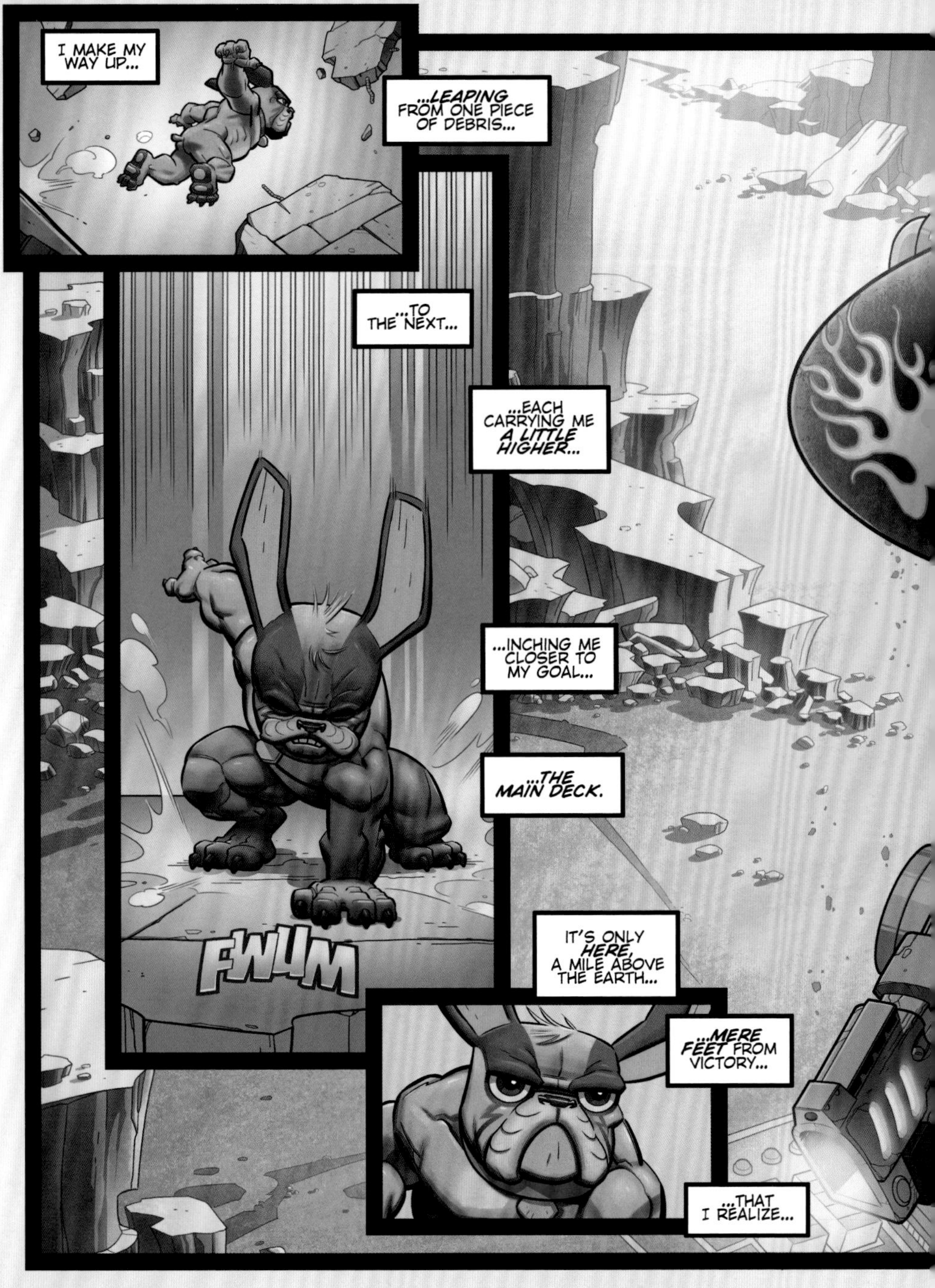
I MAKE MY WAY UP...
...LEAPING FROM ONE PIECE OF DEBRIS...
...TO THE NEXT...
...EACH CARRYING ME A LITTLE HIGHER...
...INCHING ME CLOSER TO MY GOAL...
...THE MAIN DECK.
FWUM
IT'S ONLY HERE, A MILE ABOVE THE EARTH...
...MERE FEET FROM VICTORY...
...THAT I REALIZE...

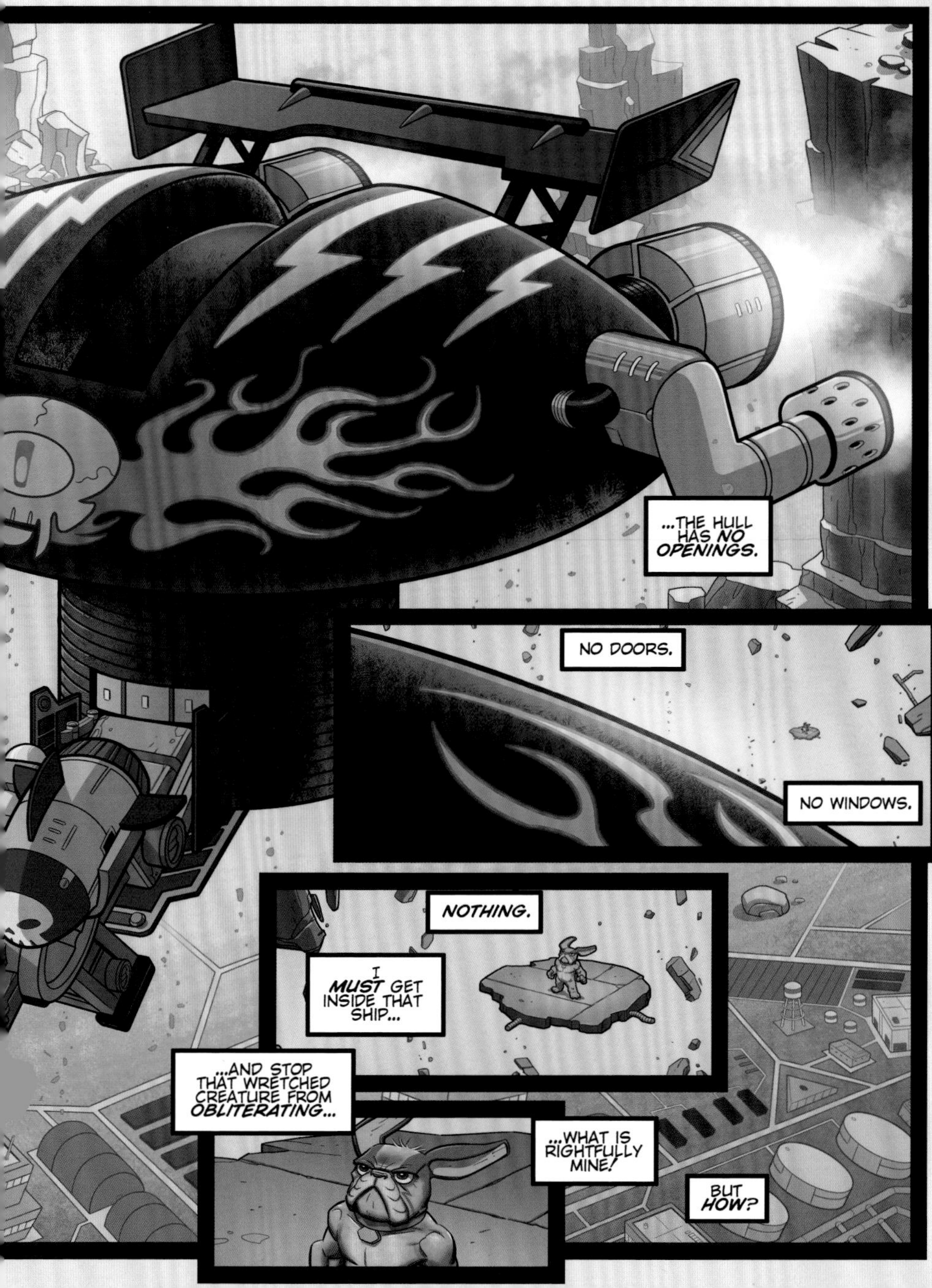
...THE HULL HAS NO OPENINGS.
NO DOORS.
NO WINDOWS.
NOTHING.
I MUST GET INSIDE THAT SHIP...
...AND STOP THAT WRETCHED CREATURE FROM OBLITERATING...
...WHAT IS RIGHTFULLY MINE!
BUT HOW?

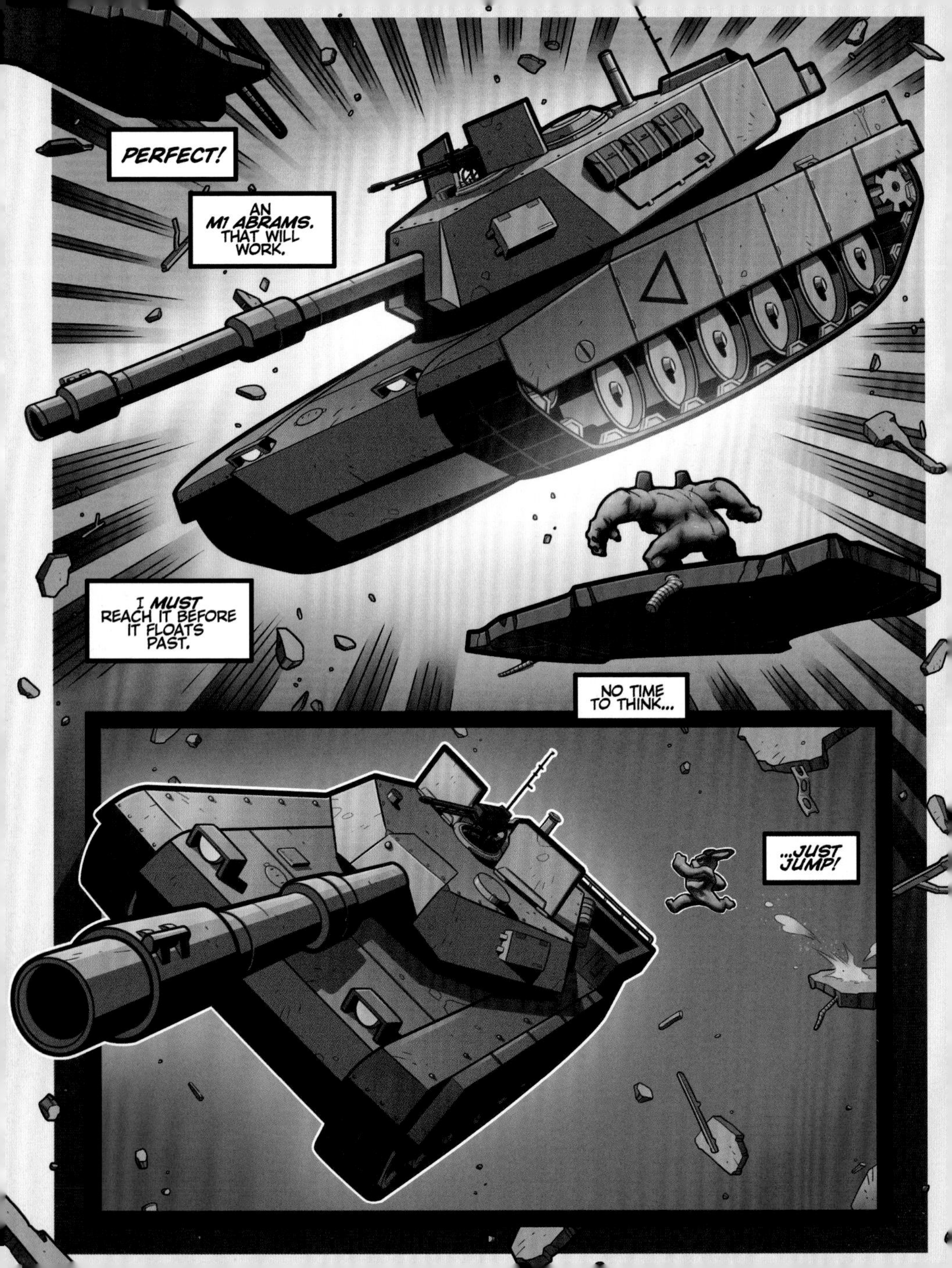
PERFECT!
AN M1 ABRAMS. THAT WILL WORK.
I MUST REACH IT BEFORE IT FLOATS PAST.
NO TIME TO THINK...
...JUST JUMP!

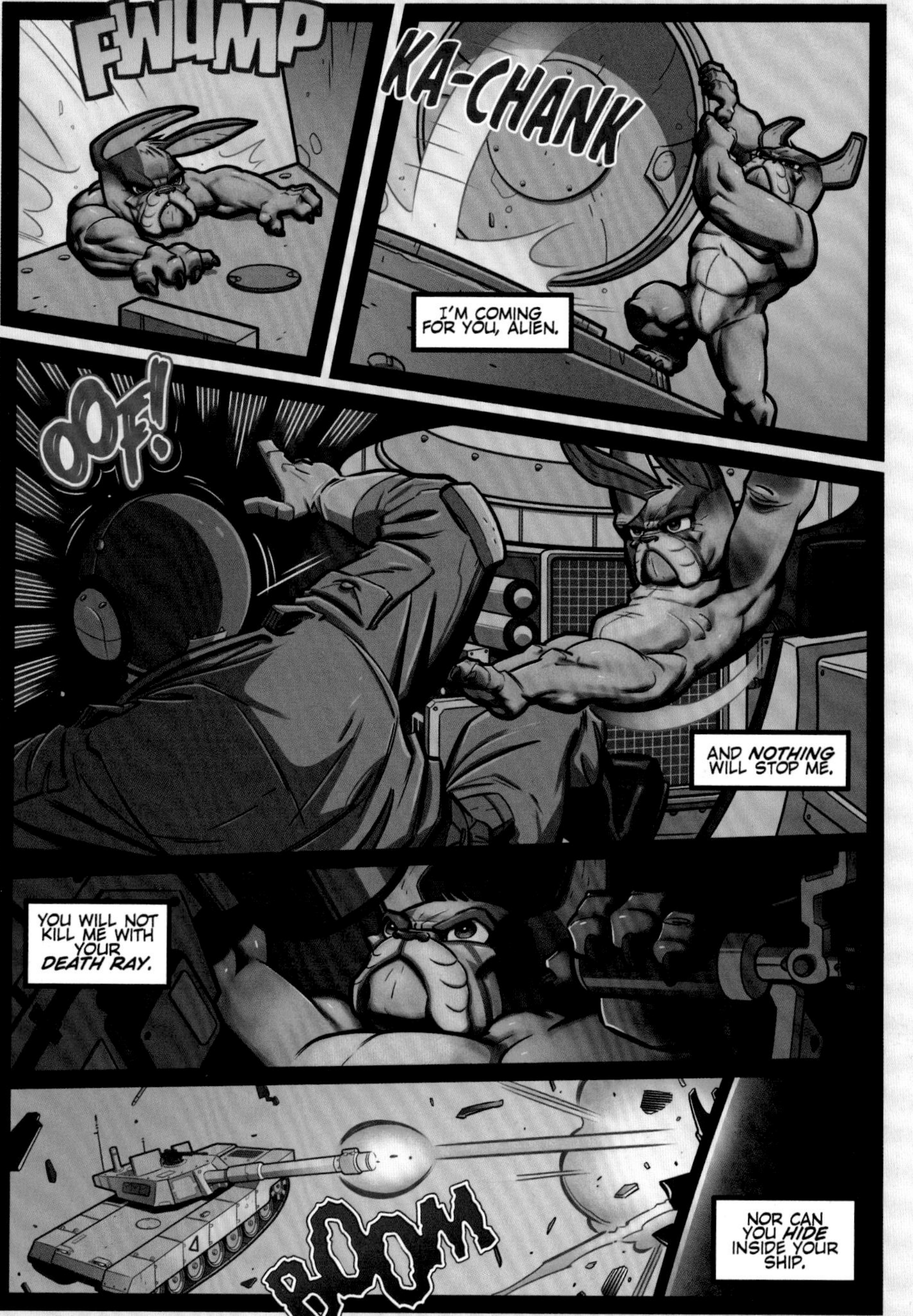
FWUMP
KA-CHANK
I'M COMING FOR YOU, ALIEN.
OOF!
AND NOTHING WILL STOP ME.
YOU WILL NOT KILL ME WITH YOUR DEATH RAY.
BOOM
NOR CAN YOU HIDE INSIDE YOUR SHIP.

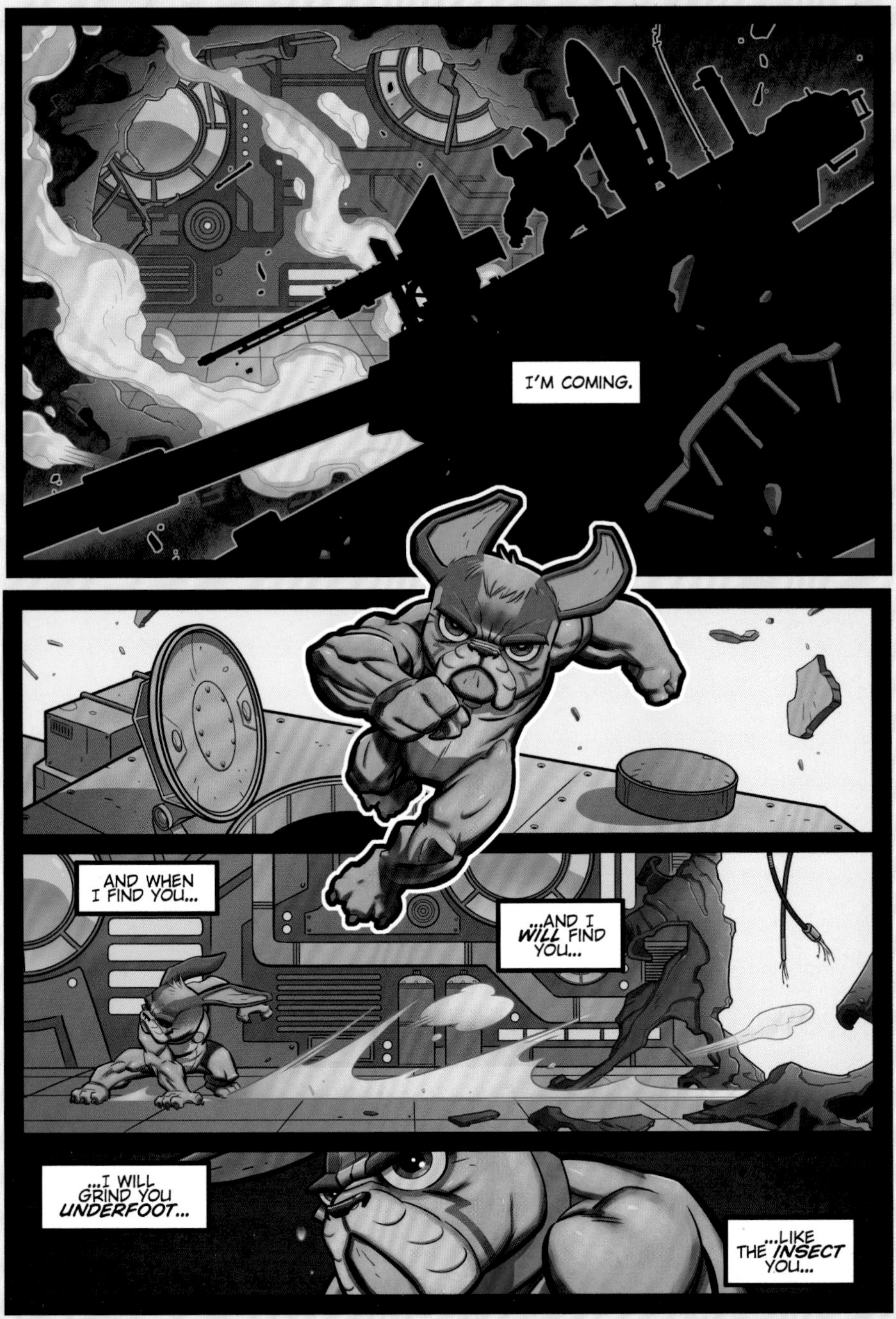
I'M COMING.
AND WHEN I FIND YOU...
...AND I WILL FIND YOU...
...I WILL GRIND YOU UNDERFOOT...
...LIKE THE INSECT YOU...

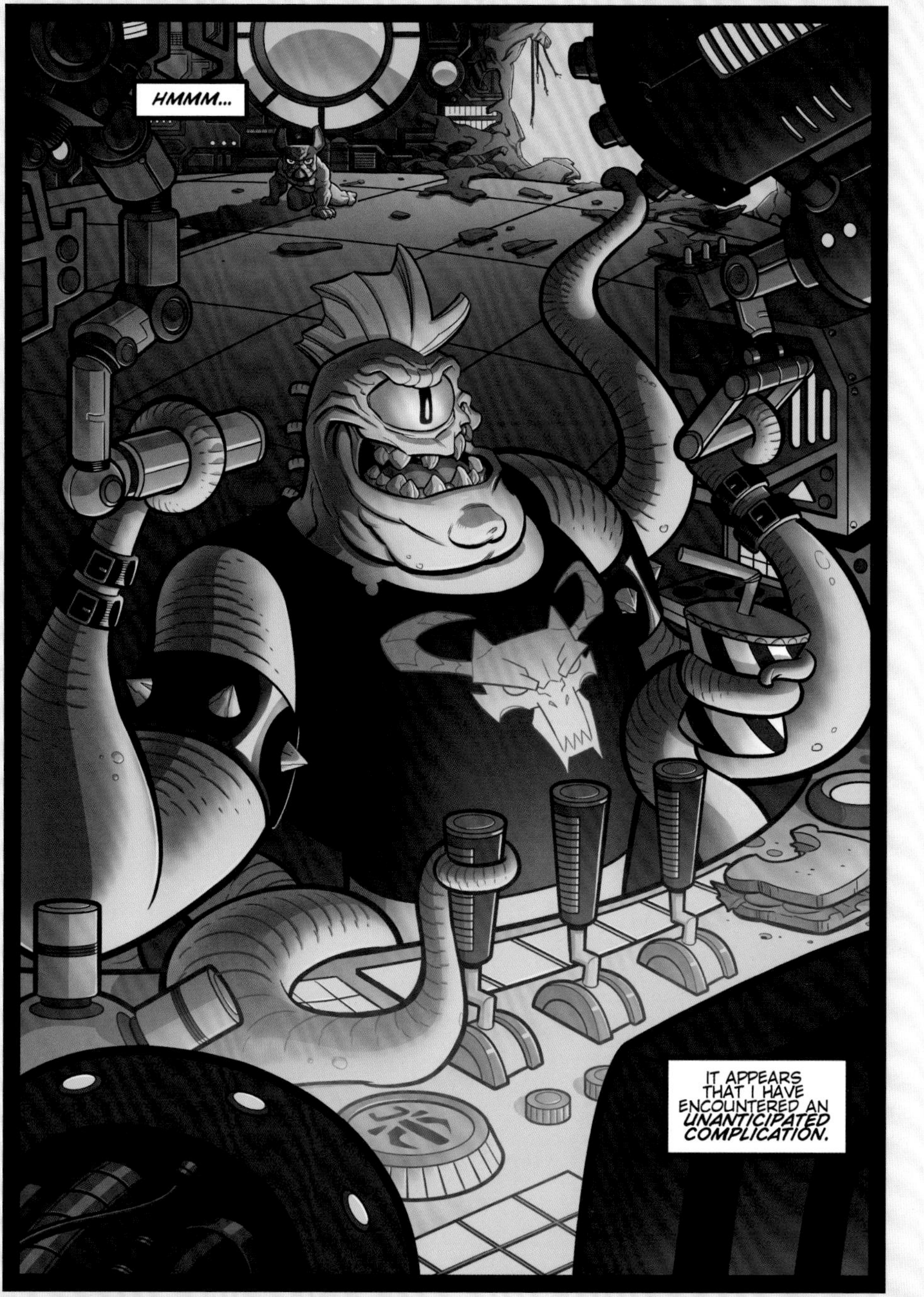
HMMM...
IT APPEARS THAT I HAVE ENCOUNTERED AN UNANTICIPATED COMPLICATION.

Would'ja look at that, Killshot thought, watching the Frenchie jump from floating object to floating object, climbing the makeshift stairs toward the hovering spacecraft.

Where Killshot wanted to go.

Inspired by the Frenchie, the colonel holstered his pistol. "Soldier!" he shouted at a private standing near a wall.

The soldier snapped to attention. "Me, sir?"

"Yes," Killshot said. "Get me a bag of ruckus."

"Bag of ruckus, sir?" the soldier asked nervously.

"You new here, soldier?" the colonel jabbed. "A bag of ruckus contains everything a soldier needs to cause some serious trouble. Do you understand now?"

"Yes, sir!" the soldier said. Immediately, he jogged over to another group of soldiers, frantic to get his commanding officer what he demanded. The others handed him what he needed and he proudly presented it to the colonel.

"Here you go, sir! Bag of ruckus."

Killshot took the pack, slid his arms through the straps, and hefted it onto his back. "Now to get myself into the belly of the beast," he said, looking up at the underside of the monstrous craft.

And then he spied it.

The bouncy house.

The inflated amusement floated in the air, held in place by support ropes to keep it from moving when in use. *If it weren't for those ropes . . .* Killshot thought, an idea taking shape.

From his pocket he removed a small pen knife, crawled onto the roof of the bouncy house, and cut the thick support lines.

Just as he suspected, the bouncy house began to float upward, toward the belly of the spacecraft.

Closer, and closer still.

The three alien sons watched the insanity around them.

"That Carl, always starting trouble," Mike said with a snarl.

"Seriously," Bill said. "All we wanted was our mother back and now look at things!"

"Nothing's changed, we still need to get her back," Supreme Leader Phil said. "Where the heck is she anyway?"

Their single eyes scanned the room, searching for their parent.

"There!" Bill yelled excitedly, pointing with a tentacle toward OB, who was climbing a staircase that could only lead up toward the open ceiling and the giant spacecraft hovering above it. "There's the strange-looking one that has her."

"And it looks like he's heading on up to Carl's ship," said Mike. "What are we gonna do?"

"What we said, boys," said Supreme Leader Phil. "We're gonna get our mother back."

They turned and started up the ramp to their ship at an awkward, tentacle-flapping run.

"Maybe if we save her, she won't be mad at us anymore," Bill said.

"Yeah, sure," Supreme Lead Phil said sarcastically as the door closed behind them with a hiss. "And Baraxian puss frogs undulate."

NINE

If there was ever a time when his enhanced Frenchie brain needed to perform at peak efficiency, it was now.

Kirby had to prevent the death ray from firing, but looking at the enormous and quite formidable form of Carl, he had no idea how he would do that.

Crouching low, just inside the vast spaceship, Kirby pondered his situation. How was he to lure the alien creature away from the death ray's complex control panel?

Kirby's eyes searched the room, finally locking on several thick tubes dangling from the ceiling. The Frenchie darted from his hiding place, moving quickly along the wall until he reached the first of the tubes. He stretched as high as he could and was just able to grab one of the thick black tubes. Pulling it closer to his ear, he listened carefully, his superior Frenchie hearing picking up the sound of rushing fluid.

He studied the tube and saw that it was actually two pieces connected by a thick nut. Carefully, he loosened the nut, creating a leak. A steady stream of fluorescent green began to flow from the tube, the sound echoing softly off the cold, metal walls of the spacecraft.

Plan in motion, Kirby moved back closer to the control panel and the enormous alien sitting there. With baited breath, he waited to see if his plan would work. It was a long shot but . . .

"Oh, Deathy, how I love the sounds you make when coming out to play," Carl gurgled in a terrible singsongy voice. "You bring me so much joy when I hear you charging out to wipe life from existence and . . ."

Kirby watched in anticipation as Carl stopped, his grotesque alien body suddenly going rigid.

"Doh! Potty break!" the alien announced. The creature slithered from his perch and undulated across the floor, humming a cheerful tune as he disappeared through a circular door in the wall.

Recognizing his opportunity, Kirby broke for the control panel and hopped up into the strangely shaped chair.

"Let's see if I can make this sing before Carl gets back."

With that, the Frenchie cracked his knuckles and went to work.

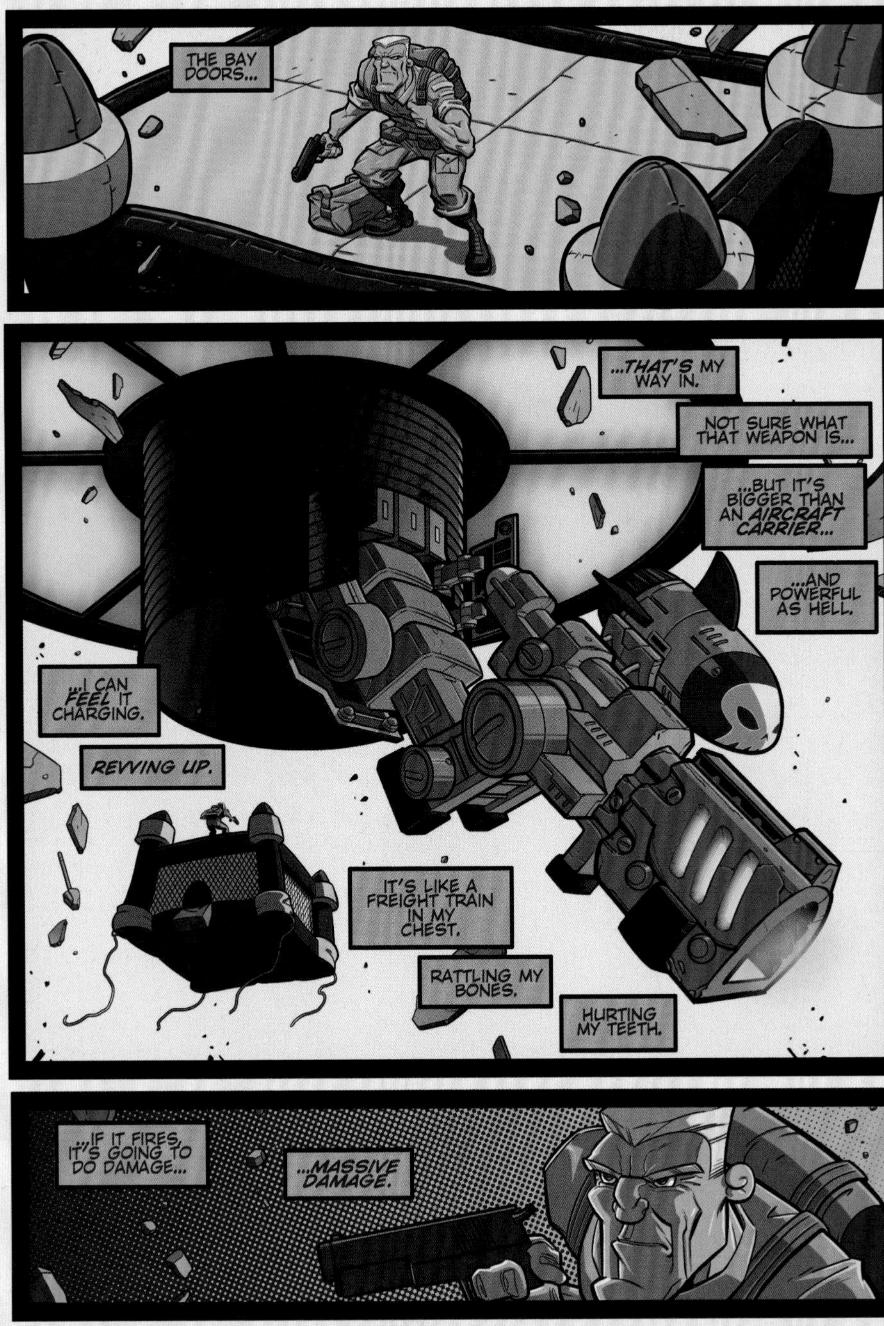
THE BAY DOORS...
...THAT'S MY WAY IN.
NOT SURE WHAT THAT WEAPON IS...
...BUT IT'S BIGGER THAN AN AIRCRAFT CARRIER...
...AND POWERFUL AS HELL.
...I CAN FEEL IT CHARGING.
REVVING UP.
IT'S LIKE A FREIGHT TRAIN IN MY CHEST.
RATTLING MY BONES.
HURTING MY TEETH.
...IF IT FIRES, IT'S GOING TO DO DAMAGE...
...MASSIVE DAMAGE.

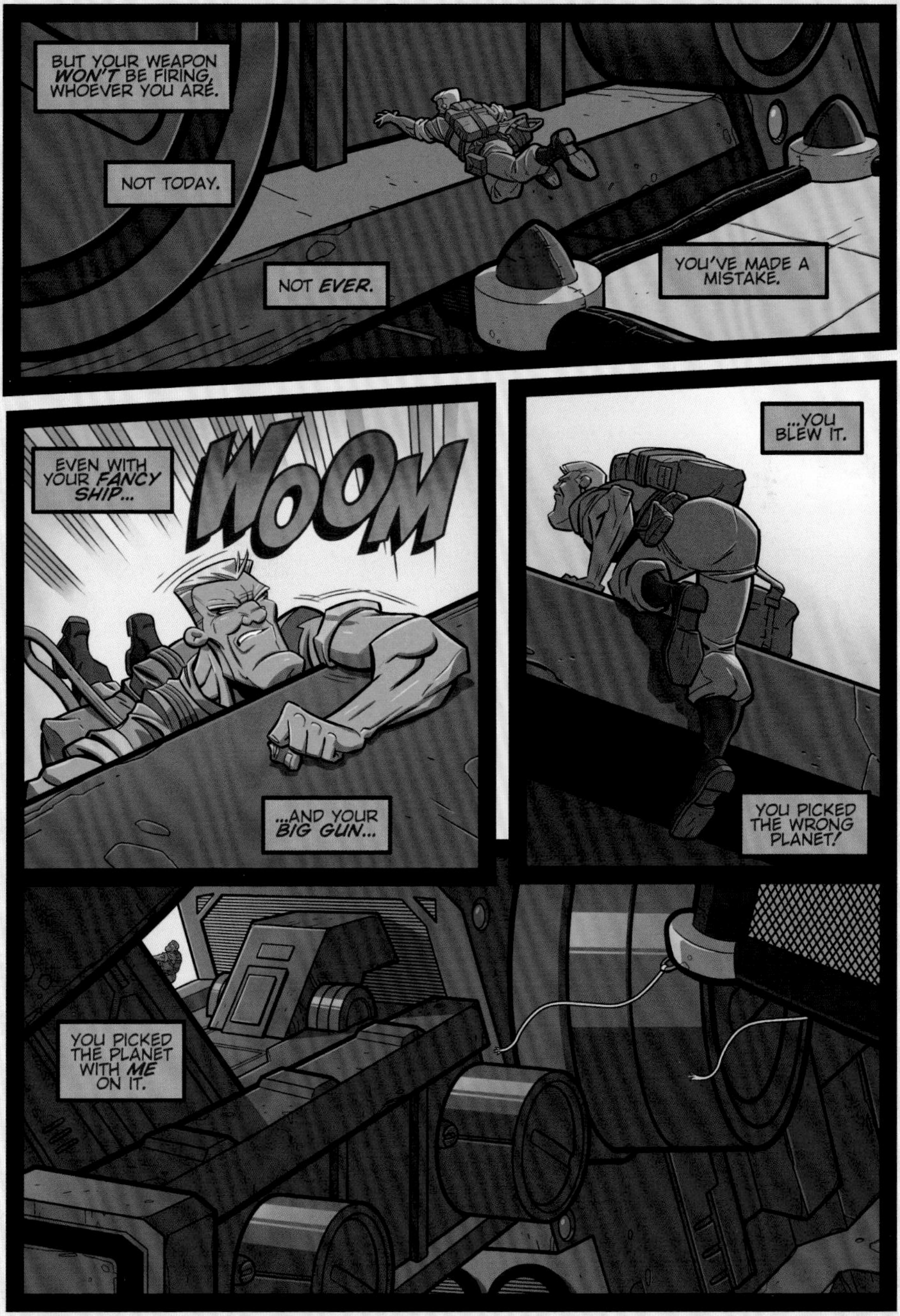
BUT YOUR WEAPON WON'T BE FIRING, WHOEVER YOU ARE.
NOT TODAY.
NOT EVER.
YOU'VE MADE A MISTAKE.
EVEN WITH YOUR FANCY SHIP...
WOOM
...AND YOUR BIG GUN...
...YOU BLEW IT.
YOU PICKED THE WRONG PLANET!
YOU PICKED THE PLANET WITH ME ON IT.

TEN

The cryo-chamber, with Erasmus and Viper still astride it, floated into the alien spacecraft, drawn inside as if the large interstellar craft had a gravitational pull all its own.

It was something that would have fascinated Erasmus Peckinpah if he hadn't been so distracted by his current predicament.

The cryo-chamber wouldn't stop spinning.

"Please," Viper cried out, holding on for dear life. "Make . . . it . . . stop!" The biker had turned a terrible shade of green.

"What do you think I'm trying to do?" Erasmus exclaimed, hands upon his ghostly hips, studying the twirling containment vessel. "Maybe if I head down to this end," he suggested, and moved to the other side of the drifting chamber.

But the weightless chamber kept on twirling round and round.

"I think Viper is gonna hurl!" the biker said, clamping a hand over his mouth.

"Well, that isn't gonna solve a thing," Erasmus chided. "Although," he began, thoughtfully stroking his ghostly chin. "Maybe if you did hurl, and hurled big in the opposite direction . . ."

The turtle's little legs weren't built for stairs.

But OB did the best he could, hopping onto the edge of one metal step and hauling himself up as fast as he could before moving on to the next, the terrifying sounds of Dr. Oddfellow grunting and wheezing behind him.

To keep himself calm, OB thought of his 20-gallon tank at home in the sunroom, the nice woodchips that coated its bottom, the plastic palm tree that added an extra dash of cheeriness, his lovely water dish always filled with the delicious nectar of life, and the sun—the glorious rays of sun that he loved so much to bask in.

He could practically feel them now, beating down upon his shell.

It was so nice.

The sudden pressure around one of his legs made OB squawk like a chicken being plucked.

"Got you!" the doctor said, a sinister smile oozing across his doughy features. "You are going to give me zhat jar or . . ."

The scientist began to pull OB from the step, and the turtle felt himself begin to panic.

And that was when it happened.

OB could never predict when or if it would happen, but sometimes, when he got really upset—

His body did weird things.

Dr. Oddfellow squeezed his leg all the tighter and tried to draw him closer, but that all came to a sudden and shocking stop when OB's leg turned to liquid.

The turtle turned to see the look of absolute surprise on the doctor's face as he gazed at his fingers and the fluid that dribbled between them onto the stairs.

OB was just as shocked as the scientist, especially when the water flowed back to his body, reforming his leg.

WHOA!

Not wanting to waste an opportunity, OB tried to quicken his pace up the stairs and . . .

"Not so fast!" the doctor growled, lunging, hands outstretched.

His arms were much longer than they looked, and OB felt the chubby sausage fingers close around his shell.

"This time I have you for sure!" the evil scientist proclaimed.

But OB's body was at it again.

Thick thorns were suddenly poking from his shell, and Oddfellow let out a bloodcurdling scream as they stabbed his hands. He dropped the turtle as he stumbled back and fell down the stairs.

OB snuck a quick look behind him and saw the man lying in a heap, blowing on his punctured flesh.

I'm startin' to like these powers, the turtle thought, climbing onto the next step, and then the next.

On his way to what remained of the roof.

ELEVEN

It did not take long for Kirby to figure out the control panel. Once his atomically altered brain had grasped the basics, everything became perfectly clear.

He was just about to begin retracting the death ray when a thick green tentacle wrapped around his body and began to squeeze. It did not take a genius, or a French bulldog with an atomic brain, to figure out that Carl had returned from his bathroom break.

The chair spun around and Kirby was suddenly face to face with the leering giant.

"Well, look at this," Carl gurgled. "Ain't you an interesting-looking bug. That's what I call you guys on this ball'a dirt planet. Bugs. I do that because we're so much smarter than you and stuff."

"And yet your mother remained hidden from you for—how many years was it? Where was your so called superior intelligence then?" Kirby asked, his intense Frenchie stare locked onto Carl's single, bulging eye.

The alien tightened his grip.

"That's just because my ma is wicked smart," Carl said defiantly.

"Smarter than you even?"

Carl considered that, then snarled, showing off rows of razor-sharp teeth as he drew Kirby closer.

"Wonder if your head will pop if I squeeze you tight enough," the alien giant pondered. "Let's see."

His grip grew tighter, and Kirby felt what air that remained in his lungs savagely squeezed out. Colorful dots danced before his eyes, and he knew it wouldn't be long before he either passed out or felt his ribs crushed to paste.

But suddenly, Carl let out a squawk of pain, and the distinctive sound of gunfire reverberated through the ship.

The creature's hold loosened, and Kirby took in a deep breath, once again providing oxygen to the most powerful weapon in the entire spacecraft.

His Frenchie brain.

From the corner of his eye, Kirby saw it. The military man—the colonel—Killshot—aiming his pistol and continuing to fire as Carl spun angrily to face his new adversary.

"Oh, look! Another bug!" the alien roared. "Only this one stings! I really hate bugs that sting!"

Carl went after the colonel, and Kirby, still wound tightly in the alien's tentacle, had no choice but to go along for the ride.

Erasmus scratched at the ghostly hair on the top of his strangely shaped head as the still out-of-control cryo-chamber continued to spin.

"Well, vomiting didn't work out," the ghostly mad scientist said to a sickened Viper, still holding on for dear life. "Wonder if we should concentrate on the other end? How's the stomach feeling?"

Viper let out a groan of despair, swearing silently to never do anything bad ever again if the chamber would just stop spinning.

"We need something with a little ooomph!" Erasmus said. "Something to counter this crazy momentum!"

Viper seriously considered letting go, to allow himself to fall from the spinning cryo-chamber into zero gravity, but the increasing centrifugal force had other plans.

He couldn't let go if he tried.

He looked at the ghostly Erasmus, who was still muttering to himself about an opposite-powered force, and that's when Viper came to the startling realization that only he had to worry about being killed.

That was the kind of incentive that Viper needed.

With great effort, Viper managed to lift his head up and look about the spinning room.

And then he saw it. Bright red and floating toward them. Viper had never seen anything quite so beautiful.

"That!" the biker yelled, pointing toward the fire extinguisher.

"Yeah, I saw a toaster oven go by a minute ago, big deal," Erasmus said. "Can't you see that I'm trying to think here?"

"No!" Viper roared. "That! The opposite force!" He pretended he was spraying a fire extinguisher.

It took a moment, but . . .

"Wait a sec!" Erasmus proclaimed, raising a finger as an ectoplasmic light bulb formed over his head. "That fire extinguisher is just what we're looking for!"

It was still just within reach.

"Grab it!" Erasmus commanded, and Viper acted, pushing off from the surface of the cryo-chamber just long enough to snag their prize.

"Got it!" he announced proudly, clutching the red extinguisher to his chest like a delicate new born. "Viper has it."

"Okay then," Erasmus said, rubbing his transparent hands together. "Point it in the opposite direction to how we're spinning and let it rip!"

Viper held up the extinguisher, checked and double checked how the cryo-chamber was spinning, then pulled the pin and pressed the metal handle.

The extinguisher roared, spewing a cloud of snow white. At first Viper didn't think anything was happening, but then, yes, yes, their spin was slowing.

"That's it, Cobra! Keep spewing!"

The cold in his hand was almost painful, but Viper kept right on squeezing the handle until their circular motion had nearly come to a stop and . . .

"Huh," Erasmus said, perched at the opposite end of the cryo-chamber. "Didn't think of that."

"What?" Viper yelled over the roar of the fire extinguisher.

"That we'd stop spinning and start moving in a linear direction."

Viper turned to look behind him and swallowed loudly at the sight.

They were hurtling straight for the giant spaceship hanging in the sky over the open roof of the research facility.

Terrified, Viper let go of the extinguisher, but it was already too late.

There wasn't time to jump off even if he could.

♣

Colonel Killshot had always imagined that he would bite the big one in the throes of battle, but never in a million years would he have thought of cashing in his chips while fighting a multitentacled abomination from beyond the stars.

Just goes to show how unpredictable life could be.

Carl bore down upon him, roaring to beat the band. Killshot could see the Frenchie clutched in a tentacle and wished there was something he could do to set the formidable canine free.

Instead, he raised his pistol and continued to fire into the alien's ugly mug. He guessed that it was probably the end, but what a way to go.

"Get ready to die, bug!" Carl threatened, tentacles reaching for the colonel.

Killshot tensed, preparing himself for the inevitable . . .

And then he saw it from the corner of his eye.

Something shooting past him.

Something traveling incredibly fast.

It hit Carl like a battering ram, throwing the alien terror across the room and into a wall.

The alien went down like a bag of wet laundry, the dog still clutched in his tentacled grip.

"Keep it up, buddy, you're doin' great!" the alien mother urged from inside the cotton ball jar tucked inside OB's shell.

The turtle had paused on the latest step to catch his breath. "I think I'd like to take a nap now. Phew!" OB said, nearly exhausted.

He could feel the vibration on the stairs behind him and looked down to see that Dr. Oddfellow had regained his footing and was again chasing after him.

"I don't think that guy is up to anything good," the alien mother commented. "Something about his beady eyes gives me the willies."

"Oh, the willies for sure!" OB agreed, turning to resume his climb. The top of the staircase was finally within sight.

"C'mon, shell-boy," the mother encouraged from her jar. "You can do it!"

Inspired by the alien's words, OB found a reserve of strength deep within his shell and pushed forward, scrambling up the last step to a small landing and a door.

"I did it!" he announced breathlessly—

Just as Oddfellow came up over the last step, his face a bright red, brow dripping with sweat.

"I . . . have you . . . gasp . . . now!" the doctor raved as he threw himself onto the landing and reached for the turtle.

OB and the alien mother screamed in unison. OB frantically dove beneath the evil scientist's grasping hands and ran toward the door. It was slightly ajar, the broken hinges allowing just enough room for a box turtle and his jar to squeeze through.

The turtle went for it, moving as fast as his tiny legs could carry him. He was almost through to the other side of the door . . . when he realized that there was no other side.

That part of the building was gone, torn to ruin when the alien craft first appeared. OB gasped. What waited for him was a long drop to the vast laboratory floor below.

"This isn't good," he said, on the verge of panic.

He heard a sound from behind him and turned just in time to see Oddfellow wrenching open the door.

"No!" OB proclaimed. Kirby had given him a job, a very special job, and OB didn't want to disappoint him.

It wasn't a good idea to disappoint Kirby.

The doctor reached for him, and OB immediately pushed the glass jar further down into his shell. It was a tight fit, but at least Oddfellow couldn't grab it.

"Ha!" OB said defiantly to the man.

In a rage, the evil scientist grabbed OB and began to shake him savagely.

"Give it up!" Oddfellow screamed.

Sheer panic took hold of OB, and his body immediately transmogrified into—

A block of Swiss cheese!

"AHHHHH!" Oddfellow cried out, throwing the block of cheese over the ragged edge of the landing. "I am lactose intolerant!"

As OB fell, his body changed back to its original shape.

"What's happening?" he heard the alien mother ask from within his shell, but OB didn't want to answer. It was far too depressing.

Depressing that they would be smushed when they hit the laboratory floor, and depressing because he would have let Kirby down.

It was all really so very sad.

THUNNK!

"Huh," OB said as he landed on something metal—and kind of warm. He rapped a tiny fist upon the hard surface and realized that he'd landed safely on top of something.

And that something was the screw-shaped spacecraft, as it gradually rose toward the gaping opening in the even bigger spaceship above.

TWELVE

Oddfellow wanted to scream, to cry out his rage to the gods of science.

He wanted that alien and he wanted her now—but how?

He watched the screw-shaped spacecraft as it continued to climb slowly.

He was tempted to jump, but it seemed too far.

And then as if his prayers to the science gods were somehow answered, he saw the solution.

The ice sculpture.

It was in the shape of a bald eagle, and it drifted gracefully in zero gravity like its flesh-and-blood feathered counterpart.

Yes, Oddfellow thought. *If it were just a little closer . . .*

As if somehow understanding, the eagle of ice drifted toward him.

"Come to papa!" the scientist said with a leering grin.

And the great ice bird did as it was told.

♆

OB peered out from the safety of his shell and breathed a sight of relief.

Carl's craft was looming closer and closer but at that moment he didn't really care. Sure he was on the roof of one spaceship flying up toward another one that had a death ray pointing down from it, but the little turtle had a good feeling.

Until a shadow passed over him, and OB felt a chill run up and down his spine. Something—or someone—was now standing behind him.

And the turtle didn't need more than one guess as to who. So much for that good feeling.

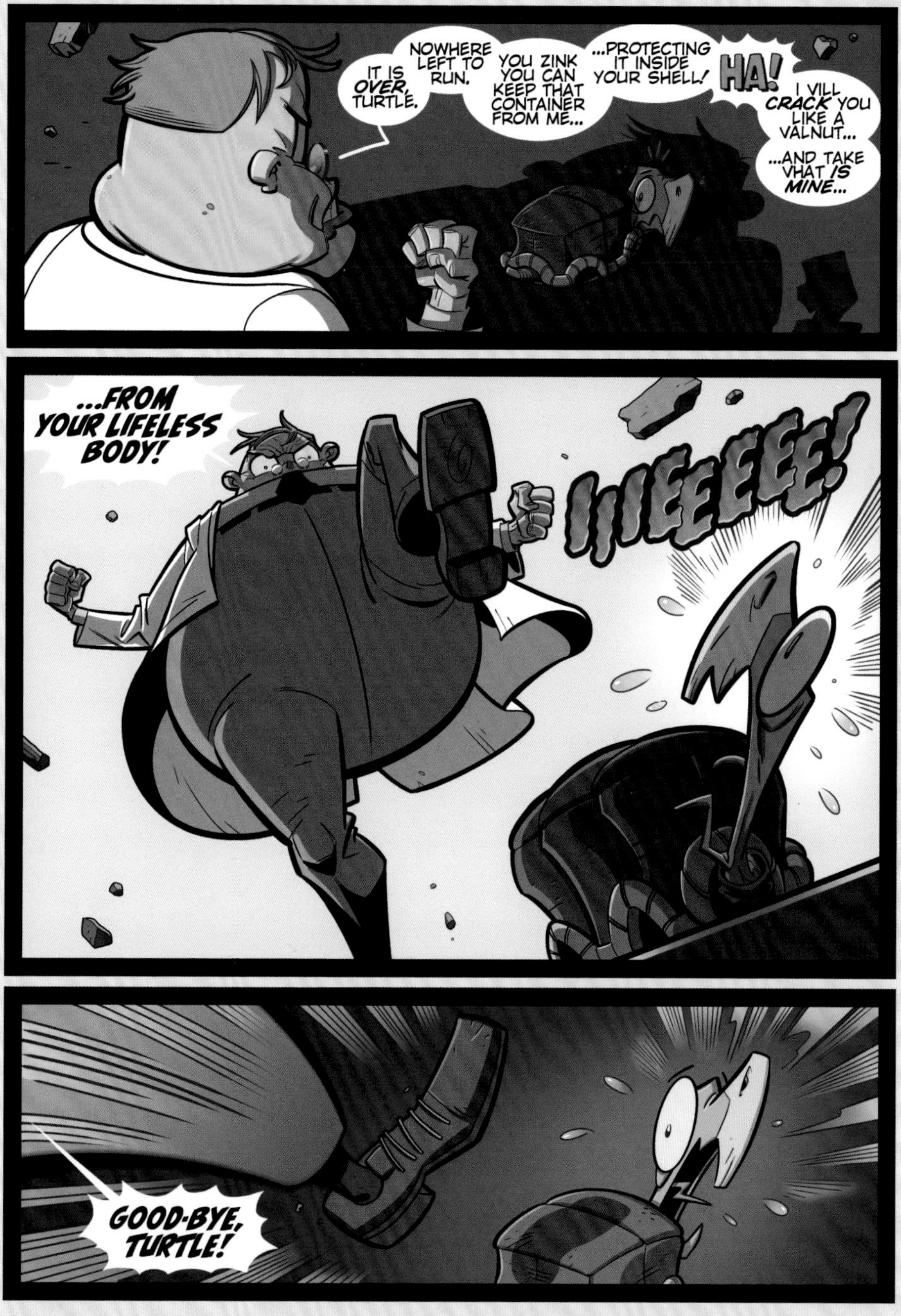
IT IS OVER, TURTLE.
NOWHERE LEFT TO RUN.
YOU ZINK YOU CAN KEEP THAT CONTAINER FROM ME...
...PROTECTING IT INSIDE YOUR SHELL!
HA!
I VILL CRACK YOU LIKE A VALNUT...
...AND TAKE VHAT IS MINE...
...FROM YOUR LIFELESS BODY!
IIIEEEEEE!
GOOD-BYE, TURTLE!

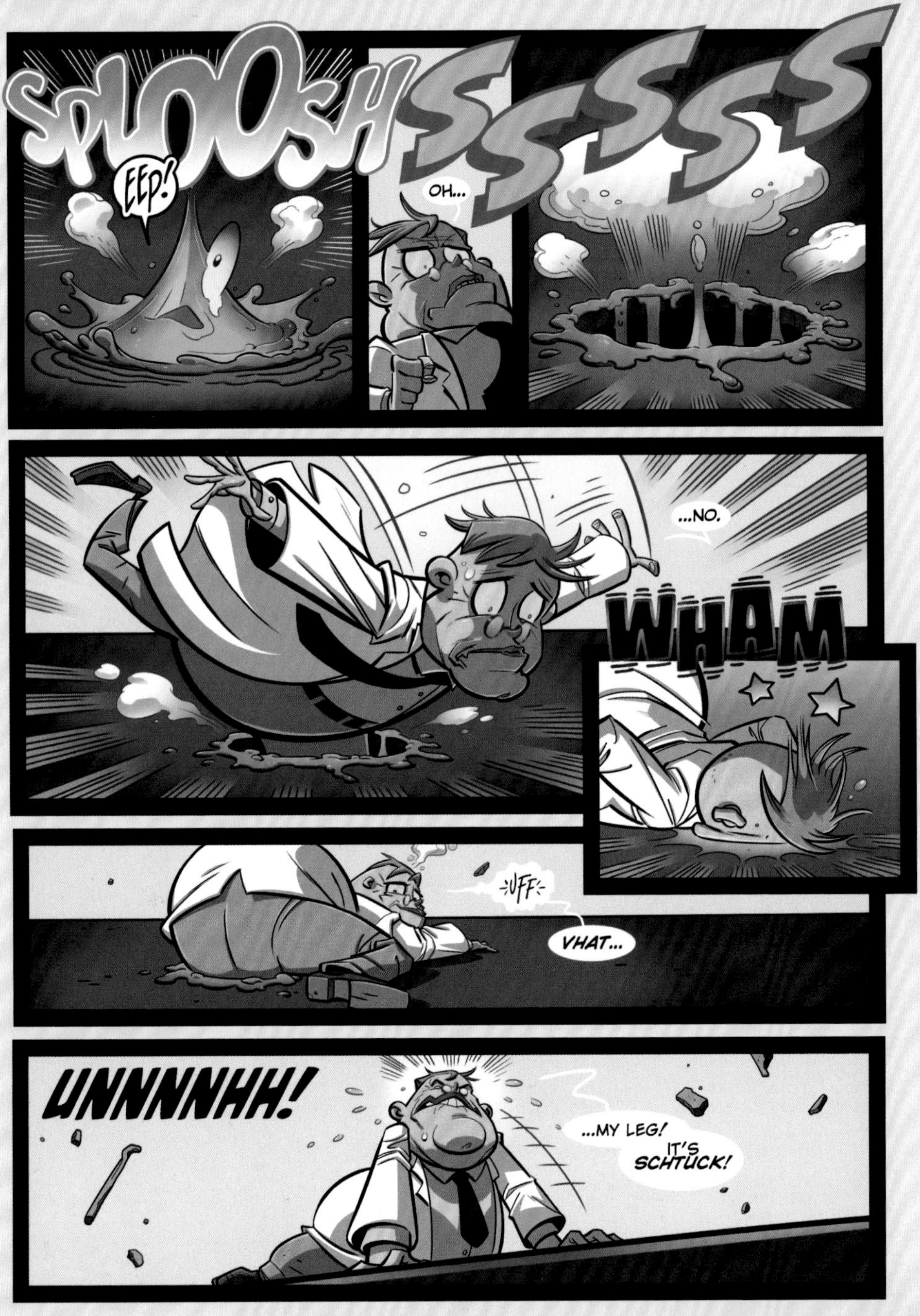
SPLOOSH
EEP!
OH...
SSSSS
...NO.
WHAM
UFF
VHAT...
UNNNNHH!
...MY LEG! IT'S SCHTUCK!

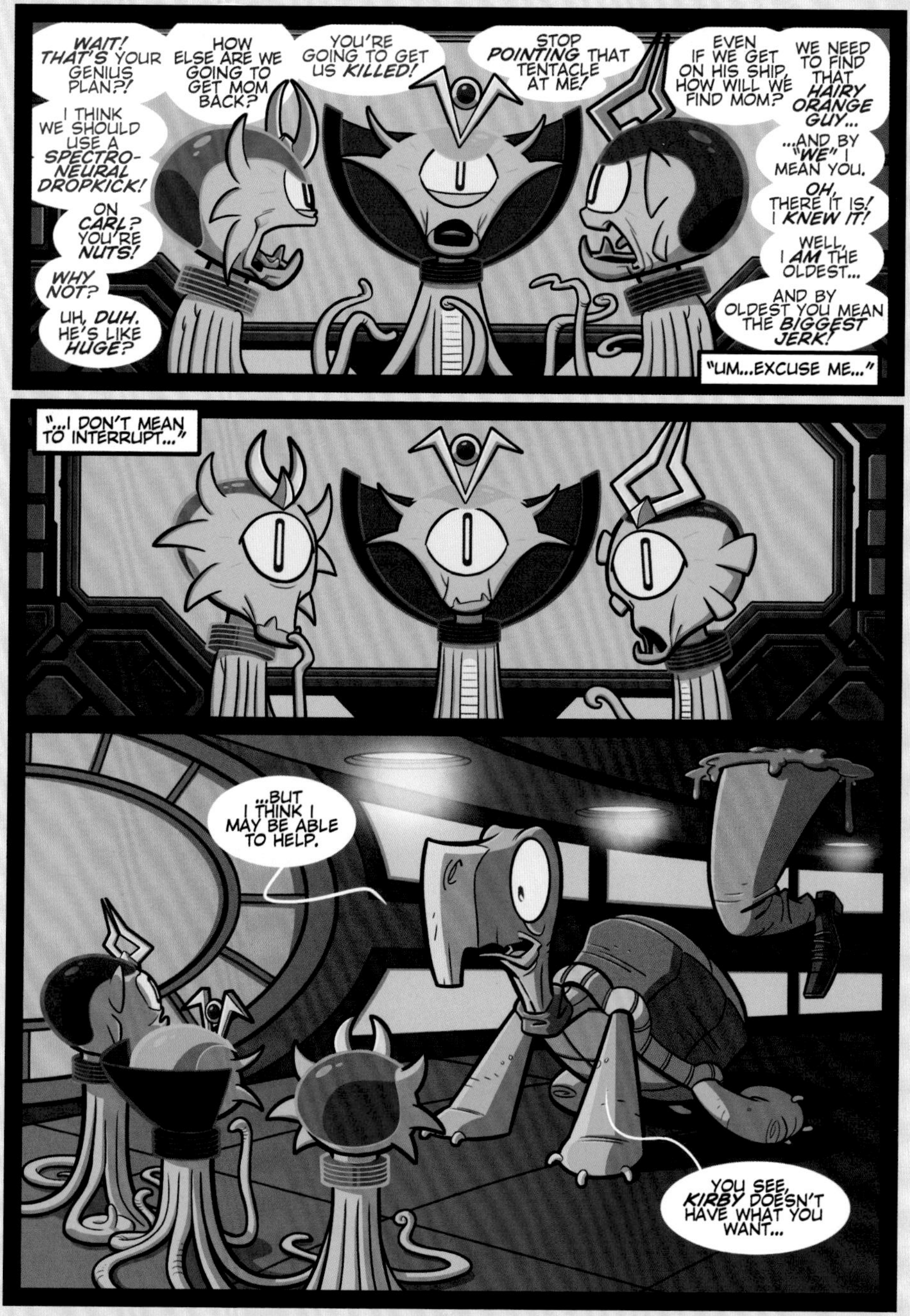
WAIT! THAT'S YOUR GENIUS PLAN?!
HOW ELSE ARE WE GOING TO GET MOM BACK?
YOU'RE GOING TO GET US KILLED!
STOP POINTING THAT TENTACLE AT ME!
EVEN IF WE GET ON HIS SHIP, HOW WILL WE FIND MOM?
WE NEED TO FIND THAT HAIRY ORANGE GUY...
I THINK WE SHOULD USE A SPECTRO-NEURAL DROPKICK!
...AND BY "WE" I MEAN YOU.
ON CARL? YOU'RE NUTS!
OH, THERE IT IS! I KNEW IT!
WHY NOT?
WELL, I AM THE OLDEST...
UH, DUH. HE'S LIKE HUGE?
AND BY OLDEST YOU MEAN THE BIGGEST JERK!
"UM...EXCUSE ME..."
"...I DON'T MEAN TO INTERRUPT..."
...BUT I THINK I MAY BE ABLE TO HELP.
YOU SEE, KIRBY DOESN'T HAVE WHAT YOU WANT...

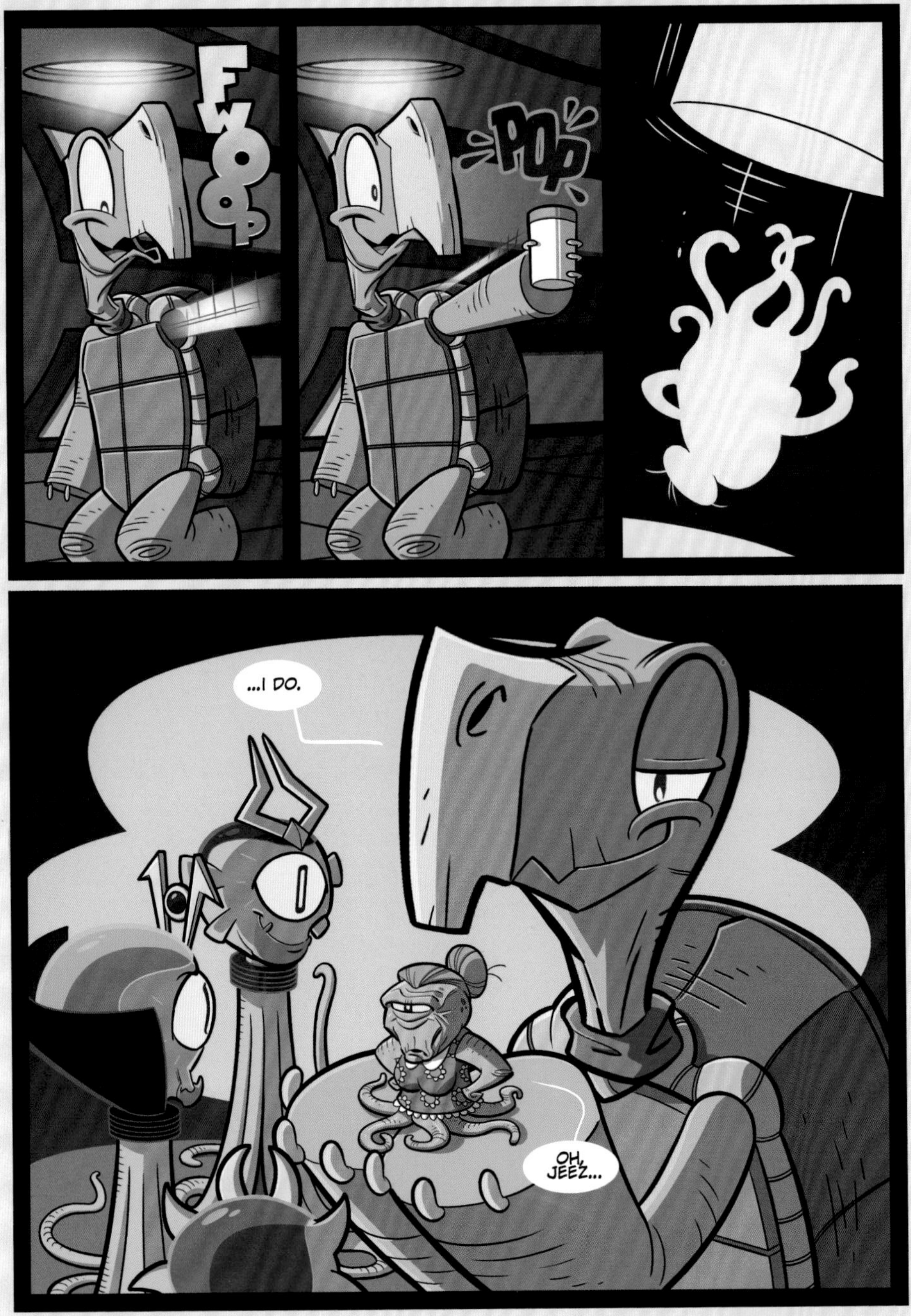
FWOOP
POP
...I DO.
OH, JEEZ...

THIRTEEN

Kirby was trapped beneath Carl's unconscious bulk.

No matter how much he struggled, the Frenchie could not free himself, but time was of the essence.

Across the spaceship floor, Kirby saw Erasmus hovering above the cryo-chamber, hands upon his hips.

"I guess any landing you can walk away from is a good one," he said. Viper moaned, attempting to sit up.

"Erasmus!" Kirby bellowed.

The ghost turned, smiled, and waved. "Hey, Konrad. Fancy meeting you here!"

"The control panel," Kirby said, pointing across the room.

"Yeah, what about it?" Erasmus said, looking where the Frenchie pointed.

"The death ray . . ."

"I know! Did you see that thing?" Erasmus said. "Puts any death ray that I ever designed to shame! If I ever made anything that spiffy I would've . . ."

"You have to shut it down," Kirby growled.

"Who, me?" Erasmus said, pointing to his bare chest.

"You!" Kirby said. "Before it's too late."

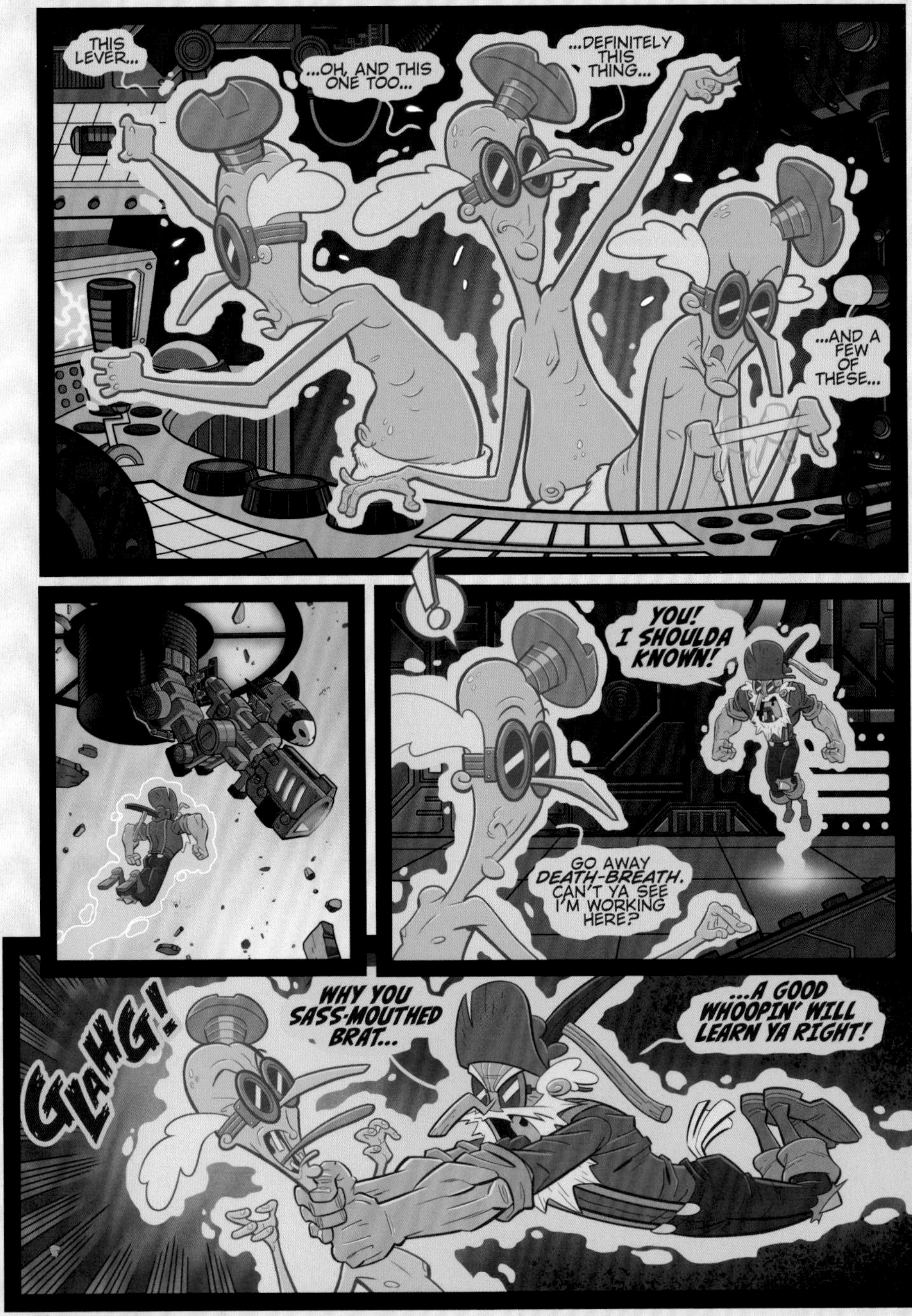

THIS LEVER...
...OH, AND THIS ONE TOO...
...DEFINITELY THIS THING...
...AND A FEW OF THESE...
!
YOU! I SHOULDA KNOWN!
GO AWAY DEATH-BREATH. CAN'T YA SEE I'M WORKING HERE?
GLAHG!
WHY YOU SASS-MOUTHED BRAT...
...A GOOD WHOOPIN' WILL LEARN YA RIGHT!

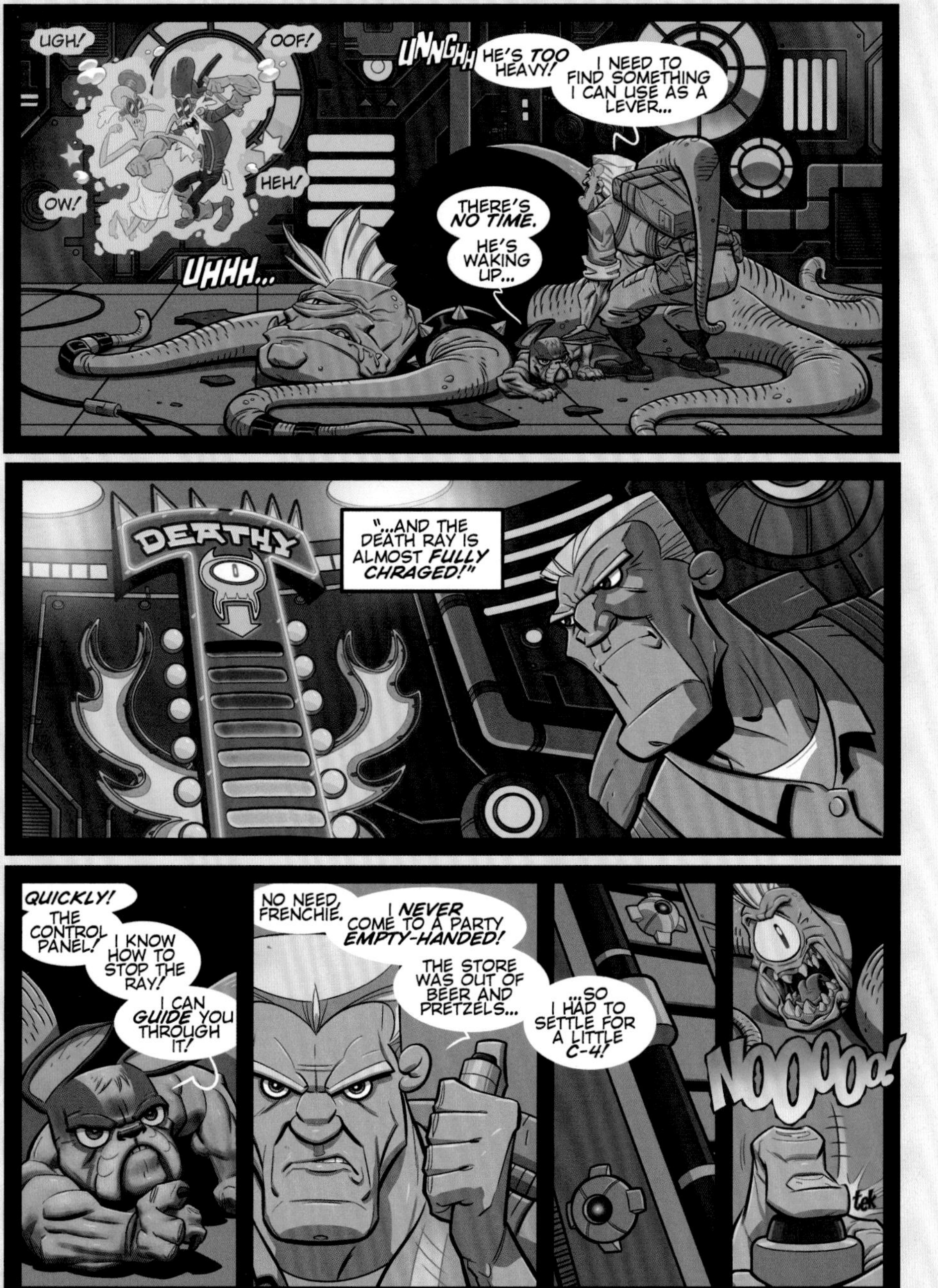
UGH!
OOF!
OW!
HEH!
UNNGHH
HE'S TOO HEAVY!
I NEED TO FIND SOMETHING I CAN USE AS A LEVER...
UHHH...
THERE'S NO TIME. HE'S WAKING UP...
DEATHY
"...AND THE DEATH RAY IS ALMOST FULLY CHRAGED!"
QUICKLY! THE CONTROL PANEL!
I KNOW HOW TO STOP THE RAY!
I CAN GUIDE YOU THROUGH IT!
NO NEED, FRENCHIE.
I NEVER COME TO A PARTY EMPTY-HANDED!
THE STORE WAS OUT OF BEER AND PRETZELS...
...SO I HAD TO SETTLE FOR A LITTLE C-4!
NOOOoo!
tek

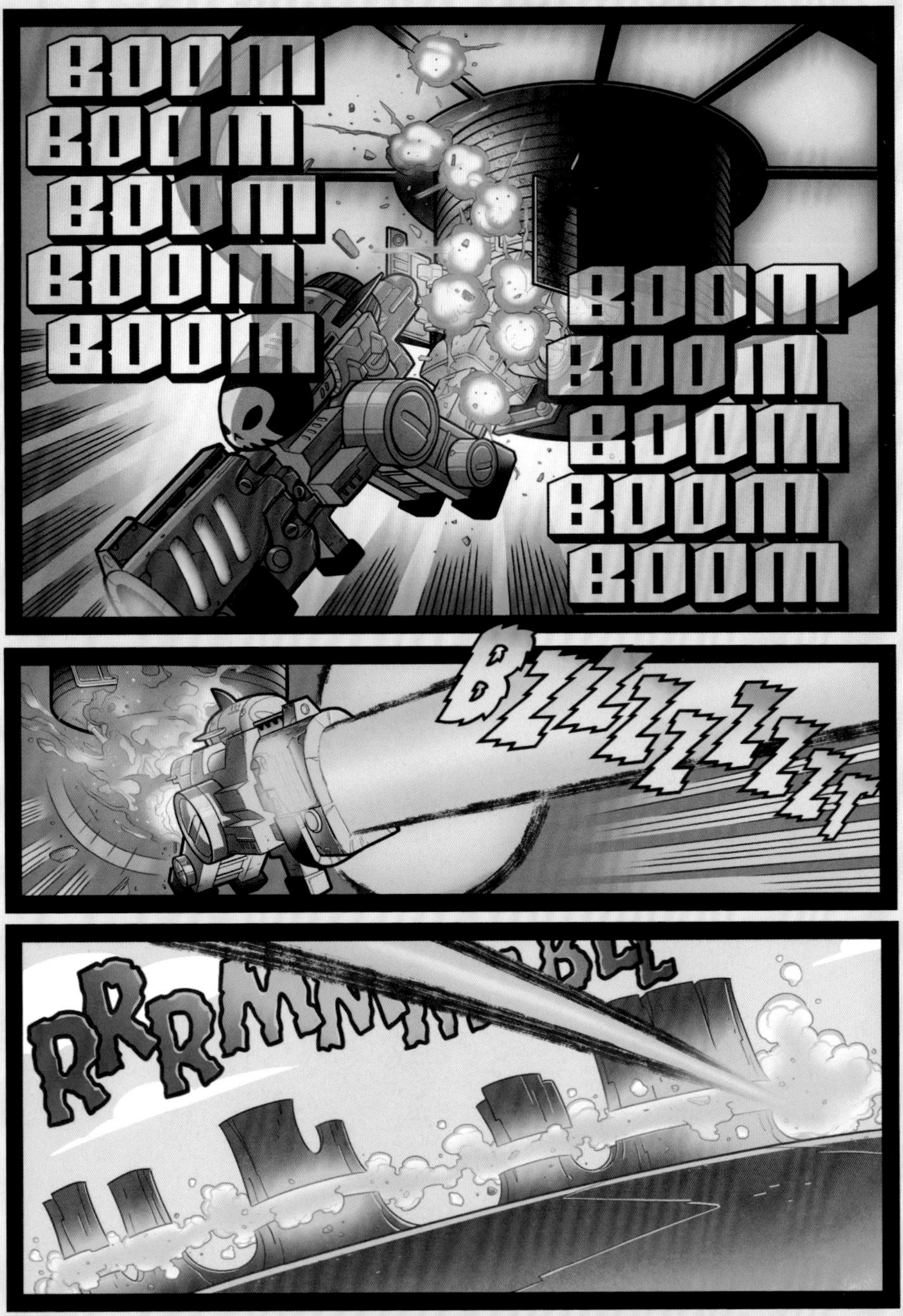
BOOM
BOOM
BOOM
BOOM
BOOM
BOOM
BOOM
BOOM
BOOM
BOOM
BZZZZZZZT
RRRMMM

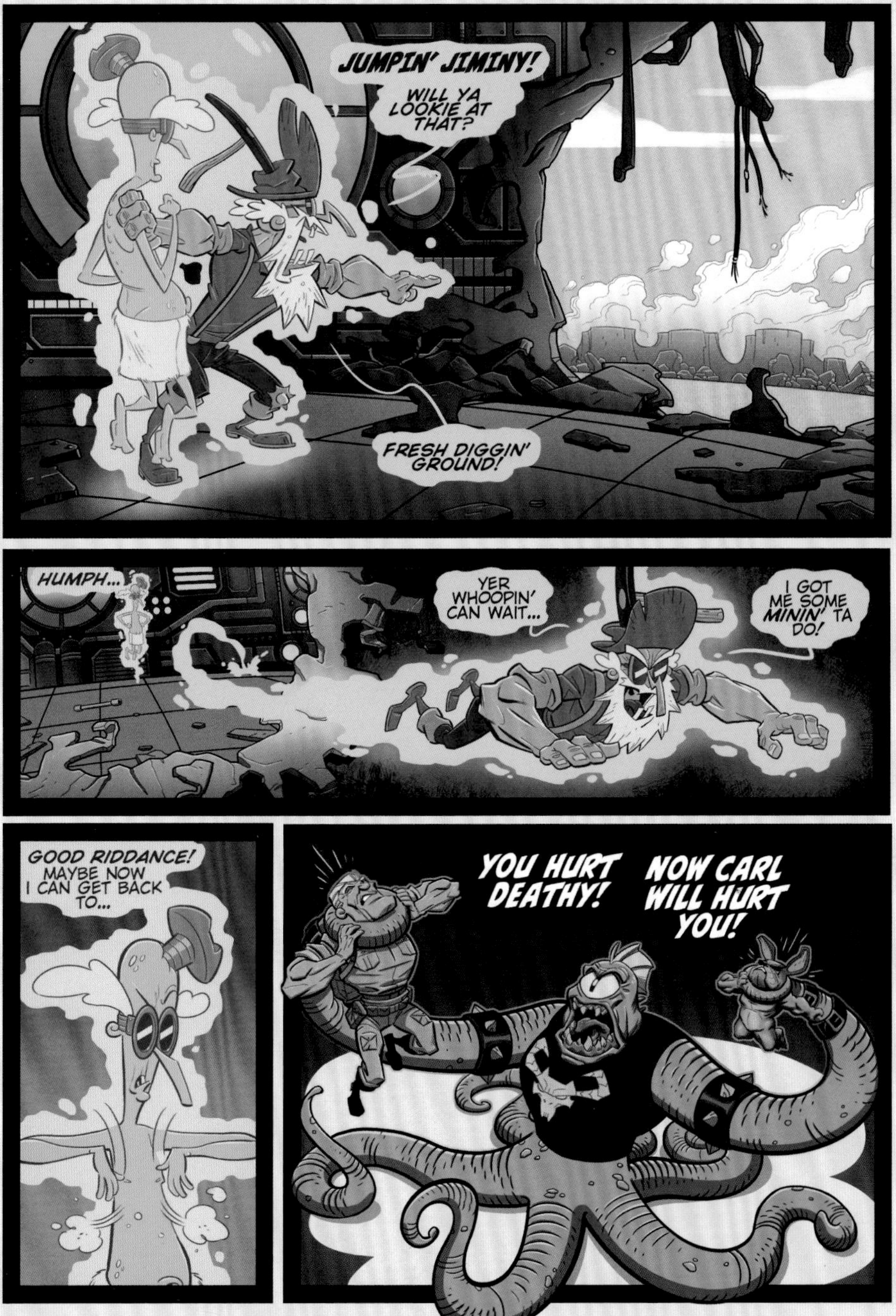

JUMPIN' JIMINY!
WILL YA LOOKIE AT THAT?
FRESH DIGGIN' GROUND!
HUMPH...
YER WHOOPIN' CAN WAIT...
I GOT ME SOME MININ' TA DO!
GOOD RIDDANCE! MAYBE NOW I CAN GET BACK TO...
YOU HURT DEATHY!
NOW CARL WILL HURT YOU!

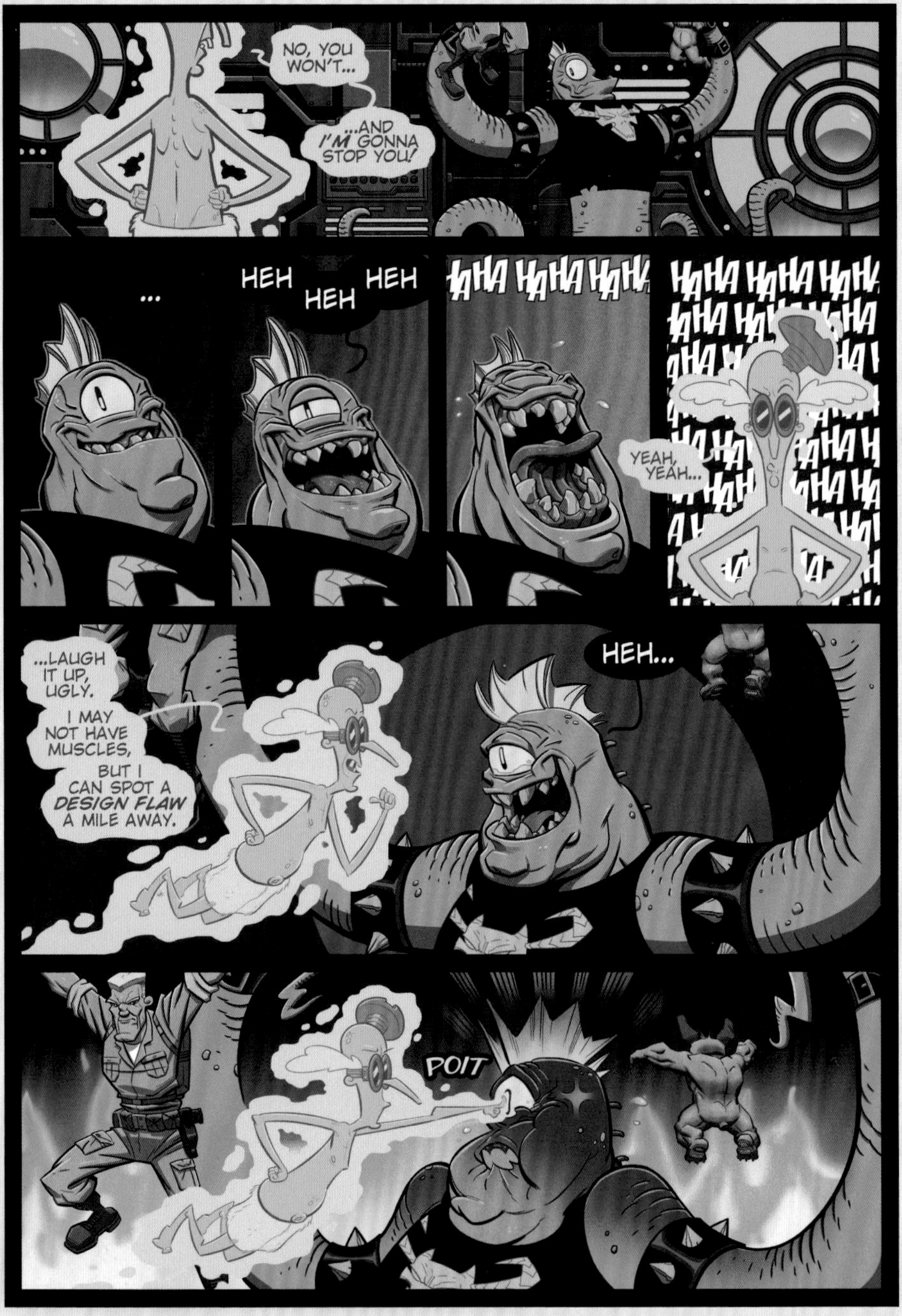

NO, YOU WON'T...
...AND I'M GONNA STOP YOU!
...
HEH HEH HEH
HAHA HAHA HAHA
YEAH, YEAH...
...LAUGH IT UP, UGLY.
I MAY NOT HAVE MUSCLES,
BUT I CAN SPOT A DESIGN FLAW A MILE AWAY.
HEH...
POIT

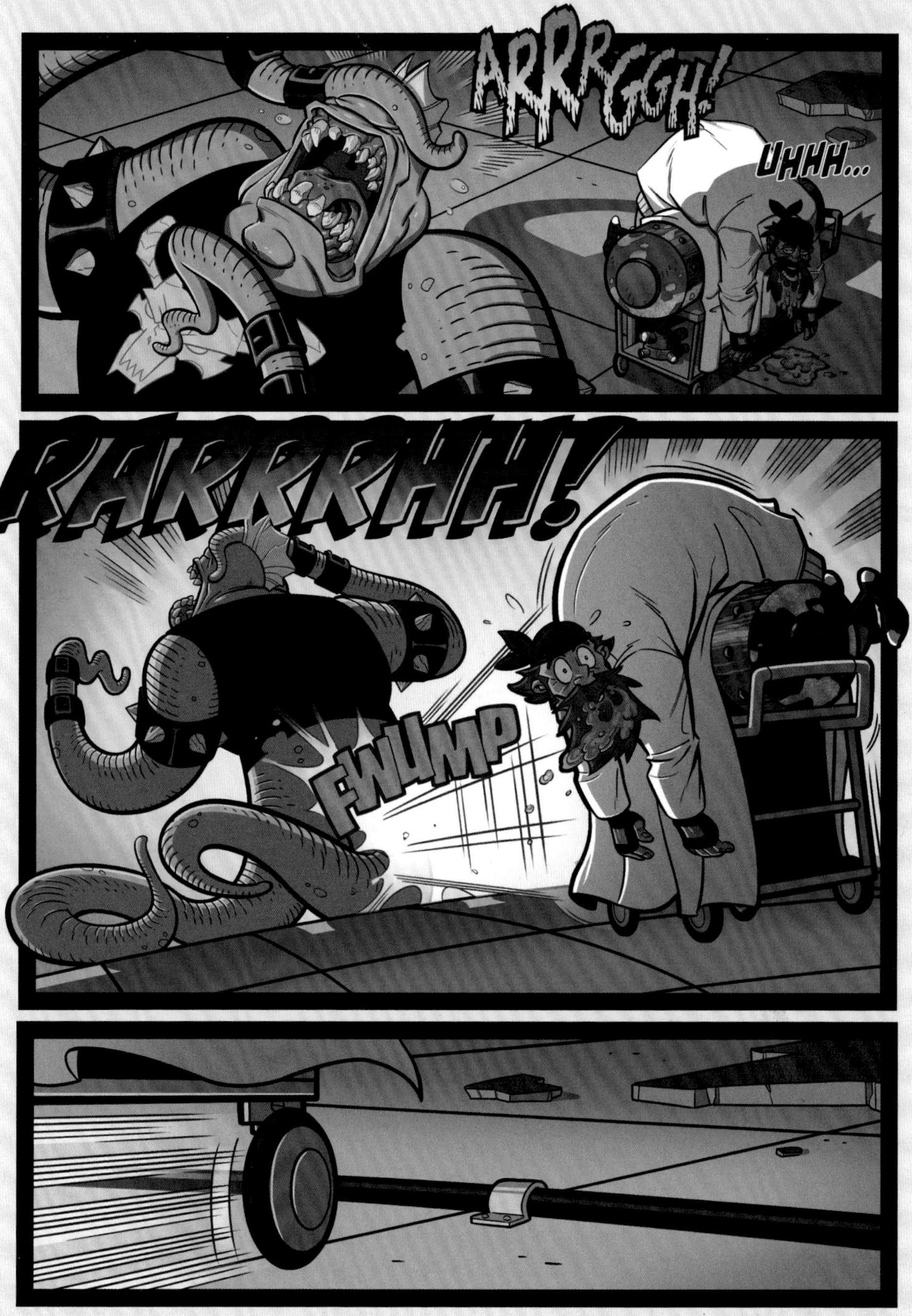
ARRRGGH!
UHHH...
RARRRRHH!
FWUMP

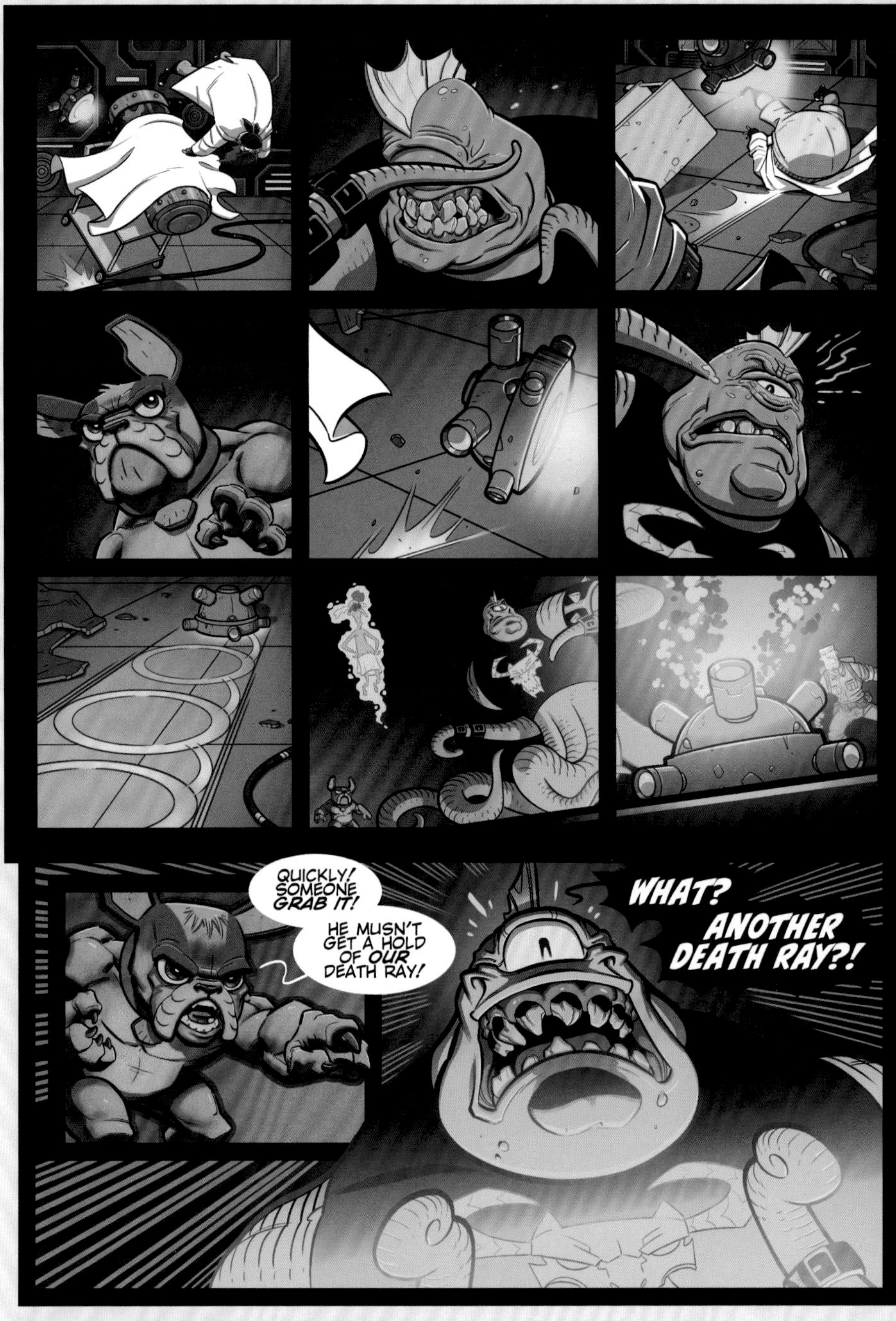
QUICKLY! SOMEONE GRAB IT!
HE MUSN'T GET A HOLD OF OUR DEATH RAY!
WHAT? ANOTHER DEATH RAY?!

Kirby couldn't quite understand how a species capable of intergalactic travel could be quite so imbecilic.

He wondered if they had perhaps borrowed the knowledge from a friend.

"Is this actually gonna work?" Killshot whispered to Kirby as they watched Carl's single gigantic eye fix upon the leaking cold fusion reactor.

"I think it just might," Kirby muttered, watching as the giant alien monstrosity undulated across the ship, snatching up the reactor in his tentacles.

"Ha!" Carl exclaimed, holding the hissing device up to his eye, turning it to study every angle. "Kinda puny for a death ray," he muttered. "I know, I'll call you Li'l Deathy. Yeah, and that's . . ."

And then his tentacles began to turn blue.

"Huh, what's up with this?" Carl asked, confused. The blue quickly spread the lengths of his muscular appendages. "I don't think I feel so goo . . ."

Carl's entire body had grown rigid, the reactor still clutched in his frozen blue tentacles.

"Would ya look at that?" Killshot said, obviously impressed. "Quick thinking, there, Frenchie."

"Never underestimate the innate power of sheer stupidity," Kirby said. "Now, I think I'll take a look at that death ray."

FOURTEEN

A snarl of disgust formed on the alien mother's features.

"Good gravy!" she exclaimed, looking around Mike, Bill, and Supreme Leader Phil's spacecraft. "I didn't think it was possible, but this place looks even filthier than before I left! What a pigsty!"

She used her tentacles to pull herself across the floor of the ship to the control room where many of her children were hanging out.

"Ahem!" she cleared her throat.

The alien children spun and their single eyes bulged as they saw her.

"Mom?" hundreds of voices said in unison.

"That's right, you filthy creatures," she said, placing her tentacles upon her hips. "And things are about to get real."

The alien children glanced nervously at each other.

"Aaron, are those your socks on the console?" Mother asked. "Put them in the hamper—NOW! Peter, get down off those induction coils! You're gonna sprain a tentacle! Who left that pizza there?" She pointed with the end of a wiggling appendage. "Greg? Was it you? That has you written all over it!"

It was an incessant barrage, her voice becoming shriller the longer she went on.

"Jimmy, I'm not gonna tell you again! Get those filthy tentacles off of my coffee table! Chet, so help me if I have to come over there! Ted, you're grounded! Henry, you're grounded too! You want to join them, Gabe? Keep smirking!"

The alien children appeared stunned, beaten into silence by the words of their mother.

The three emissaries that had first communicated with the outside pushed their way through nearly catatonic brethren.

"Mother!" Supreme Leader Phil cried. "It's so . . . nice, to have you back!"

She fixed him in a steely gaze and again placed her tentacles upon her hips. "Oh ya think so? Well, if that's the case, you won't mind helping me take a hose to this armpit," she said.

She waited.

"Well?"

"Yes, Mother," the three emissaries said in unison.

"That's more like it."

Meanwhile, Killshot's explosives had done more damage than Kirby had originally believed, and the spacecraft violently lurched to one side.

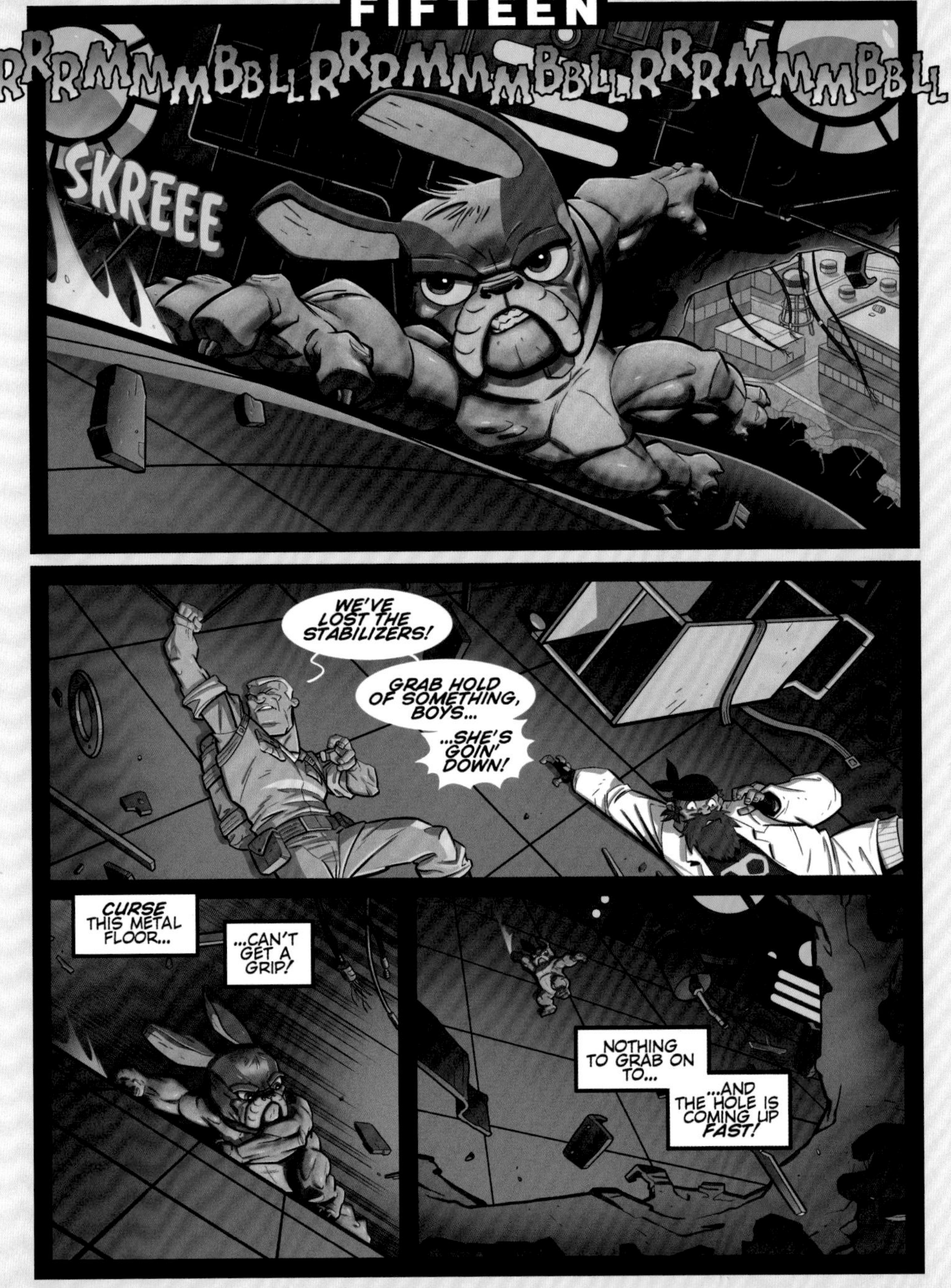
FIFTEEN
RRRMMMMBBLLRRRMMMMBBLLRRRMMMMBBLL
SKREEE
WE'VE LOST THE STABILIZERS!
GRAB HOLD OF SOMETHING, BOYS...
...SHE'S GOIN' DOWN!
CURSE THIS METAL FLOOR...
...CAN'T GET A GRIP!
NOTHING TO GRAB ON TO...
...AND THE HOLE IS COMING UP FAST!

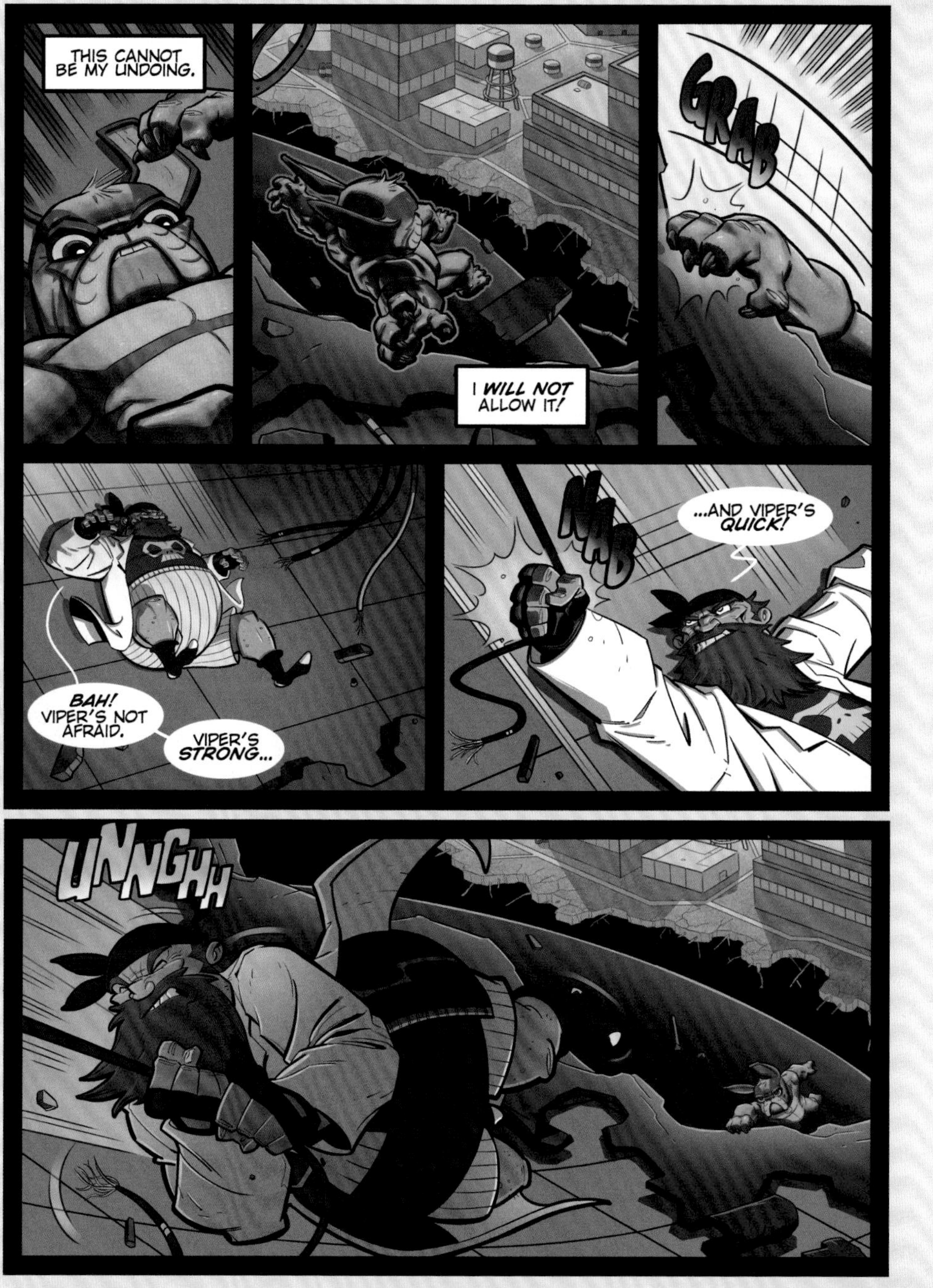
THIS CANNOT BE MY UNDOING.
I WILL NOT ALLOW IT!
GRAB
BAH! VIPER'S NOT AFRAID.
VIPER'S STRONG...
NAB
...AND VIPER'S QUICK!
UNNGHH

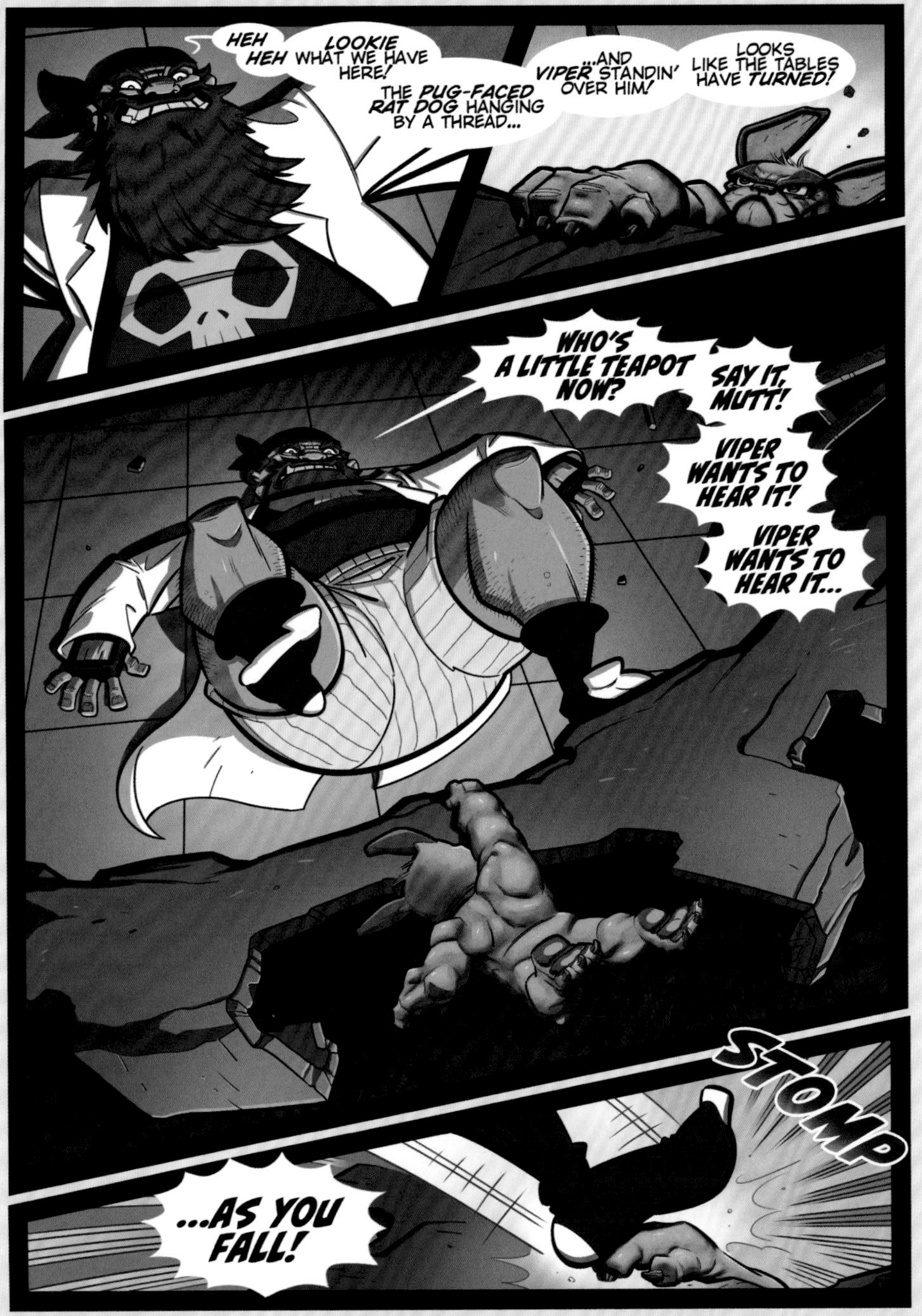

HEH HEH
LOOKIE WHAT WE HAVE HERE!
THE PUG-FACED RAT DOG HANGING BY A THREAD...
...AND VIPER STANDIN' OVER HIM!
LOOKS LIKE THE TABLES HAVE TURNED!
WHO'S A LITTLE TEAPOT NOW?
SAY IT, MUTT!
VIPER WANTS TO HEAR IT!
VIPER WANTS TO HEAR IT...
STOMP
...AS YOU FALL!

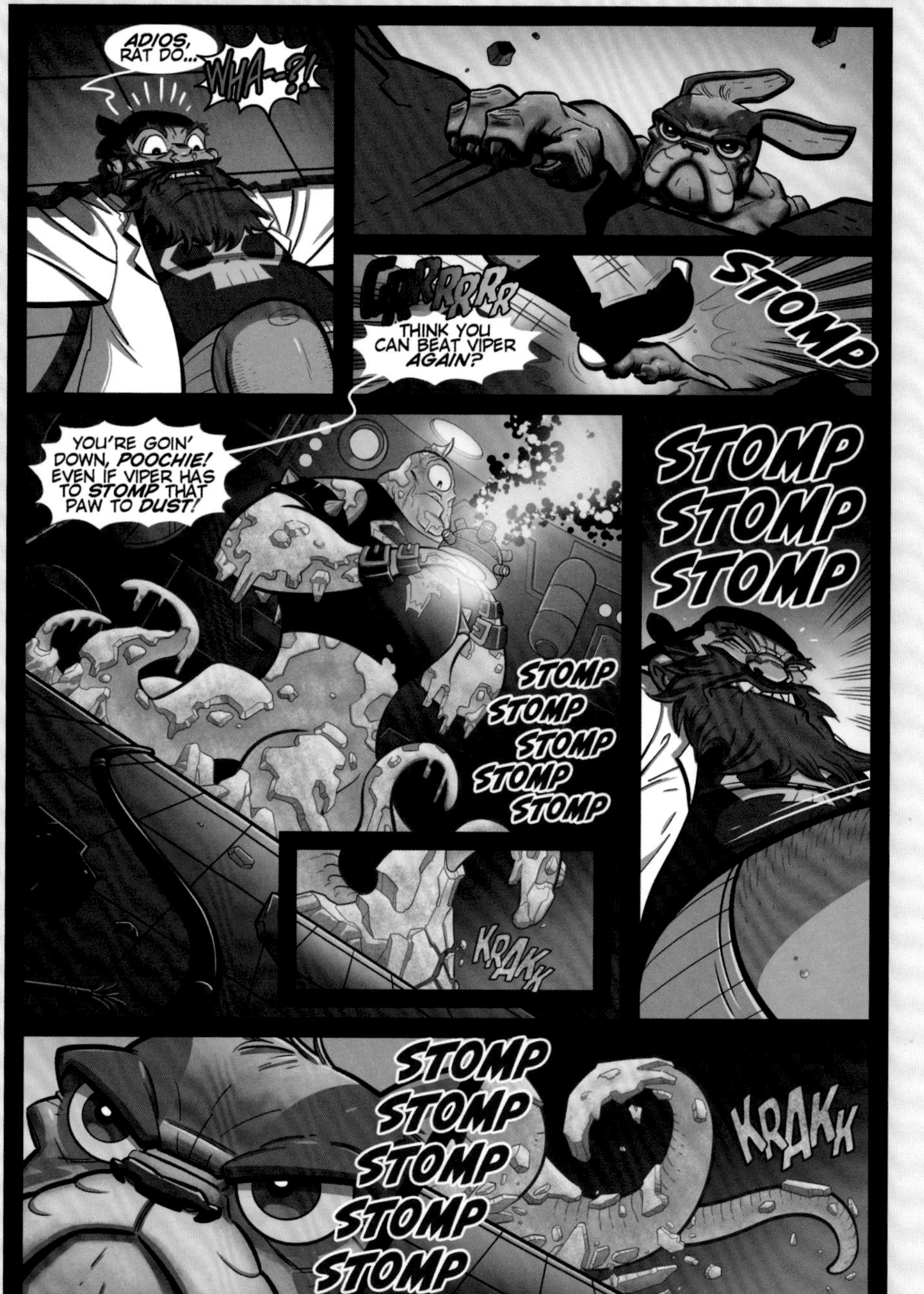

ADIOS, RAT DO...
WHA--?!
GRRRRRR
STOMP
THINK YOU CAN BEAT VIPER AGAIN?
YOU'RE GOIN' DOWN, POOCHIE! EVEN IF VIPER HAS TO STOMP THAT PAW TO DUST!
STOMP STOMP STOMP
STOMP STOMP STOMP STOMP STOMP
KRAKK
STOMP STOMP STOMP STOMP STOMP
KRAKK

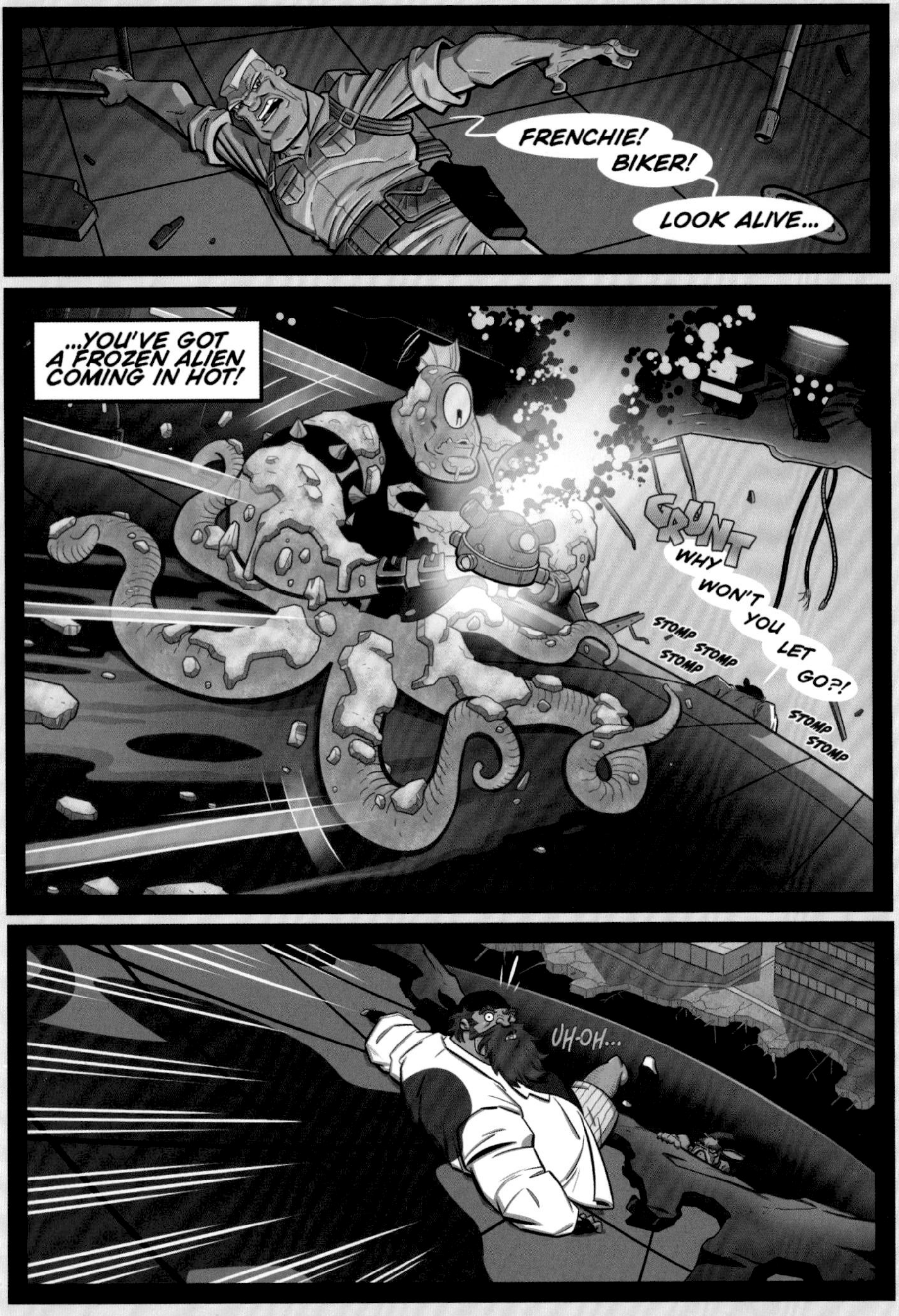
FRENCHIE!
BIKER!
LOOK ALIVE...
...YOU'VE GOT A FROZEN ALIEN COMING IN HOT!
GRUNT
WHY WON'T YOU LET GO?!
STOMP STOMP STOMP
STOMP STOMP
UH-OH...

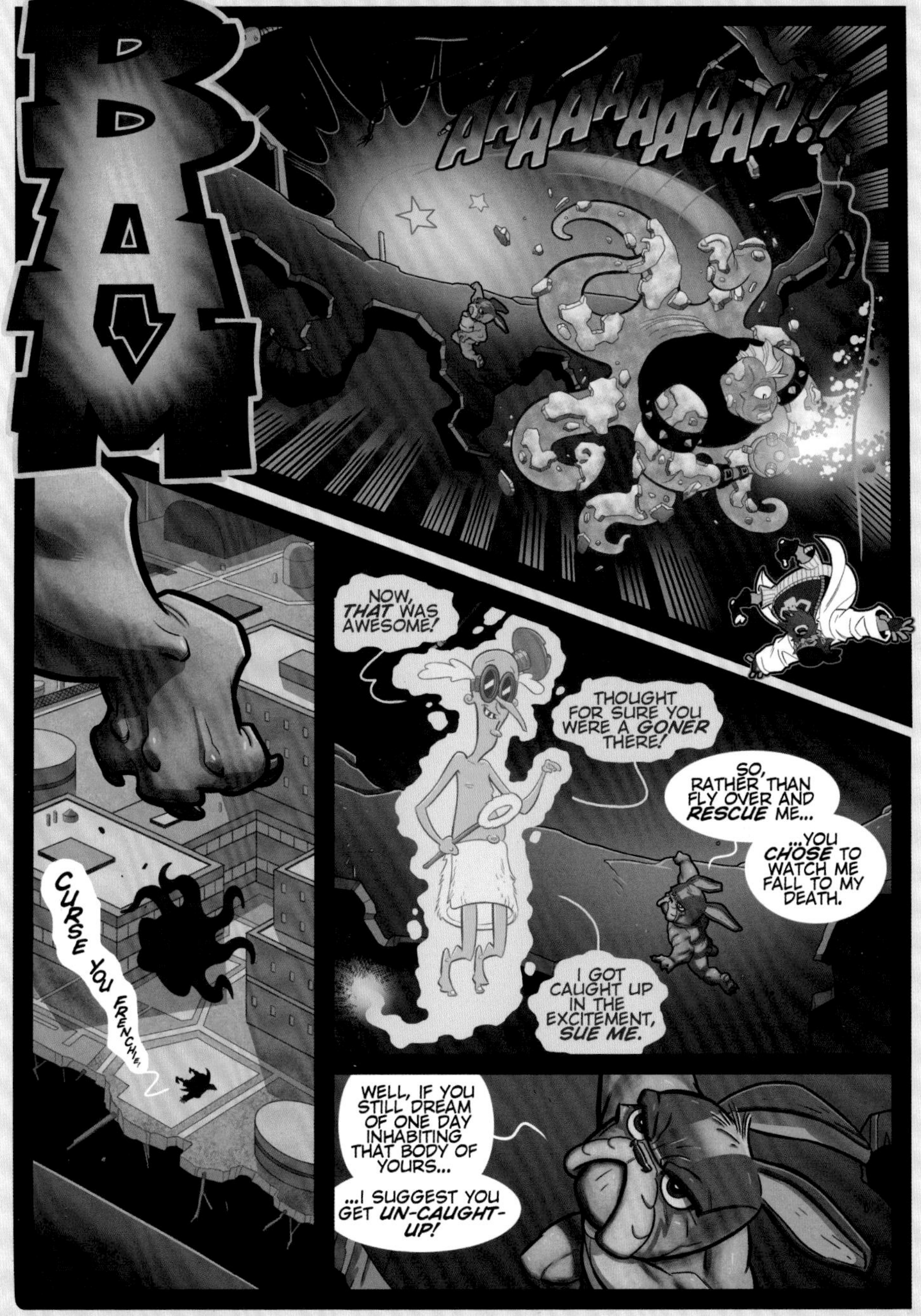
BAM
AAAAAAAAAAAH!!
NOW, THAT WAS AWESOME!
THOUGHT FOR SURE YOU WERE A GONER THERE!
SO, RATHER THAN FLY OVER AND RESCUE ME...
...YOU CHOSE TO WATCH ME FALL TO MY DEATH.
I GOT CAUGHT UP IN THE EXCITEMENT, SUE ME.
CURSE YOU FRENCHIE!
WELL, IF YOU STILL DREAM OF ONE DAY INHABITING THAT BODY OF YOURS...
...I SUGGEST YOU GET UN-CAUGHT-UP!

Erasmus, Kirby in his arms, passed one of the spacecraft's circular windows, and something caught the Frenchie's keen eye.

"What'cha lookin' at, Kort?" Erasmus asked, noticing Kirby's stare.

The bouncy house, looking somewhat the worse for wear with a rip in its body, was floating dangerously close to one of the ship's exhaust ports.

Erasmus connected the dots. "What do you think the odds are that it's gonna end up inside the . . ."

"Very high," Kirby said, eyes riveted to the inevitable.

"If we didn't have bad luck on this trip, we wouldn't have any luck at all," Erasmus said, just as the bouncy house was sucked into one of the spinning fans of an exhaust port and flames exploded.

Carl's ship lurched, and Erasmus dropped Kirby as alarms began to blare loudly.

⌁

"Looks like the engines are failing," Killshot said.

"And that's the least of our problems," Kirby said.

"Oh?" Killshot asked. "Don't sugarcoat it, Frenchie, let me have it."

"When your men removed the reactor from the cryo-chamber, they cracked the housing. The crack has grown more severe with all the recent . . . activity."

"And that's a bad thing, I'd wager?"

"Very," Kirby said. "The reactor is unstable and will explode."

"And here I was thinking that the news was gonna be bad," Killshot said with a grimace. "I don't know what Washington's beef with you is, Frenchie, but right now I really don't care." The colonel patted his backpack. "Got myself an emergency chute. I suggest we use it and get the heck out of here before we don't get to choose."

Kirby searched for his spectral compatriot and found him with the cryo-chamber, looking down at his still unliving body.

"Erasmus, we're going," Kirby said.

"What?" the ghost asked. "But we can't leave me behind!"

Kirby looked at Killshot and shook his head.

"That's your choice," the colonel said. "But I have a duty to my men out there, and the US of A."

"Perfectly understandable," Kirby said. "Don't let me keep you."

Colonel Killshot made his way to where the tank blast had left a gaping opening in the side of Carl's spaceship.

"If I had a pistol and 10 of you, I could take over the world, Frenchie," Killshot said with a smile. Then he saluted Kirby and turned to the opening. "And thanks for the best birthday ever," he yelled, leaping into the void outside the ship.

"I thought he'd never leave," Erasmus said. "So, what are we gonna do about him?" he asked Kirby, pointing to the body inside the cryo-chamber.

Kirby had no time to explain. There was only so much time remaining before the spaceship faltered from the exhaust port explosion and the core of the cold fusion reactor broke down and ignited another explosion of incredible ferocity.

"So, what's the scoop?" Erasmus asked. "The suspense is killing me . . . if I could be killed, if you know what I mean."

Kirby began to haul the cryo-chamber across the floor.

"Careful there, Kong," Erasmus said. "All I need is a concussion to go along with that alien shuttle craft lodged in my noggin!"

"Help me push this over to the opening," Kirby said.

Reluctantly, Erasmus began to push from the other end. "Why aren't I liking this plan so far?"

"Silence, specter," Kirby barked.

The Frenchie stood at the edge of the jagged tear in the spaceship wall, peering out onto the laboratory floor far below. It appeared the gravitational anomaly caused by the alien ships had started to weaken, the floating detritus gradually drifting toward the ground.

And then he saw it: the Cadillac Eldorado.

It was a distance from Carl's spacecraft but not entirely impossible to reach.

If he were to give the cryo-chamber a good enough push . . .

It just might work.

The angry alien children converged upon OB as he slowly backed away from them.

"This is all his fault!" one screamed.

"I . . . I thought you wanted her back!" OB cried, his shell hitting a wall.

"She took my phone!" an alien child raged.

"She's your mother," OB said. "I mean, technically it's her phone."

"And technically, you need a good beating!" another of the children shouted.

The aliens rushed him, their slimy tentacles reaching out to enwrap him in their constricting grip. OB tried to swat them away, but there were too many.

If ever there was a time he needed a superpower . . .

And then he felt it.

At first he thought it might be hunger pangs. After all, he hadn't had anything to eat since some Fritos in the car before Viper and his gang attacked.

But no, this was different.

He hoped that, whatever it was, it would be useful.

The alien children were close now, the smell of their breath terrible, their tentacles grabbing and squeezing, and then . . .

He was gone.

A little turtle moving through time and space.

From here . . .

♥

. . . To there.

OB appeared in the front seat of the Cadillac Eldorado with a crackle of electricity and the smell of bacon.

"Oh," the little turtle exclaimed, knowing exactly where he was. "How convenient," he said, gripping the steering wheel in both tiny claws.

Then he saw where he really was, a good 100 feet off the ground, with Carl's spacecraft, clearly in trouble, above him.

The ship was leaning to one side, smoking holes scattered over its surface.

He wondered if a certain French bulldog might have had something to do with it, and that was when he saw it: a tiny, almost undistinguishable shape falling—no, launching itself from a large hole in the hull of the alien ship.

"What the heck . . ." OB said, squinting his eyes for a better look.

"Is that . . ." he began, not sure if he should trust his eyes.

"Maybe . . ." It was kinda impossible, but then again, life with his best pally in the whole wide world often was.

"It is!" OB exclaimed, a smile on his face.

It was Kirby for sure, riding what looked to be the cryo-chamber like a surf board.

OB started to turn the wheel back and forth, moving his small body up and down and side to side to maneuver the floating car toward Kirby.

"Hey, Kirby!" OB screamed at the top of his lungs. He was waving wildly. "Over here! I'm over here!"

OB turned the steering wheel sharply to the left and looked up again, trying to find Kirby among the other gradually falling debris.

The turtle thought he'd somehow missed his friend when he felt something heavy wedging itself into the back seat and then saw Kirby land in the passenger seat beside him.

"OB," Kirby acknowledged with a slight nod, as if nothing truly incredible had just occurred.

"Hey, K," OB said, tiny claws still clutching the steering wheel.

"Well, that certainly was somethin'," Erasmus said from the back seat, his spindly arms wrapped around the cryo-chamber.

"Where'd you come from?" OB asked.

"I was inside the chamber with Stiffo here, didn't want me getting lonely."

"OB," Kirby said sharply.

"What's up, K?" OB asked, turning his attention back to the Frenchie, who was staring intently at the spaceship above them.

"It is only a matter of minutes before the fusion reactor explodes," Kirby said. He looked over the side of the passenger door and saw that they were close to touching ground. "Be prepared to hit the gas as soon as we touch the ground."

"Will do," the turtle said, gripping the steering wheel and readying himself.

The Cadillac touched ground with a bounce, and OB stomped the accelerator, tires screeching and back end fishtailing as they rocketed their way toward their exit, a jagged section of missing wall.

"This driving thing isn't so hard," OB said. "If I'd known that, I would have learned to do it years ago!"

SIXTEEN

The road leading away from Area 51 hummed beneath the tires of the old Eldorado. Ahead of them, Kirby could see the military convoy making its escape before the inevitable.

"Pass them," Kirby ordered the little turtle still behind the wheel of the modified Cadillac.

OB obediently slid the Eldorado to the left, its tires kicking up clouds of desert dust as he sped up to pass the line of military trucks.

The canvas cover over the back of one of the trucks flapped in the breeze, revealing the cow whose heart had been the object of their mission.

"Hey, there's Marie-Claire!" OB said, waving happily at the cow.

"Marie-Claire?" Kirby asked.

"Yeah, that's her name."

Kirby was going to ask the turtle how he knew that but decided that it just wasn't worth it.

As they passed the transport truck, Kirby saw that Colonel Killshot was behind the wheel. The man acknowledged the Frenchie with a slight nod.

"Get ahead of them," Kirby commanded. "I'm eager to be away from here."

"Yeah, let's get back to the lab," Erasmus said from the back seat, his ghostly arm slung over the back of the cryo-chamber that held his thawed but still lifeless body. "We got some things to discuss."

Kirby was about to agree when the air was suddenly filled with a sound like the buzz of a billion bees. He turned to see that the screw-shaped spacecraft was rising from the damaged installation from which they'd escaped. It hovered for just a moment as a small projectile shot from its underside, and then the main craft flew straight up, gone from sight in the blink of an eye.

They hadn't gone too much farther down the road when they saw him standing by the side of the road, still wearing the tattered lab coat and no pants.

"Hey look!" cried Erasmus. "It's Python!"

OB slowed down as he pulled the car over.

The biker was muttering beneath his breath as he stared off into space. "French bulldogs! The devil in disguise, that's what they are!"

"Hiya, pal!" Erasmus called out. "We was wondering what happened to you!"

Viper stopped, and his eyes began to focus on the old Eldorado.

Kirby knew that he shouldn't, but he couldn't help himself. He gave Viper a little wave.

The man spun around and ran off into the desert, screaming at the top his lungs as if the devil himself were chasing him.

"Huh, wonder what got into him?" Erasmus pondered as the shape of the biker grew smaller.

OB pulled back onto the road, and then it happened. It wasn't as if Kirby hadn't been expecting it—a sort of strange punctuation to the end of the sentence that defined this most bizarre mission.

A sudden flash of bluish light shone in the rearview mirror. Kirby moved the mirror enough to be able to see the roiling mushroom-shaped cloud as the cold fusion reactor in the belly of Carl's spacecraft finally exploded.

"Whoa!" Erasmus exclaimed from the back seat. "Would you look at that!"

And look they did.

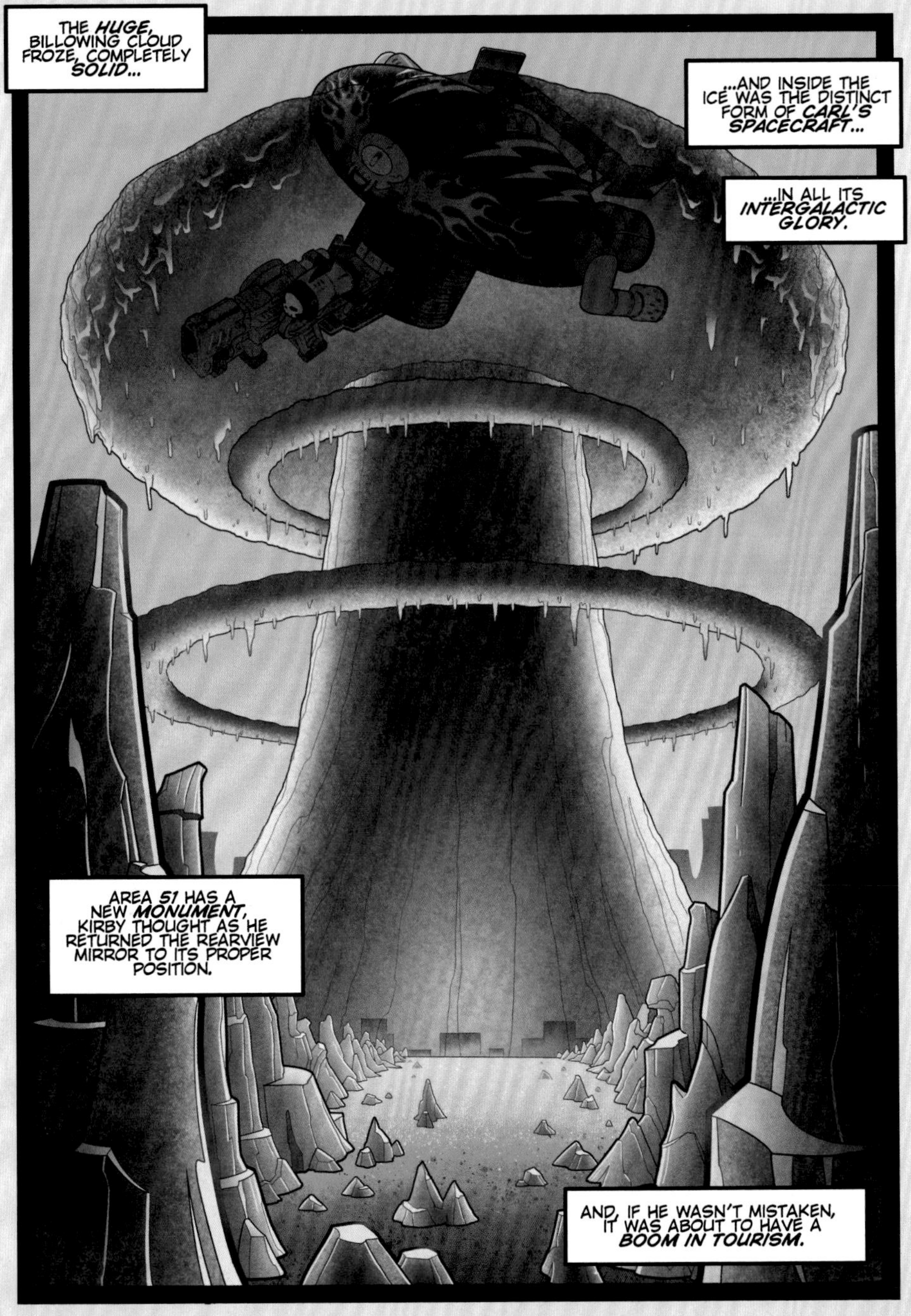
THE HUGE, BILLOWING CLOUD FROZE, COMPLETELY SOLID...
...AND INSIDE THE ICE WAS THE DISTINCT FORM OF CARL'S SPACECRAFT...
...IN ALL ITS INTERGALACTIC GLORY.
AREA 51 HAS A NEW MONUMENT, KIRBY THOUGHT AS HE RETURNED THE REARVIEW MIRROR TO ITS PROPER POSITION.
AND, IF HE WASN'T MISTAKEN, IT WAS ABOUT TO HAVE A BOOM IN TOURISM.

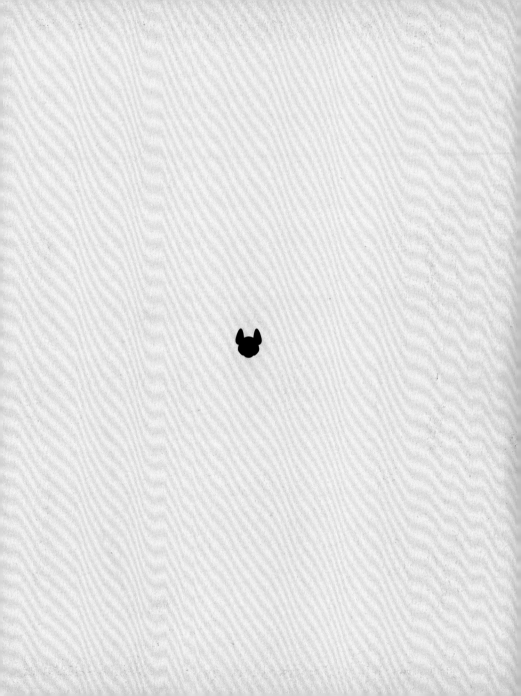

EPILOGUE THE FIRST

Supreme Leader Phil, his brother Mike, and his other brother Bill stood impatiently waiting, tentacles twitching and tapping.

The three were standing in front of a device that resembled an oversized microwave oven. It hummed ominously.

"I don't know about this," Mike said.

"Relax," the Supreme Leader told him. "This is a great idea. Trust me."

"Yeah," said Bill. "We need a mother, right? Otherwise we've got no mothership. Besides, this one will be much easier to handle."

"True," Mike said. "Do you think it worked?"

The strange machine stopped with a resounding DING!

"Of course it worked," Supreme Leader Phil said confidently. "Who got the A in genetic biological modification class?"

The door of the machine swung slowly open.

Dr. Oddfellow was aware that something had happened to him . . . that something was different.

But what was it exactly . . .

The former doctor staggered out of the machine, seeing the three aliens waiting just outside and countless more behind them. They all seemed to be waiting for . . . something.

When they saw him, they all began to cheer, tentacles waving in the air as they whooped and hollered their excitement.

Oddfellow had no idea what was going on.

"Vhat . . . vhat is going on?" Oddfellow asked the three tentacled beings standing before him. They too seemed very excited.

"You're magnificent!" one of the aliens said, clapping his green tendrils together. There was a tear in his single, bulging eye.

"I'm already in love," said another of the three.

"And look at her eye!" announced the alien leader.

Oddfellow's brain raced. *What are zhey talking about?*

He spun around to see if there might be someone sneaking up behind him and caught sight of his reflection in the glass window of the machine he'd exited.

"Vhat iz zhis?" he asked, raising his hands to his face . . . but they weren't hands at all.

"No!" Oddfellow shrieked looking down at his tentacles. "How . . . how can zhis be?"

He looked at his reflection again, at the single eye in the center of an enormous head.

"Vhat have you done to me?" he screamed, turning back to the three aliens. "Vhat have you done?"

"We needed a new mom," said the leader of the aliens.

"Yeah, a little genetic manipulation here, some gene splicing there, and boom! New mother! And may I add, you look adorable!"

Oddfellow, now more like strange-mom, stumbled forward on shaky tentacles, his brain on fire with the hideous revelation.

He—or was it she now—looked out over the vastness of the waiting alien children. They were all smiling at him adoringly.

"Hey guys!" the Supreme Leader said, saddling up beside Oddfellow to put a thick tentacle around his shoulder. "Check it out—new mom is a green-eye, and you know what that means!"

"Sisters!" they roared with excitement.

EPILOGUE THE SECOND

Jedidiah Peckinpah reclined on one of the many bags of gold strewn around his desert camp and gazed up at the stars.

"This is the life, eh, Petunia?"

The ghostly mule that had been his faithful companion in life—and death—listened intently.

"All that gold just waitin' to be found, and me not lookin' in the right place all this time."

The ghostly mule nibbled at some scrub brush as the prospector continued to speak.

"Who'da thunk meetin' up with a weird-lookin' dog, a guy with no pants, and my lily-livered great, great, great nephew would lead to me finally bein' able to achieve my heart's desire," the ghostly prospector said wistfully.

Petunia looked at him, slowly chewing the scrub.

"Don't tell me you've forgotten what I've always wanted," Jedidiah said, looking to his companion. "The whole reason I got into prospectin'? The thing that makes my heart go pitter-pat?"

The mule continued to chew. Listening.

"Why it's farmin', girl!" the ghost said excitedly. "But not just any old crop, no sir."

Petunia bored with the prospector's ravings, slowly wandered off into the desert.

But Jedidiah didn't notice. He was on a roll, talking about the thing that would get his blood a'pumpin', if he had any blood.

"I ain't interested in your corn, or wheat, no sirree, Bob," Jedidiah proclaimed. "I'm gonna have me the biggest farm in all of the U-nited States to grow me the greatest vegetable in all the land."

Jedidiah's ghostly eyes twinkled as he thought of this special crop.

"The twinklin' jewel in the vegetable crown," he said, rubbing his thick hands together. "The one veggie above them all."

Petunia ambled back just in time to be reminded of the prospector's most favorite vegetable.

Jedidiah locked eyes with the mule and whispered the name of the thing that even in death filled him with passion.

"I'm gonna grow me some sugar beets," Jedidiah Peckinpah whispered enthusiastically while slowly nodding. "That's right, sugar beet fields as far as the eye can see . . . which wouldn't look like much because the beet is a root and grows underground, but you know what I'm gettin' at!"

The ghost prospector again surveyed his vast fortune of gold and turned his gaze to the heavens and thought about the future.

And as he thought of the limitless bounty that he would grow, what he believed to be a falling star flew across the sky, and he took it as a sign of good things to come.

Sugar beets, yes sir.

As far as the eye can see.

But the falling star the ghostly prospector thought he saw wasn't a falling star at all.

The alien spacecraft rocketed across the sky.

The alien mother was quite happy with her new ship, this one being much larger and less cramped than the one that she had used to escape her children all those years ago.

She was thankful there had been a relatively comfortable sleep chamber on board the original escape pod, imagining that she probably would have lost her mind trapped and awake for all those years stuck inside the skull of the human.

But now it had all changed. Now she could get down to living the way she'd always wanted, away from the needs and demands of her children.

It'll do them good not to have me around, she thought. *Maybe it'll help them build some fortitude.*

They'd depended on her long enough.

Now was her time.

Reclining in her chair, the alien mother reached across to the control console and picked up a large brochure, her single eye reading about the best places to visit in Hawaii.

She smiled with the thought of a very long and well-deserved vacation.

She'd always wanted to try poi.

EPILOGUE THE THIRD

Kirby had returned the Eldorado to the garage—and to its previous non-working condition.

OB and Erasmus were busily applying a thick coating of dust and dirt to the vehicle to give it back that special unused look.

"It appears you two have things under control here," Kirby told them. "I have work to do back at the house."

"Don't worry about us!" Erasmus said as Kirby left the garage. "We're just a couple'a artists at work!"

"Yeah, we're like the Michelangelo of filth!" OB said, whipping a handful of mud at the car's door and smearing it around.

Kirby hadn't expected the mission to go as long as it had. The weekend was nearly over.

He climbed the stairs, entered the home, and went to the kitchen where his machine was still working—still freezing time to the moment just before they'd departed.

Tom and LeeAnne were still at the kitchen sink, wrapped in each other's arms. The Frenchie squatted down at his complex device and prepared to allow time to begin flowing again.

But he had to be very careful; time was not something to be trifled with casually. Once the machine's effects were reversed, time would fall into place with a vengeance—the whole nature-abhorring-a-vacuum thing.

He wondered how Tom and LeeAnne would comprehend the missing time and determined that they would likely deal with it the way they dealt with all the bizarreness that had been going on around their new Strasburg home.

They would simply shrug their shoulders, then continue on with their mundane lives.

Kirby flipped a switch and watched as a distortion in the air, a wave of rushing time, passed through the kitchen and over his owners. The second hand on the kitchen clock started to move again, as did Tom and LeeAnne.

Quickly, the Frenchie picked up his device and headed for the back door.

"Man," he heard Tom say behind him. "My head is fuzzy."

"Your head is always fuzzy," LeeAnne answered snidely. "Hey, what day is it anyway?"

Kirby didn't hang around to hear the answer.

It was good to be back in the lab. There was so much that needed to be done, and Kirby still hadn't been granted access to Erasmus's world domination files.

OB was back at the house, resting peacefully in his aquarium, and Kirby decided that now was as good a time as any to get some questions answered.

"I know you're here," he announced, as he filed some notes and sketches he'd made of Carl's death ray.

Erasmus's ghostly form manifested. He was eating what appeared to be a ghostly hot dog, smothered in ghostly mustard, relish, and onions.

"I've never been a quiet chewer," he said through a mouthful of ghostly dog.

"Are you going to tell me?" Kirby asked.

"And what would I be telling you?"

"About that." Kirby pointed to the deactivated cryo-chamber that still held the living, but not yet alive, version of Erasmus Peckinpah.

"Oh," Erasmus said. "That guy."

"Yes, that guy," Kirby said. "Why didn't the nuclear heart restore it to life?"

Erasmus finished the hot dog and licked his fingers.

"You're right about that, Konan," the ghost said. "Not one of my better decisions, if you catch my drift."

"I do not catch your drift," Kirby stated flatly. "Explain."

Erasmus looked at his wrist. There was a watch there now where there hadn't been before.

"Is that the time?" he asked. "I gotta hit the sack, got a busy day tomorrow if . . ."

"Explain!" Kirby barked, his patience with the specter on the wane.

Erasmus sighed. "All right, all right. The reason my flesh-and-blood body didn't come back to life might have something to do with the demon monkey."

"Demon. Monkey," Kirby repeated, not quite sure if he'd heard the ghost correctly.

"Yeah, see, back when I was still alive, I kinda knew that my days were numbered and couldn't bear the thought of not being around anymore, so . . ."

Kirby waited.

"So I sold my soul to a demon monkey from the underworld," Erasmus said. "In exchange to keep on existing."

Kirby glared, fire in his eyes.

"But you call this existing?" the ghost asked, arms spread as he hovered over the laboratory floor. "Personally I think I got the poop end of the stick."

Kirby began to massage his temples, feeling as if his head very well might explode.

"So you sold your soul to this . . . ," he said.

"Demon monkey. That's right," Erasmus said. "Personally I think he got a bargain."

"And that is why, even though your human body has received a nuclear heart, it does not live."

"Yeah, I think so," Erasmus said, gazing over to the cryo-chamber propped in the corner of the room.

"It's because you no longer have a soul," Kirby said.

The ghost hung his head and sighed. "Not the kinda thing one likes to be reminded of, thank you very much."

"So your human form will not live unless . . ."

"I get my soul back," Erasmus said.

Kirby put a paw over his eyes and attempted to think of a time when all this has passed and the world answers to his every whim.

"And in order to do that, we have to make a trip to the underworld," Erasmus finished.

Kirby sighed.

"Of course we do."

THE END OF BOOK TWO

KIRBY
A BIOGRAPHY

Kirby "Crackle-Lockjaw" Sniegoski was born on January 23, 2010, in Secaucus, New Jersey—

And the world was changed forever.

Even at a very early age, Kirby knew he was destined for bigger things—important things—and he chose Mr. and Mrs. Thomas E. Sniegoski to aid him on this journey.

While living in Boston, Kirby began to cultivate the ideas that would eventually mutate into his plans for world conquest.

A graduate of a plethora of online college-level courses such as *Fascism for Fun and Profit, A User's Guide to Weapons of Mass Destruction, Ninjutsu: With an Eye Toward Contract Killing, World Domination in Three Easy Steps, Making the Perfect Omelet, The Dark Arts: Making Friends and Influencing People Through Black Magic*, Kirby began to accumulate the knowledge necessary to make his plans a reality.

After relocating to the suburbs south of Boston, Kirby discovered the last pieces of the puzzle that would set his grand schemes in motion.

Kirby currently resides on the South Shore, with his people, a box turtle named OB, and the ghost of the previous owner of the house in which he lives.

His plans for planetwide subjugation are moving along quite nicely.

ABOUT THE CREATORS

Thomas E. Sniegoski is a *New York Times* best-selling author who has written for children, young adults, and adults, and has also worked in the comic book industry. He has written characters such as Batman, The Punisher, Buffy the Vampire Slayer, and Hellboy. He is also the author of the groundbreaking YA series *The Fallen*.

Tom McWeeney is a cartoon illustrator veteran with a comic book and toy design background. He has served as a writer/artist on projects for DC Comics, Dark Horse, and WildStorm, as well as a product developer for Hasbro, Fisher-Price, and Nickelodeon.

An Imprint of Insight Editions
PO Box 3088
San Rafael, CA 94912
www.insightcomics.com

Find us on Facebook: www.facebook.com/InsightEditions
Follow us on Twitter: @insighteditions
Follow us on Instagram: Insight_Comics

Library of Congress Cataloging-in-Publication Data available.

ISBN: 978-1-68383-643-8

Publisher: Raoul Goff
Associate Publisher: Vanessa Lopez
Designer: Evelyn Furuta
Executive Editor: Mark Irwin
Assistant Editor: Holly Fisher
Senior Production Editor: Elaine Ou
Production Manager: Sadie Crofts

ROOTS of PEACE · REPLANTED PAPER

Insight Editions, in association with Roots of Peace, will plant two trees for each
tree used in the manufacturing of this book. Roots of Peace is an internationally re-
nowned humanitarian organization dedicated to eradicating land mines worldwide
and converting war-torn lands into productive farms and wildlife habitats. Roots of
Peace will plant two million fruit and nut trees in Afghanistan and provide farmers
there with the skills and support necessary for sustainable land use.

Manufactured in China by Insight Editions

10 9 8 7 6 5 4 3 2 1